Ask for Blues

ASK FOR BLUES

Malcolm Walton

Matador
9 Priory Business Park,
Wistow Road, Kibworth Beauchamp,
Leicestershire. LE8 0RX
Tel: 0116 279 2299
Email: books@troubador.co.uk
Web: www.troubador.co.uk/matador
Twitter: @matadorbooks

ISBN 978 1788038 058

British Library Cataloguing in Publication Data.
A catalogue record for this book is available from the British Library.

Printed and bound in Great Britain by 4edge Limited
Typeset in 11pt Adobe Garamond Pro by Troubador Publishing Ltd, Leicester, UK

Matador is an imprint of Troubador Publishing Ltd

To Miranda
who encouraged me to keep writing –
because she wanted to know what happened next!

Author's Note

Having read many musical memoirs in recent years, I decided to adopt a different approach by writing this book as a novel. Nearly everything really did happen as chronicled but, in the words of Eric Morecambe, 'not necessarily in the right order'. Very little fictional material has been created apart from, out of necessity, some of the dialogue. The encounters with well-known musicians all happened as described. I have borrowed just two pieces of conversation from more recent times: the limerick recited by Ted in the Rising Sun, courtesy of George Walker, and the conversation in the lock during the Riverboat Shuffle, attributed to Bob Taylor.

I would like to thank Jonathan Horne and Quentin Bryar for their invaluable help during the editing process.

Contents

Prelude
1944

The green and orange Halifax Corporation bus was making its way from Mile Cross towards the town centre. Martin was sitting next to the window which, due to the blackout, was more or less covered by a concertina-style leather blind. Jack Hellowell, Martin's grandad, had promised him a surprise this Sunday evening but despite constant questioning would not reveal what sort of a surprise. They got off at Corporation Square, Martin holding his grandad's hand. "Now, we are just going to cross the road. See over there?" asked Jack. He was gesturing towards a little gathering in the centre of which were about fifteen people, all wearing a kind of military uniform. There were holding an assortment of silver objects, some quite small, some enormous. They glinted in the reflected light of the moon.

"Who are they, Grandpa?"

"Just you wait and see!"

They crossed the road and joined the onlookers. Suddenly, the Halifax Salvation Army Band burst into life with a rousing march. Martin could not contain himself. He jumped up and down, waved his little arms about and looked at his grandad, his face radiating unadulterated pleasure. It was the first time that he had heard such a thing. It was nothing like the music that he had heard on the wireless. It was a brass band, full of lovely rich sounds, from the highest soprano cornet to the lowest double B-flat tuba. This was for Martin, a two-and-a-half-year-old wartime child, the best thing that had ever happened.

From that moment, while he was still living in the north with his grandparents, he pestered Jack to take him to hear the band every Sunday. Jack often complained that, had he known what this was going to spark off, he would have had second thoughts about it. But, had he lived long enough to see Martin's progress in the world of music, he would have been pleased with what he did.

CHAPTER 1

Overture

1957-58

'One, two, three o'clock, four o'clock rock
Five, six, seven o'clock, eight o'clock rock...'

Bill Haley and his Comets were straining the fragile loudspeaker cone to its very limit. Martin Weston had just bought his very first 78 rpm record from Curry's Cycle and Gramophone Shop in Barnet High Street. This record was dynamite. All the lads at Martin's school were singing it, generally accompanied by the sound of wooden rulers beating time on the classroom radiators, when the master was out of the room. The spectacular opening lines were more a declaration than a song, almost yelling from the rooftops 'just listen to this!' For the first time since the 1930s' swing bands, there was a new music. Something urgent and exciting had burst the protective bubble around Doris Day, Jimmy Young, and other respectable 1950s' hit parade artistes. Rock and roll's seminal recording, 'Rock Around the Clock' was destined to become a massive hit for the most unlikely teenage hero: a middle-aged, portly guitarist with a kiss curl, shaped like a question mark, flopping limply over his forehead. This tune, with its pile-driver beat, had achieved notoriety when, before the record was released, it was featured in *Blackboard Jungle,* a film that was forever associated with irresponsible teenage behaviour: dancing in cinema aisles and 'Teddy Boys', with flick knives and bicycle chains ripping up the seats. Such vandalism, luridly written up in the national dailies, had received universal condemnation. It brought all the 'Colonel Blimps' out of the woodwork, after they had been silenced by the Second World War. Eventually, it came to Barnet and, for one week, was the main feature film at the Odeon. Some of Martin's circle of friends had seen it; others, including Martin, had not been allowed to go. This, Martin thought to be very unfair and restrictive on the part of his parents.

Nevertheless, it was their pre-war gramophone that, under duress, was doing its level best to cope with this ground-breaking record, although his parents were blissfully unaware because Martin had the house to himself. When the record reached the point where the band riffed 'Da-da-da, dada-da-dadada...' the loudspeaker added its own contribution: a buzzing sound, indicating that some integral component was giving way under the strain. It was as if this respectable, mahogany-cased machine had sided with its owners and was therefore adding its own voice of disapproval to what it was being forced to play.

It was the summer of 1957 and Martin, a fifteen-year-old grammar school boy, had just spent his earnings from that week's paper round on Bill Haley's record. Up until then, as a rule, this regular source of income financed bits and pieces for his bike, such as a Brooks saddle, yet more carriages and track for his model railway, electronic components for the making of crystal sets and books by Arthur Ransome. But this was not destined to continue, now that he had discovered the joy of owning 78s. His parents possessed a few, including 'When I'm Cleaning Windows' by George Formby, the majestic 'Orpheus in the Underworld' by the Black Dyke Mills Band and Maxine Sullivan's 'Loch Lomond'. This had become Martin's favourite, for no other reason than something about it was different. It had a compelling rhythmic pulse and a saxophone solo. It was a jazz record; not that he knew anything about jazz, nor even what it was, back then. The repetitive playing of it must have planted a seed in Martin's subconscious, which bloomed later that year.

These well-played records were bought by Martin's parents shortly after they married in 1940, and the floor-standing, electric gramophone came as a wedding present. On all bar one, 'The Holy City', a present from one of Martin's ancient relatives which was probably only ever played once, there was too much surface noise for comfortable listening, the grooves having been ground down, time after time, with steel needles. But Martin had a brand-new disc and, as he made his way home from the shop, having read, and re-read all the small print on the Brunswick black and silver label, even including the matrix number, the patent number and the words *Made in England*, he couldn't resist sliding it from its paper sleeve to gaze admiringly at the virgin, black shiny grooves. By holding it at a certain angle, he could make out the wavy contours of the sound vibrations, transferred from the wax master onto the shellac disc. Totally unnecessary; a kind of foreplay with an inanimate object!

Thus began Martin's lifelong love affair with music. His grandad, Jack, had taken him to hear the Salvation Army band during the last year of the war, which had left an indelible impression on one so young. But, in recent years, his encounters with music were more parental driven than by free choice. He used to sing in the church choir, and had been subjected to piano lessons with Miss Baillie-Smith from the age of eight. However, his interest in formal lessons was no more than lukewarm and, with some sense of relief, he was eventually able to persuade his parents that he could not fit in both piano practice and homework, once he was at the grammar school. Nevertheless, disinterested or not, under Miss Baillie-Smith's tutelage, he did manage to attain Grade 5 before the age of twelve.

Things seemed so different now, and from that day in 1957 Martin stopped spending whatever money came his way on model railways and crystal set components, and started saving up for one of those stylish red and white, Rexine-covered Dansette record players. He had seen one in Curry's window priced at eighteen guineas. Owning it would mean emancipation. He would never again have to ask whether he could use the family gramophone, but could play his records in his bedroom, whenever, and for how long he wished. All of this was soon realised, but only after having sold all of his Hornby-Dublo. He was too frustrated to wait for the accumulation of a few shillings week by week. His father was not particularly impressed by this action, having bought Martin the train set as a series of Christmas presents, but this was nowhere near the level of disgruntlement that he reached when Martin, some five years later, had his first suit, in charcoal grey (again bought by his father), converted into a tuxedo by his then girlfriend in order to play in a dance band.

Linda was a friend from early childhood. They had grown up together, lived in the same road, been to the same primary school, and their parents were friends. They all came from the north, not that common in a Hertfordshire dormitory town back then; northerners tended to stay put in 'God's own country' and had an inbuilt mistrust of 'soft' southerners. Martin's parents were from Yorkshire, Linda's from Derbyshire. She was also fifteen and had recently turned from a tomboy into a boisterous teenage girl, not exactly pretty – but attractive in a sturdy kind of way. She had a great love of all sporting activities and in due course became a PE teacher and married an athlete. But back in 1957, Martin had a crush on her and was always trying to find ways to impress – especially now that he was into music and had the edge on her when it came to knowing a little bit about Bill Haley and Tommy Steele. The two families occasionally met up for afternoon tea on a Saturday or Sunday. Martin looked forward so much to this that he would cancel anything pre-arranged with his mates, such as cricket in the park, or the cinema, just to make sure that he could see Linda.

Still awkward and a little shy, he could not pluck up the necessary courage to make any headway with the opposite sex and, even though Linda and he were close friends, felt unable to either say or do anything even slightly demonstrative; he was rather hoping that she might make some sort of a move. As childhood had progressed into adolescence, bringing with it a new awareness of girls, and vice versa, he couldn't pick up any clues as to whether she now had any affectionate thoughts about him. He looked in vain for any visual hint no matter how slight, but nothing appeared on his radar. At least he didn't feel uncomfortable in Linda's presence, because he had known her since she was five years old. Other girls, whom he hardly knew but would have liked to know much better, and even relatively mature women in their twenties, like a friend of his mother's, produced a much more visible sign of embarrassment. If he fancied them, it made him blush when in their proximity. So much so in fact that on one occasion he crossed to the other side of the road to avoid having to pass close by his mother's friend, as he felt his cheeks had become uncontrollably hot. Imagine how he then felt, a little later, when she was appointed lab technician at the grammar school. Martin's obvious discomfort during chemistry lessons did not go unnoticed by Mrs Gray (Martin never did discover her first name), and she herself even went a little pink. In later life Martin often wondered whether, with the wind in the right direction, he might have been introduced to carnal delights by this older woman. He was able to reflect, ironically, that the teenagers of the sixties, only ten years later, would have had no difficulties whatsoever.

Linda had an elder brother, Jonathan, a tall, blonde, gangling youth of seventeen, who Martin looked up to as a sort of hero. Jonathan had in the past taught Martin and a few other younger boys how to climb massive oak trees, construct bows and arrows, matchstick guns and fishing rods. He was also the first of the group to get the *Eagle* comic every week, featuring Dan Dare, pilot of the future. This always guaranteed an after-school visit to his home by Martin and a few others on Friday, the day the comic came out. He was extremely popular, and his height ensured his role as leader of the pack.

At one of those family teas (a social event carried over from pre-war days, still in vogue during the 1950s but not destined to last much longer), Martin's musical aura was just about to experience another massive jolt, more intense than his discovery of 'Rock around the Clock'. Jonathan had acquired a 10-inch LP entitled *New Orleans Joys* by the Chris Barber Band, and was allowed to play it during tea. In addition to the jazz tracks, were a couple of skiffle numbers. This was a hybrid, new kind of music: part folk song, part rhythm and blues. A nasal-voiced guitarist called Lonnie Donegan sang 'Rock Island Line' and 'Diggin' My Potatoes'. Martin had a feeling of déjà vu. He was back in wartime Halifax having his senses awoken by something new and exciting. It was precisely the same sensation. Both the jazz and the skiffle captivated him to the exclusion of all else, so much so that he temporarily forgot about Linda, who was sitting next to him. He knew from that precise moment that he was going to have to learn how to play this skiffle thing himself, and as soon as possible. Teenage obsessions are accompanied by an overwhelming sense of urgency, and this was no exception.

He thought about the piano lessons that he had managed to wheedle out of over three years ago and wondered if anything that he had learned would be of any use. At that stage, he could only recall having to learn such pieces as *The Merry Peasant* and *The Harmonious Blacksmith* and for all the world could not see any points of coincidence with 'Diggin' My Potatoes', with its blues structure and undoubted sexual innuendo. But it would not be long before he came to recognise the importance of this early but unloved training. Melody, harmony and rhythm are the building blocks for *all* forms of musical expression. Sometimes one's parents have their uses!

So how on earth was Martin going to become a skiffle musician, and on what instrument? Lonnie had become his new number one idol, and every time his latest recording was issued Martin would find some way of buying it. He quickly decided that he needed a guitar. Lonnie sometimes used a pianist, but only as an afterthought. Martin didn't wish to be an 'afterthought'. At school, two of Martin's close friends, Doug Fisher and 'Josh' Whitely, found Martin's enthusiasm for this new music compelling. So, having agreed among the three of them that they just had to become part of this musical revolution, how were they to go about equipping the group? Josh unexpectedly declared that he had a snare drum. Then Doug managed to buy a guitar and learned the requisite three chords needed to play 'It Takes a Worried Man', their first ever foray into song. Martin, in sheer desperation, made a tea chest bass… a tea chest, a piece of string and a broom handle was all that you needed for this basic piece of kit. At last they were a skiffle group! Learning the words and the three or four chords to the Lonnie Donegan repertoire was not that difficult as Martin had devised a three-colour system. The lyrics were written out in blue for the root chord, red for the median and green for the subdominant. On the rare occasion that there was a fourth chord, this would be black. The change in colour was aligned precisely where it happened on the record; often between syllables.

Their very first public performance at a youth club, early in the new year, was enthusiastically received. After all, in 1958 skiffle was constantly in the hit parade and even had its own Saturday morning radio programme. But Martin desperately wanted to be the centre of attraction, and he still had no guitar. Eventually, after a holiday job washing cars at a second-hand car lot, he achieved his dream, nurtured since that teatime with Jonathan and Linda. It was an archtop, *f*-hole style guitar, like those used by all the professional dance bands and jazz players. He got it from a junk shop in Wood Green near where he was working, and it cost him three pounds, ten shillings. Their skiffle group now had a name, The San Hillbaro Ramblers. This was an amalgam of two local telephone exchanges – Hillside and Barnet. The 'San' bit was added on to give it a Spanish-American flavour, and the 'Ramblers' bit was borrowed from a well-known London-based skiffle group, The City Ramblers.

They played as often as they could at youth clubs in the Barnet and Totteridge area, usually in a side room of the inevitable church hall but, sometimes, in the main hall, competing with the badminton. It was at one of these youth clubs that the skiffle phase started to fizzle out for Martin, and what was destined to become his lifelong love of jazz, kicked in. It was at St Marks Club, New Barnet, that a clarinet, trombone and bass player were trying, in a very enthusiastic manner, to play some simple jazz tunes, much in the same way as Doug, Josh and Martin had initially approached skiffle; bags of determination but noticeably light on musical proficiency. Technical deficiencies would have to be ironed out before any fame or fortune, but right then that was not their biggest problem. The poor bass player, the sole member of what should have been the rhythm section, had an impossible, lonely task; the band clearly had an urgent need of either a piano, guitar or banjo to provide some sort of harmonic structure. Martin was no slouch when it came to getting what he wanted, other than things to do with the opposite sex.

"Can I join in?" he asked. "I know a few chords... what do you think?"

The trio looked at each other, then at Martin. The clarinet player spoke: "I saw you playing last week with your skiffle group. Do you know any jazz?"

"Well, I have heard Chris Barber's LP, *New Orleans Joys*, and this new bloke, er, is it Acker Bilk?"

So they let him sit in with his guitar and, mercifully, played a couple of simple tunes to which Martin managed to find the right chords purely by ear. As the youth club evening came to an end, the clarinettist, whose name was Jimmy, said, "If you can learn a few tunes, maybe off that Barber LP if that's the only record you have, come and join in next week. We could really do with a guitar."

Great! Martin was over the moon. Going home, he kept telling himself 'this is it, this is it'. His thoughts moved into the realms of fantasy; this youthful quartet morphing into a tremendous jazz band, in great demand, and with him, at the age of only sixteen, their guitarist. Woe betide anyone pouring cold water onto a teenage daydream such as this, for the short time it will last. Reality will kick in quite soon enough, without any help. This first band that Martin joined became before long 'Monk Hadley's Jazz Friars', another product of creative thinking. Its genesis was derived from a little hamlet on the outskirts of Barnet called Monken Hadley. In due course, someone had the idea of drawing cartoons of stout monks clad in habit and sandals playing musical instruments, their very own band logo.

Martin still went to the teatime rituals with Jonathan and Linda's family, but now he made sure that he always took his guitar with him. He was, of course, showing off, unashamedly parading his credentials as a musician. Usually he made a great effort to impress Linda with a song or two but despite everything never did find out whether this was all in vain. There were still no clues forthcoming, visually or otherwise. It would be another couple of years before he had a proper girlfriend, and by then Linda was no longer in the running.

Almost overnight, the average adolescent's lifestyle can go through paradigm shifts, as each new experience replaces the last and, with these changes, new friends come along and sometimes the old ones get left behind. By the age of eighteen Martin hardly saw Jonathan or Linda any longer, except by chance. His more recent friends had more than adequately filled the void. By the time he reached twenty-three, he had experienced similar changes of direction quite a few times.

"How do you feel about switching to piano?" enquired Jimmy Prior, the leader of Monk Hadley's Jazz Friars, having discovered that Martin had had four years of piano lessons when younger. Martin's guitar playing was adequate, but the British Trad movement preferred the clunking banjo. So, if they could enlist a banjo player, and there was one who had recently become a club member, this seemed like a good idea and they would then become a seven-piece band. More importantly, it would give the band the commercial sound that was all in vogue. They had, over the last year, managed to add a drummer and a trumpet player to the original line-up and the consensus of opinion from their peers was encouraging. They were not at all bad. They had already made a private recording on the drummer's reel-to-reel Grundig tape recorder, and frequently went to his house to listen to it. It was a bit of a trek to where he lived in East

Barnet, but back in those pre-cassette recorder days there was no known way of making copies, other than by placing a microphone against the speaker of one tape recorder and re-recording with another tape recorder. Nobody had one.

Martin was now in his element; he was living the dream. School became a place of extreme boredom. There was absolutely no contest between completing the barest minimum of academic work that he could get away with, and the coming evening's jazz – the jazz won by a mile. One or two of the band members had recently finished their schooling and had money of their own. Martin had more or less given up any aspirations to go on to university. He wanted to be out in the big wide world just like his friends.

CHAPTER 2

Doug

Spring, 1959

"What would you chaps like to drink? You can have anything you like," Clive, Doug's father, offered, much to the astonishment of Doug and Martin, both now aged seventeen. The three of them were sitting on a bench, in the early evening sunshine, outside The Beehive at Little Berkhamsted. They had got there in Clive's brand-new Hillman Minx, following a fruitless afternoon tinkering with a non-running moped that Doug had just acquired. Clive, noticing the futility of their efforts, had said, "Come on, put it back in the shed and I'll take you for a drive as it's such a nice afternoon."

Doug's mother, Alison, an extremely attractive woman in Martin's opinion, declined the offer to join them all for a spin in 'the old girl'. Sadly, it wasn't long before it became common knowledge that their marriage was on the rocks, so her reluctance to accompany her husband that afternoon was, in hindsight, predictable. It seemed to Martin that both Doug's parents were a sight more interesting than his own. Alison had worked for a theatrical promoter before the war and had personally looked after Fats Waller during his 1939 British tour. When she had told Martin about this, he had found it nigh on impossible to get his head around it. He had only just bought 'When Somebody

Thinks You're Wonderful', by Fats Waller and his Rhythm, recently reissued on a 45rpm single. And now he was just one step removed from having been in his presence. He had bombarded Alison with a stream of questions, most of which she couldn't answer as they were all about music. But she did tell Martin that Fats was always the perfect gentleman. Had Martin at that time known about the great man's legendary appetite for food, drink and, in particular, women, he might have considered such a beauty as Alison to have been lucky to have escaped 'the perfect gentleman's' clutches, spending, as she had, so much time in his company. Or maybe she hadn't? She was hardly likely to admit to an indiscretion in front of her own son and his friend! To cap it all, Clive had been a Battle of Britain pilot, one of 'the Few'. Martin could not imagine anything more glamorous and daring. But like so many heroes of the war, Clive was reluctant to talk about his exploits. The job had been done, it saved us from Nazi tyranny, and that was that. True to type, he still retained his handlebar moustache. Martin could not help reflecting upon the difference between Clive and Harold, his own father. True, Harold had had an interesting war as a research chemist, designing a new high explosive called RDX, later to become known as Semtex. Also, Harold had always said that the casualty rate at the Government Munitions Factory in Waltham Abbey was higher, pro rata, than members of the armed forces because of it being a priority Luftwaffe target.

That day, sitting outside a sleepy Hertfordshire country pub, Martin and Doug were happily drinking their shandies, while Clive was ensconced somewhere inside, consuming pints of McMullen's bitter. It would still be another few months before the two of them could legally drink in a pub.

Of course, this was not the first time that they had tasted beer, but it was the first time that an adult, indeed a parent, had actually condoned it. Martin was acutely aware that Harold, in comparison almost teetotal, would have never done such a thing, and he felt a pang of envy for Doug and his liberated parents, as he saw them.

"Do you remember our last skiffle group gig?" asked Doug. This had been six months ago, in the autumn of the previous year. "I thought we played well and I was a bit surprised that you packed it in. Josh and I both reckoned that we had a good thing going for us." Martin did not respond immediately. That gig, in the evening, by a bonfire on a little bit of green at the top of Totteridge Hill, had been the cause of a sore point with Martin, of which now Doug had unwittingly reminded him. They had been playing in near total darkness, lit only by the flickering embers of the fire, which had the effect of colouring everyone's face an unnatural brick red. Martin had thought that he recognised, across the other side of the semicircle of onlookers, a girl from one of the Barnet youth clubs.

The San Hillbaro Ramblers were going through their repertoire of Lonnie Donegan numbers, and at the end of one number Martin simply waved across and said "hello". It wasn't long before they had to give up, when the fire finally died and they could no longer see what they were doing. The girl had gone by then. Then, a few days later, a hand-delivered letter had arrived from this girl, but she was not who he had thought she was. The letter said something along the lines of: *You said hello to me the other night. My name is Marion and I know your friend Douglas. Perhaps we can meet.* Martin pumped Doug for what he knew about this girl, but it turned out to be very little other than that she played tennis nearly every Saturday afternoon at the public courts in Totteridge. The next Saturday found Doug, Martin, and a couple of others, spending the morning at Finchley Swimming Pool. In North London, this was a top-of-the-list attraction for teenagers during the summer and autumn terms. Well aware of this, the manufacturers of Brylcreem had spotted a golden sales opportunity by placing a dispenser of their product right outside the men's changing cubicles. Nearly everybody wanted a one penny dollop of the stuff, having just towelled their hair dry. It was widely advertised on billboards, generally featuring a picture of the great Dennis Compton swinging a cricket bat over his shoulder, hair glistening and sleek. Sometimes it featured a shocked lady, stroking her boyfriend's hair, saying, 'Oh no, dry scalp!' Martin, in all innocence, thought that this was another name for dandruff. (In hindsight, why should the prospect of a greasy scalp have been in any way appealing?)

Doug, who was not averse to practical jokes, used all his powers of persuasion to deter Martin from using any Brylcreem. He had said that the latest trend, one that all the girls liked, was the unkempt straggly look. This he claimed to have gleaned from reading a hairdressing magazine in the barber's. "You shouldn't comb your hair, or put any kind of dressing on it. It's very bohemian and will be sure to impress Marion," he went on. Martin was not at all happy about this since he had always thought, contrary to what Doug had just told him, that his normal, groomed hairstyle *was* what the girls actually liked.

As they walked towards Totteridge, he had been having second thoughts and attempted without success to comb his sun-dried matted mess of hair. Then, beginning to feel embarrassed, he got cold feet and said that he was not coming with them. The persuasive Doug won the day, however, and then Martin saw Marion in broad daylight. She was nothing like the girl that he had mistaken her for and, worse still, did not find her particularly attractive, so any potential future meeting was very quickly ruled out. Later, what made Martin so irritated, was the feedback that Doug received from Marion, saying that she did not find Martin attractive – there was something odd about his hair! This was entirely Doug's fault. What if he *had* fancied Marion after all; where would he have been then, eh? Up the proverbial gumtree!

Martin was jolted out of his reverie back to the question that had been asked.

"Well yes, I agree we did have some fun with the skiffle group, and it was all bloody good in its day but, you know how it is, this new jazz band I'm in has got a lot more going for it and I reckon, when all's said and done, skiffle may be on its last legs. Lonnie has become a bit of a music hall turn. Look at the stuff he's churning out: 'My Old Man's a Dustman', 'Chewing Gum on the Bedpost'. You're not going to tell me that this rubbish is skiffle, I hope, and where have all the other groups disappeared to?"

Doug somewhat reluctantly agreed that this was so, thought a bit more about it and then finally admitted "You know, I don't know why I ever thought that I was cut out to be a musician. It was all your doing! You got me into it, and now you have got me out of it! But I guess I'm not like you, I never wanted to go any further than we got. I was happy just strumming along, you know. Bugger all that learning about music theory stuff, and practising things! And as for jazz, I wouldn't even know where to start. You're probably better off doing your own thing. You're obviously keen enough to spend the time needed. Don't think I am, to be honest."

Martin, feeling a little guilty about having abandoned his mates Doug and Josh in order to play jazz, said that loads of people had jumped on to the skiffle bandwagon a few years ago, all because of Lonnie Donegan. Virtually none of them had any musical training and who knew what they were up to, now that it had as good as fizzled out? As for himself, Martin said that he felt that he wanted to continue in music and it obviously had to be something a bit more challenging than skiffle. Jazz was exactly the direction that he needed to move towards. Doug replied that it was pretty obvious that Martin was determined to do what was now driving him, regardless. And he added, to show that he bore no grudge, "Good luck, no hard feelings." He went on to say that he himself knew absolutely nothing about Martin's new heroes: Louis Armstrong, Bix Beiderbecke, King Oliver and all the others whose names he could not remember. "In all honesty, I just saw playing in public as a very good way to get the girls. A very good way indeed!"

Martin reflected that Doug, with his dark saturnine looks, was already streets ahead of the rest of them in this department, with or without a guitar around his neck. Doug was soon to leave school, become a film cameraman for ITV and get more than his fair share of willing women. Their paths rarely crossed again.

CHAPTER 3

Monk Hadley gets paid

1960

"What numbers shall we play at Southgate?" asked Jimmy Prior. The four of them were sitting in Martin's mum's Ford Anglia. This was the model that looked the same from the front and back; like half a Mars bar on top of a whole one. It was raining outside and they were discussing the forthcoming 'proper' gig as the interval band during a Saturday dance at the Standard Telephone and Cables Social Club. Sarah, Martin's first girlfriend, and Pam, who was engaged to Jimmy, both went to the same youth club where Monk Hadley's Jazz Friars was formed eighteen months ago. The band had improved during that time to the point where they thought that they could try their luck in the world beyond youth clubs, and the first engagement was looming; secured after a bit of begging by Dave, their trombone player, who happened to work for Standard Telephones.

During his last year at school, eighteen-year-old Martin had finally broken his duck as far as girls were concerned and had one significant advantage that most of his contemporaries did not. He had access to his mother's car, having passed his driving test before his eighteenth birthday at the first attempt. He did this without any practising between the weekly driving lessons paid for by his father.

Even though the driving instructor urged him to do so, his father was not going to allow a learner driver behind the wheel of his precious Daimler. In any event, the process for gear changing was entirely different, the Daimler being equipped with a Wilson pre-selector box and a fluid flywheel. Martin's mother was taking driving lessons at the same time (a package deal) and upon her surprising test success, Harold bought her an Anglia as it was identical to the driving school car and therefore would not involve any learning curve. This, the 100E model, had a remarkable vacuum-operated windscreen wiper mechanism. It was quite possible to get the wipers to slow down to a dead stop when accelerating hard – just when you actually needed clear vision ahead – and, perversely, when the engine was idling the wipers went back and forth so fast that it was almost a blur.

On Sunday evenings Martin used to take Sarah for a drive in the countryside, and eventually park down a quiet lane in a farm entrance or such, wait for the windows to steam up, lock the doors and engage in a prolonged session of light petting. Before long, in gradual stages, this moved forwards to the heavier variety. It had to be admitted, though, that Sarah made the final empowering move by checking, in the middle of a tickling session, how far Martin's vest went down inside the waistband of his trousers. One thing led to another and Martin sensed that he had been given the green light. Left to his own devices, he would still have been worrying about the next move come Christmas! Sarah had suspected this and felt he needed some help. From that moment on Martin considered that he had at last joined the adult world and, for the first time in his life, began to feel more confident with women. It would still take a few years before his level of confidence matched that of some of his contemporaries but, nevertheless, it was a good start.

Sarah was a shorthand typist and had volunteered to type and bind the band 'arrangements'. These consisted of little more than a list of the order of soloists and some commentary. Some of the commentary was not what you would ever find on proper printed orchestrations – 'kick it hard' or 'flare' for example – but it meant something to the band.

"Whatever we do, I think we should include the numbers that we have got routines for; you know, 'Maryland', 'Indiana', 'Ice Cream', 'Delia Gone'," Martin said in reply to Jimmy's question about what to play.

This last one was copied from an Acker Bilk EP that had come out that year and had five vocal choruses that Jimmy took it upon himself to sing. The band members had differing tastes, but one thing they agreed upon was that Acker was deservedly popular. Very conveniently, he appeared regularly at Barnet Jazz Club, so they were able to watch and learn at the master's feet, so to say. He proved to be an interesting role model, given to enthusiastic grunts, ramblings about key signatures, which no one understood, and dubious taste such as the use of the microphone to amplify his belches. A little later, Kenny Ball caught their attention, particularly Martin's, in a big way. He could actually play Louis Armstrong and Bix Beiderbecke solos, note for note! Martin thought, not for the first time, that what *he* really wanted to do was to play the trumpet. When Doug Fisher brought an old bugle to school one day, Martin spent the entire morning, lunchtime and afternoon breaks down the bottom of the rugby pitch, out of sight of prefects and masters, experimenting with it and managing, in the end, to produce a few proper notes.

Monk Hadley's Jazz Friars was now one of about four or five traditional-style bands playing in the Barnet area. There was The Cardinal Jazz Band, possibly the longest established, The San Jacinto Stompers, Mr Benjamin Farr's Jazz Orpheans and Ted Nottage's All Stars. Seeing a fly poster for Benny Farr's band in Barnet, Martin asked Jimmy Prior in all innocence what an Orphean was. Jimmy replied, incredulously, "someone who lives in an Orpheanage of course!"

The great day of the Southgate engagement arrived. The seven members of Monk Hadley's Jazz Friars waited for the professional dance band to finish their first set. Jimmy had asked his band to wear white pocket handkerchiefs. This, he said, would show the other lot that we are a proper band, because we have a uniform. They discovered, on the night, that the 'other lot' wore white trousers and blue blazers with open neck shirts. Hardly a sartorial contest at all. Jimmy made no comment.

As the last few bars of the interval waltz came to a close, the saxophone player grabbed the microphone and said, "Ladies and gentlemen, we now have a special treat for you." He paused momentarily, clearly trying to remember something. "Please welcome Monk Friar and his Jazz Band to the stage." Ah well, so much for the clever play on words that Martin and Jimmy had spent some time formulating.

The self- assured, gig-weary musicians left the stage and were replaced by seven nervous young men. Jimmy, even though the leader, from whom an example might have been expected, found himself playing with his back half-turned towards the audience. It was the only way that he could develop any confidence. But all things considered, the half-hour set went quite well. Some of the audience had disappeared in the direction of the bar. This was not a commentary on the music, but simply because they needed to. The rest of them, ballroom dancers to a man (or woman) did, it had to be admitted, find it difficult to execute, with any degree of confidence, the recognised movements for the quickstep or the foxtrot. The tempos were either too fast or too slow. In fairness to the band, they had only previously played for jiving at the youth club, and this was alien territory.

But it was, for each of them, their very first paid gig. Ten shillings each! At that time, 1960, this would have been enough for four packets of cigarettes or eight pints of beer. The band was very shortly going to embark on a series of changes that would both secure its future and, contrarily, bring about its eventual demise.

CHAPTER 4

Ted

1960

"Do you know 'Sweet Lorraine'?" asked Ted Nottage.

The Rising Sun in Barnet High Street was a Victorian boozer that time had left alone, sandwiched between a bakery and an estate agent. In the public bar, Martin was playing the piano, squeezed in the alcove next to the front door. It was a Saturday lunchtime, and Martin had plucked up the courage to ask the landlord whether it would be all right 'just to have a little go on your piano?' It happened to be Ted's local, and a popular meeting place for Barnet jazz and folk musicians. Martin didn't know Ted, but was aware of his local celebrity status as a trumpet player and an artist. In his early thirties, he had a round, florid face crowned by a mass of unkempt curly brown hair. He was wearing a corduroy jacket with an open-neck checked shirt. A large, old leather belt encircled his ample waist, and his shirt was half in, half out of the waistband of his baggy trousers. Ted had a reputation as someone who went out of his way to be deliberately outrageous and he derived much pleasure from shocking middle-aged ladies at art classes with his sometimes pornographic oil paintings, boldly executed in his own highly original 'brutalist' style. You wouldn't find a Nottage original on any self-respecting living-room wall, but you may have possibly found one as a centrepiece in student digs, provided they were studying the arts or PPE.

Martin had already started playing when Ted made his entrance, heralded by a loud salutation to the whole pub. Having bought himself a pint, he stood next to the piano; seemingly appreciative, while silently assessing Martin's abilities. He took out a packet of Woodbines and offered one to Martin while he was still playing. Martin nodded and Ted placed it in position, then lit it for him. The smoke went straight into Martin's eyes but he was not going to remove the cigarette from his mouth. From his perusal of old black and white photographs featuring jazz pianists such as Art Tatum, Willie 'the Lion' Smith and Fats Waller, he had noticed that playing the piano with a fag dangling from the lips was de rigueur, and he was desperate to make the right sort of impression. He could hardly see any longer due to the smarting and watering, but at the end of the piece he was playing he modulated, more by touch than sight, into 'Sweet Lorraine'. Afterwards, while Martin was surreptitiously wiping the tears from his face, Ted asked whether he played with anybody and Martin told him about Monk Hadley's Jazz Friars.

"Where do you rehearse?" asked Ted.

"We used to rehearse at St Mark's Youth Club, but now that we are all at work and one or two of the band are over twenty, we're maybe a bit too old for youth clubs? We need to find somewhere else."

Ted grinned. "Go on, you surely haven't got anyone over twenty! Bloody hell!"

Martin found himself, not by any means for the last time, the unwitting victim of sarcasm and resolved to be less open-eyed innocent with his future pronouncements.

"Look," said Ted, "there's an upstairs room here which I sometimes use to rehearse my crew. Do you want me to find out when it could be free for you?"

So the Jazz Friars moved their base to the Rising Sun, rehearsing on Sunday mornings before the pub opened at noon. Passers-by would stand outside on the pavement and get some free entertainment. Ted often popped in to listen, sometimes with his wife – who was always clad totally in black – sometimes with another woman, more arty in her choice of attire. "What a guy!" they all thought. "How does he get away with it?" It seemed that he was determined to be as unconventional in his personal life as in other aspects of his flamboyant existence. It all paid off in the end though. Ted, a founder member of CND who was highly visible blowing his trumpet on marches, in due course managed to catch the attention of the media and during the 1970s he was often to be seen on TV, still scruffy, still smoking his Woodbines, still outrageous. That's what the producers wanted, and he was only too happy to just be himself.

At one of these rehearsals, the trumpet player, Bill – who was very different from Ted – made a suggestion. "I don't think that we are going to get anywhere with this name of ours. I can't see the jazz clubs putting it on posters. It *is* a bit of joke, isn't it?"

Martin and Jimmy, having been there at the birth, felt somewhat let down. How ungracious; not everyone was blessed with the gift of inspiration! Ted threw in his two-pennyworth by pointing out that most bands used the bandleader's name, even if they had a made-up name as well. He listed a few well-known bands, and added, "You know, I bet Acker Bilk realised, quite early on, that just continuing to call his band 'The Paramount Jazz Band' wasn't going to pay his mortgage."

So, after a very short debate, the band became Jimmy Prior's Jazzmen, just in time for the summer of 1960.

Martin had left school in April that year and, although he wanted to do something glamorous, such as working for an advertising agency, ended up working for Lloyds Bank, partly due to inertia and partly due to a parental steer endorsed by his headmaster. His headmaster had even gone so far as to advise Martin's father that advertising was a very dubious sort of a career, and certainly not suitable for an ex-pupil of Queen Elizabeth's Grammar School!

CHAPTER 5

An agent, a cornet and a rebellion
Late 1960

"Well, I can get some posters printed, and you need to think about a uniform."

Jeremy Turton was addressing the band at the Rising Sun, standing, as if to emphasise his status, a little way apart from the others, and wearing a suit and tie. To Martin it seemed faintly ludicrous that here was this guy, a stranger to most of them, holding forth in a dusty room above a basic pub, as if this was some sort of business meeting. It was all the more amusing because there was what looked like, and very possibly was, an ancient dog turd on the unswept floor, near his polished brogues. Martin's indoctrination into the world that jazz musicians inhabited had already conditioned him to be deeply suspicious of the motives of those who didn't play anything trying to muscle in.

Jeremy had been appointed band agent by Jimmy. In some respects, it was a good idea, as none of the band had any contacts with clubs, pubs and other likely promoters of their talents, whereas Jeremy said that he did. The first gig that Jeremy obtained for the band was in a pub in Tottenham, renowned for the occasional bit of bother on Saturday nights. Jimmy had adapted the uniform idea, worn by the Jazz Friars earlier that year, by arranging to have seven white handkerchiefs embroidered with the legend 'Jimmy

Prior's Jazzmen'. Jeremy, not unreasonably, failed to notice this and enquired politely whether they had forgotten about his request for some sort of uniform? Jimmy, without saying a word, pointed to his pocket handkerchief. Jeremy didn't seem to be impressed. "At the very least you should all wear the same coloured shirts," was his considered advice.

So, in this rather grand but faded Victorian gin palace surrounded by condemned terraced housing, Jimmy Prior's Jazzmen made their debut, to a lukewarm reception. The pub's built-in clientele was more used to hearing rock and roll than jazz. Afterwards Jeremy gave his verdict. "Well, this was considerably better than what happened here last week – that band didn't get paid!" Out of his earshot, and after only one gig, a couple of the band could be heard muttering about agents. After all, these were the people who would send you anywhere, maybe even as far as Watford, to meet whatever fate awaited, and would then deduct 10 per cent or more from the fee. Also, Jeremy had not exactly filled their diaries with future engagements.

Over the preceding few months Martin's obsession with becoming a trumpet player had continued to gnaw away. This was bolstered by the painful truth that all the action took place in the front of the band, both musically and socially. He had noticed how the girls looked up in admiration as the clarinet, trumpet and trombone players launched into their solos. Sometimes the admiring glances led to the promise of more to come later. No such luck for the four guys at the back of the band! He was determined that his days as a mere member of the rhythm section were going to be numbered. He would, somehow, be out in the front, enjoying the benefits. At times like these he seemed to conveniently forget that, for the last few months, he had a permanent girlfriend.

But, another huge factor was the state of some pianos that he was expected to perform on. They were almost unplayable; and this was worse than being totally unplayable because anything that sounded wrong was assumed to be the fault of the wretched pianist. In his dreams, he could see himself, shining trumpet in hand, sounding like an amalgam of all his trumpet heroes: Louis Armstrong, Bix Beiderbecke, Bunny Berigan and Kenny Ball; the star of the band, admired by the other musicians and adored by the fans. In a more realistic mode, he did not imagine that this fantasy could become reality very quickly. It would require a concerted effort on his part; a demanding but necessary learning curve requiring months (years? *no!* not years) of dedicated practice.

Jeremy, having become aware of Martin's obvious fixation, approached him after the Tottenham gig: "I have an old cornet at home. I had a few lessons but never really got on with it. Do you want it? I could sell it to you for £5, if you are interested."

Martin, without a second's hesitation, plunged straight in. "Oh really? Yes, great! – if it plays all right. When can you bring it along?"

Bill, the band's trumpet player, chimed in and said that he would have a look at it for Martin when it arrived. And so, one week later Martin was the owner of a very old silver-plated ex-Salvation Army cornet in high pitch. He did not then know that to play with any kind of musical formation, from a rock and roll band to a symphony orchestra, since around 1921 you needed to have an instrument built in concert pitch. But neither did he have any idea that this cornet was in fact in high pitch. None of this really mattered anyway, because Martin's first attempts at producing notes were not really in *any* kind of recognisable pitch. Anybody who has lived in close proximity to an embryo trumpet player will understand that their early efforts can be truly horrible, and uncontrollably loud to boot! Martin's father was no martyr in this regard and, after a short while, banished him to the greenhouse when he wanted to practise. Ironically, he had to relent and allow Martin back indoors after receiving complaints from the neighbours.

Jimmy Prior, having observed all this, advised Martin that he should not have any expectation of becoming the band trumpet player for, perhaps, a very long time, if ever, and gave him the benefit of advice from one who is both older and wiser. "It took me five years to learn the clarinet … so just think about that. Anyway, we need you as the pianist. Where would we get another one?" Martin was not about to give up though, as we shall see.

The gigs that Jeremy obtained were infrequent, low paid and in venues that were not necessarily looking for a jazz band. The band was beginning to get used to audience requests for pop tunes of the day and having to explain that they didn't play that kind of music. They did, though, have to learn 'Happy Birthday' and 'God Save The Queen', both of which they played in the wrong key, which found the audience switching their voices down an octave, halfway through, as to continue in an upwards direction would have been impossible.

It was not long before rumbles of discontent were becoming a regular feature of band chit-chat and, though neither Jimmy nor Martin were aware of it, there was even talk of a coup. But then, as is sometimes the case with tricky situations, chance made the difficult thing easy. Jimmy suddenly contracted a virulent flu virus which kept him out of circulation for the best part of a month. The bass player, Steve, had recently played with another band and Geoff, their clarinet player, had impressed him. So, on a purely emergency basis during Jimmy's absence, he was drafted in. Steve, without opposition or discussion, also took it upon himself to run the band on an interim basis. It wasn't long before rules were being proposed.

"I want to see all the brass instruments polished before the gig," said Steve. "I think that we should look smarter on stage too and, by the way, I don't think that we should take our drinks up with us."

It had to be said that none of these, especially the last one, was ever seriously considered. Jeremy, who perhaps should have been saying these sort of things, stopped looking in at the weekly rehearsal and only now appeared at the gigs to make sure that he was the one collecting the fee. There were, therefore, many opportunities for talking behind his back.

"Why do we need an agent?" asked Bill. "For what little he does, I'd rather take our chances and save ourselves 10 per cent. In any case, we have now been to a few places that might have us back. We only have to ask them."

One day, Steve announced, "I have been talking to the College of Fred, and they will give us a trial gig which, if it goes well, could become monthly!" The College of Further Education, to give it its proper title, had a Tudor hall within its campus built in 1573 that had been the original Queen Elizabeth's Grammar School, prior to the replacement building of 1932 that Martin had attended. This magnificent hall, with its original high raftered ceiling, oak beams and that lovely light red sixteenth-century brickwork, had started to be used, on a weekly basis, by the College Jazz Appreciation Society. It was becoming a great success with the students, and the place to be, and be seen, on a Friday evening.

"Great," said Martin. "I'll tell Jimmy when I call round to see him tomorrow."

There was a moment of silence, then: "Martin," said Steve. "We have had a discussion and decided to strike out on our own with Geoff instead of Jimmy. We're going to come up with a new name for the band, and Jeremy will become history. It's a bit awkward because we all know that you and Jimmy are great mates, but we would love you to come on board as our pianist."

Martin was shaken. He had always looked up to Jimmy as the driving force behind the band. These guys owed him a lot. Where would they have been otherwise? And the bugger was too ill to be there. Martin tended to wear his heart on his sleeve and, when faced with emotional upsets, this always made him too hot and bothered to collect his thoughts. This occasion was no exception.

He spluttered. "*What!* You can't do this. Jimmy doesn't..." He left the sentence unfinished, and then continued with more unfinished sentences. "How did this...? *Look!* It's just bloody not... Well, sod you lot, I'm not leaving Jimmy. You're all rotten bloody..."

Gradually, he regained some degree of self-control. "OK, I've calmed down a bit now. Yes, get rid of Jeremy, great idea but, come on, I just don't get it, what's all this about Jimmy?

The poor bloke's been ill for a month. You can't sack him for that – you can't sack him anyway, can you?!"

Bill, rather than Steve, provided the answer. "No, we can't sack him; we're all resigning. I find that I play better with Geoff next to me. Jimmy is a loud player and I can't compete. I'm not the only one who thinks this either."

Martin looked at them with incomprehension. He thought them all traitors, cowards and bastards. But he just confined himself to saying, "Right, you do what you want. I'm sticking with Jimmy. I'm going to call in on him on my way home, so you can all hand back the band arrangements and the handkerchiefs. They don't belong to you, they are his."

He added, as an afterthought, "Jimmy will finish up with a better band than you lot. Just you wait and see."

CHAPTER 6

The band re-forms

1961

"I say, I say, I say, my dog has no nose."

"How does he smell?" chanted the band.

"Bloody awful," said Benny.

It was another room above a pub, this time the Railway Arms next to New Barnet Station. Mr Benjamin Farr's Jazz Orpheans were doing an evening gig and their esteemed leader had decided to regale the sparse audience with one of his well-worn bits of music hall repartee. This he generally did when things were not going too well on the musical front which, on a typical Benny Farr gig, was more often than not.

"That's the second joke of the evening," Martin said to Jimmy. "The first was the trumpet playing!" They had come to see for themselves what the local competition was like, as they had not so far managed to form another band.

Benny Farr was of the same generation as Ted Nottage, probably in his early thirties, and had earned a reputation within the local musical fraternity as someone with whom you would only work as a last resort. They were wary of him; he was given to gross exaggeration, particularly when it came to the actual fee they might expect for the gig. This, coupled with the fact that his trumpet playing was not wonderful, had in the past made it difficult for him to honour bookings, as it was never certain how many band members would turn up. Once bitten, twice shy! In the end, he played safe by booking two clarinets, two trombones, etc. When, as often happened, both players turned up, he would let them both play, but halve the fee!

His saving grace was his charisma, and his self-cultivated image. This tended to impress those who did not yet know him. He had lank black hair, angular features with an aquiline nose and his accent was slightly 'public school'. He generally wore a blazer, with some sort of a badge on the breast pocket and a cravat. He owned a Triumph Roadster and this was often put to good purpose when offering to drive young ladies home after the gig. Often, the unsuspecting females thought that this was being done for purely altruistic reasons.

During the interval, Jimmy and Martin introduced themselves to the other band members. Benny was busy at the other end of the room trying to impress a prospective lady passenger by offering a ride home in his open-top car afterwards (the term 'ride' was a good one in this instance). The guitarist, Owen Meadowcroft, was an intriguing character. He looked for all the world like some kind of lounge lizard straight out of the 1930s. His hair was Brylcreemed and parted in the centre, he had a moustache and his smile was reminiscent of Terry Thomas. They were both expecting him to say, 'Good show' or 'Hard cheese, old man', but in the event, he disappointed them by turning out to be just an ordinary product of north London, much like themselves in fact. His playing was not at all bad so Jimmy decided to tell him about the recent demise of the Jazzmen, and then asked whether Owen fancied joining as part of a new line-up. He thought for a moment and said that he could not see why not; as all he had on, at present, was Benny Farr and this, he confided, had no recognisable future.

Owen continued: "Have you found a bass player yet? Because, if not, I'm sure Brian would like to do it. We are old mates and often play in the same bands."

Brian was summoned and said that yes, he would like to have a go as he too was disillusioned with the prospect of becoming a permanent fixture within Benny's band. He recalled one of their recent gigs, in a private house somewhere in Bayswater. The band had not long set up before it became apparent that there were only male guests present. This seemed odd, and then a couple of blokes were spotted in an amorous embrace in the corner of the room. Homosexuality was illegal at the time, so the musicians told Benny, quite seriously, that they should pack up and go home. Benny seemed unable to see why there was a problem and, after unsuccessfully pleading with them to stay, remained all on his own. Whether he was paid never came to light. No doubt he could have told jokes all evening rather than play trumpet all on his own although, should all else fail, he would have even done just that; no doubt preceded by some witticism such as 'I am now going to play the trumpet voluntarily.'

The following weekend Jimmy found a drummer, quite by chance, living in his own street. Now they just needed a trumpet and trombone. Martin's family was on the telephone, although it was not considered to be a necessity for every household back in the 1960s, nor was owning a car. So Jimmy and Martin drafted an ad which was sent to the *Melody Maker*, the essential weekly publication for jazz and dance band musicians.

It said: *Wanted, Trumpet and Trombone for Jimmy Prior's Jazzmen. Auditions, Sunday 3rd March at The Rising Sun, 71 Barnet High Street from 10 AM. Please telephone BAR 4636 if interested.*

"Mr Weston, there is a personal telephone call for you," said Mrs Darcey, the senior clerk on the foreign exchange desk at Lloyds Bank, Knightsbridge. There was a distinct emphasis on the word 'personal'. The bank did not officially allow personal calls to be received, other than in emergencies. It was Martin's mother at the other end: "Is there something that you forgot to tell me?" she said. Without waiting for an answer, she continued, "I have had call after call from trumpet players replying to an advert with our telephone number on it."

"Ah, sorry, Mum, I did forget to tell you. Actually, I thought they would ring in the evening when I was in."

Martin had been transferred from his first branch in Potters Bar to the prestigious Knightsbridge branch during that same year, following a very pleasant six weeks' residential training course at a converted country house in Hindhead, deep in the heart of the stockbroker belt. This had been more like a holiday than work, and provided for at Lloyds Bank's expense. Entirely different from Martin's experience at school, where he had been conditioned to be eternally grateful; just for the privilege of being educated! You weren't supposed to be enjoying yourself. The Hindhead centre had dormitories, a restaurant, a bar, a vast main hall with stage and grand piano, a gymnasium and a sports ground. The course work was thorough, but pleasant and with no pressure whatsoever (unlike the constant stress of trying to satisfy a queue of customers in the branch, and not knowing what time you would finish in the evening). Furthermore, the social side of the course was a definite plus. Most of the new entrants were in Martin's age group, male and female, and they had extra money to spend as all accommodation, meals and travel costs were paid for. In the evenings, Martin and a few new friends, including a jazz drummer who happened to be there, used to go into the main hall. Martin played the grand piano and Fred beat out a rhythm on the radiator. He had brought his sticks and brushes with him, but no drum kit. The others listened or jived for a bit. After that they would all walk into Hindhead's town centre and visit one or other of the pubs. Walking back in the dark there were many opportunities for mild flirtation. Yes, more like a holiday than work!

At his new branch, which was conveniently situated next door to Harrods, he had been put onto the foreign exchange counter – just Martin and another clerk, Stephen, working for Mrs Darcey. It was a self-contained little unit, screened from the main cashiers' area by wood panelling on all three sides. The Knightsbridge branch was one of the largest in London and had a staff of well over a hundred. On Friday nights, after the books had been balanced, all the younger staff, Martin included, used to go to Tattersall's Tavern, drink copious quantities of draught bitter and then make their way home. In Martin's case, this often meant catching the very last Tube from Knightsbridge Station. On one such journey, Martin found himself, still a long way from Barnet, and in desperate need to empty his bladder. He knew he could not get off the Tube, otherwise he would never get home. The carriage had emptied by the time it reached Kentish Town. Martin seized his one opportunity, opened the connecting door at the carriage end and mercifully relieved himself on to the track while the train was on the move. Later, he broke out in a cold sweat when he remembered, with much horror, what can happen when water makes contact with high-voltage electricity.

One of the other great things about working in the West End of London was that Sarah worked for the Country Gentleman's Association, not that far away in Jermyn Street. Sometimes, on a summer evening, they would meet in Green Park and perhaps walk down to the Embankment, cross Waterloo Bridge and have a coffee in the foyer of the Royal Festival Hall, soaking up the atmosphere. They both smugly felt that, for a while, they had become part of sophisticated metropolitan life.

Martin and Jimmy went to the Rising Sun early next Sunday to be ready for the auditions. No trombone players had answered the ad, but six trumpet players had said that they would be coming. Martin's mother had scheduled them in at fifteen-minute intervals. This was something that she had done on her own initiative, without consulting Martin, who hadn't been there to ask, in any event. Before the war, she had been the 1930s equivalent of a PA to one of the senior managers at Paton and Baldwin's Wool Factory in Halifax, so had been well trained in such matters.

Ten o'clock passed and no one had arrived. Jimmy asked Martin what he had told them and Martin had to explain that his mum had taken the calls. "Then they probably thought we were a kids' band, I expect," was Jimmy's somewhat unfair conclusion. By eleven, they had resorted to rehearing some new numbers with Jimmy, as the sole front line, when footsteps were heard coming up the stairs.

Then a familiar figure put his head around the door. "Where are all these bloody trumpet players then?" said Ted Nottage. "Even though unasked, unwashed and unwanted, I came here out of the goodness of my heart to give you the benefit of my vast experience and help you avoid picking the wanker."

They were all delighted to see him and stopped the rehearsal for a chat. "Looks as if no one is coming now," said Jimmy. "And we didn't get one reply from a trombone player."

"You know, I used to play in a Trad band before I saw the light," Ted mused. "My lot have not got much on right now. I could maybe help you out for a bit, if you want." To a man, they were gobsmacked. The legendary Ted Nottage was prepared to front their band. Gosh!

"I can do vocals as well. You ain't heard nothing like it! Look, I'll just pop back and get my hooter. Might as well not waste what's left of your rehearsal." Later that morning Ted told them that he had heard a very good trombone player over in East Barnet, and he didn't think he was in anybody's band at present. "Shall I get in touch with him for you?" he asked. "I don't have a telephone number, but I know someone who might. I'll ask around and let you know next week."

By next week, Donald 'Gus' Grimshaw had joined Jimmy Prior's Jazzmen on trombone. A phoenix had risen from the ashes of treachery; what would prove to be a much better band by far.

CHAPTER 7

The big time

1961

"Can you teach me how to play tenths?" Martin and Sarah were enjoying Saturday night drinks in the Alex, as it was known locally. Len Adams, the resident pianist in the Alexandra Hotel, New Barnet, for many years, had been a dance band pianist in the late 1930s and 1940s and was now, aged about fifty, to be heard every Friday, Saturday and Sunday in the saloon bar playing a selection of tunes from the 1920s up to, more or less, the present day. Martin thought that he sounded like Teddy Wilson, Benny Goodman's pianist, who had become Martin's latest hero thanks to Brian, the bass player in the new band. Brian had played him the Benny Goodman Trio recording of 'Time on My Hands' and Martin considered the four-bar introduction by Teddy Wilson to be absolute pianistic perfection. So much so that repeated listening to the first few grooves of the LP, followed by Martin trying to reproduce what he had just heard on Brian's family upright, had damaged the record and caused the needle to skip.

Len spread his left hand, from thumb to little finger and invited Martin to match his own spread with Len's. There was a good half-inch difference in favour of Len.

"You can probably do it, but you may have to jump the gap in some keys, particularly the flat keys, which a lot of jazz tunes are written in."

"How do you mean jump?" Martin asked. Len proceeded to demonstrate by showing how the little finger hits the bass note, lifts off, and the thumb hits the tenth above, a fraction of a second later.

"Do you know, Fats Waller had such an enormous hand that he could stretch to a twelfth?" added Len. "He never had the need to jump, and neither did Art Tatum!"

Martin had discovered the Alex a couple of months earlier after Jimmy Prior mentioning that a good pianist played there over the weekends. It had become a regular Saturday event for Martin and Sarah when there were no gigs to take him away. The pub, built in the 1930s, had a wood-panelled saloon bar where the piano was situated, and the vast majority of the weekend clientele went specifically to hear Len play; quite a few of them hoping to be able to sing their party pieces. Len had a sidekick, Tommy Taylor, who acted as a sort of unpaid master of ceremonies. He usually dressed in a dark suit which had seen better days, patent leather shoes and, even though he had divested himself of his outdoor coat, a long white silk scarf. His own contribution consisted of the sort of songs that you could hear on *The Good Old Days,* a TV programme broadcast from a music hall. He was not particularly good, but he managed to establish some rapport with the customers by doing a bit of a Max Miller – risqué jokes, suggestive comments, winks and leers. His favourite song concerned a woman who, before getting into bed with her lover of the evening, removed her glass eye, dentures, unscrewed her wooden leg and took off her wig. That was his forte! Tommy's main function, however, was to allocate a slot for every would-be singer. Having called them up, he used to announce: "First time's the singer's, second time's yours." This always meant that the song finished up with everybody joining in, and the guest singer being drowned out! Martin always got onto the rota as a guest pianist, and made sure that the chances of anyone knowing the words to his selection of jazz compositions was very remote. He did not want to be part of a sing-along.

At the end of this particular evening, Len made an unexpected gesture: "Would you and Sarah like to come round to our house on Wednesday evening? I expect Ivy will provide a little snack, you and I can have a tinkle on the piano, and we'll see if you can get the hang of playing tenths."

So began an association between Len and Martin that was to last for many years. Under Len's tuition, Martin did – fairly quickly – master the art of playing tenths, or stride as it is also called, and this did not go unnoticed within the ranks of Jimmy Prior's Jazzmen. They did not actually know what had changed, but could hear the obvious improvement. At home, even Harold, after hearing Martin practising on the family piano, was moved to comment favourably on what he heard. Of course, he himself knew all about stride piano, having grown up in the era of Carrol Gibbons and other household names of the day; a time when every dance band pianist played that way.

Jimmy Prior and Ted Nottage managed between them to obtain quite a few interesting and varied gigs throughout the summer of 1961. "We're doing a Riverboat Shuffle and another evening gig on the same day," announced Jimmy. "We have to get to Tower Pier for ten o'clock and we should be back around five. Then we will have to get the Tube to Southgate and we're on at eight." Only Brian, the bass player, owned a car, a rather wonderful 1934 Triumph Gloria. Martin was not allowed to use the Ford 100E for band purposes, so the rest of the band were totally reliant upon public transport, and the willingness of the others to carry bits of the drummer's equipment as well as their own instrument cases.

The great day arrived. Brian drove down to Tower Pier and parked on the cobblestones. It seems incredible now that parking in central London in the early 1960s was free. No yellow lines anywhere! Martin had brought his guitar along as there was no piano on board. He would double up with Owen. In the open air, the sound of an acoustic guitar can get lost, so this was a good idea. But, in any event, Martin wasn't going to miss out on this one, needed or not! Riverboat Shuffles on the Thames were prestigious events. All the main bands were doing them: Barber, Ball, Bilk, Lightfoot, Welsh, etc. Usually more than one band was booked so that they could have an on-off rota. Sometimes the boat went to Margate, sometimes up and down the Thames. The bar was opened just as soon as the boat set sail, and remained open all day!

The sound of music played over water has an ethereal, almost haunting quality of its own. It's very difficult to explain, but it can't be replicated indoors. On this sunny day, Jimmy's band was sharing the musical duties with another band. It was a trio: clarinet, banjo and sousaphone. One hour on, one hour off. This way, there was never a time without music except when entering a lock. A British Waterways bylaw forbids music in locks, presumably on the basis that a boat could spend up to half an hour navigating the lock and the music might upset the nearby residents. On this day, the boat arrived at the first lock in the middle of Jimmy's stint, thus cutting short their set. Ted Nottage was delighted with the unexpected extra drinking time.

"Why you no pray in rock? Why you no pray in rock?" an extremely agitated Japanese gentleman demanded, having forced his way through the throng and confronted Ted.

"Risten, pirrock," said Ted. "Not arrowed to pray in rock, sirry Blitish byraw!"

The afternoon wore on; by now it was half past three and the boat was nearing Hampton Court. "When are you going to turn around?" Jimmy asked the captain.

"Oh, in about another two hours. We're aiming to get back by about ten." There followed an anxious discussion between Jimmy, most of the rest of the band, the captain and the representative from the booking agency, who was there, enjoying a free day out, as his company had arranged the event.

"We were told that we would be back by five, and we *do* need to be, because we have another gig to get to." Usually, under these sort of situations, musicians are treated as no more significant than hired casual labour, rather than the star entertainers they believe themselves to be, and as a rule get nowhere at all by complaining. Amazingly, against all their expectations, the guy from the booking agency told the captain that the original arrangement was as Jimmy had stated, and that he had not thought it necessary to advise Jimmy of the changed timings, being unaware that the band had a later gig to get to. So, could the captain please pull in at Hampton Court so that the band could find their own way back? He then was left with the unenviable task of asking the clarinet trio whether they minded playing for a bit longer, and with reduced breaks, probably for no more money. Support and assistance such as this from the generally untrusted 'parasites' was, as Martin and the others would come to realise over the years, exceedingly rare, although in this instance they all had to pay for their rail fares back to central London, so it wasn't exactly unbridled generosity. Somehow, they did manage to get to the evening gig. This involved humping an entire drum kit and a double bass on and off trains, and up and down staircases and escalators. Thankfully, back in 1961, there were no automatic barriers to navigate.

There were lots of good gigs; some well-paid, some not so well. The band was doing all right, without any help from an agent, but with considerable help from a short-lived phenomenon known as the Trad Boom. They just could not lose out that year. Trad Jazz was being played on all radio stations, it was in the hit parade, and its hour had definitely arrived. It was suggested back then, without too much exaggeration, that if you knew the right way to hold your instrument you would probably get some work.

The most prestigious gig they ever obtained was in the late summer. They were to play for an evening barbecue at a country club in Hertford. The tickets, as they subsequently discovered, were £7 each, the equivalent of half a week's wages for a good deal of the population. The band had been offered a fee of £35, plus free food and drinks for a four-hour gig. This was a fortune for bands at the level of Jimmy Prior's Jazzmen. The chaps were under instruction to get there with plenty of time to spare, and to dress smartly. Ted exercised his discretion when it came to the last instruction, and took no notice of it at all. He had his reputation to preserve; they could take him as he was, or not at all. The organisers had decorated a very large outbuilding, not far from the clubhouse, with banners, balloons and bales of hay for the seating. They had built a stage and had provided a piano and PA.

Martin removed the front panel from the piano, to give more volume. The band experienced great difficulty in tuning to it, as it was a quarter of a tone flat. They were not at all happy with having to pull their tuning slides out a long way, and retune every string on the guitar and bass, but what else could they do about it? Eight o'clock arrived. "Right," said Jimmy, "we'll kick off with Indiana." He banged his right foot on the floorboards; one, two, one two three four. Within the first few seconds, one of the hammers, having been struck, detached itself from the piano mechanism and flew away over Martin's right shoulder. By the time the tune had progressed as far as the trumpet solo, a further three hammers had suffered the same fate. When the tune had ended, Martin picked up the truncated hammers and discovered that they had been broken at an earlier date and glued back on to the remainder of the stems. After further inspection, at least ten more hammers were seen to be in this condition; all ready to part company with the piano, any minute now. It would not be long before Martin had not only an out of tune instrument, but a completely unplayable one. Jimmy, supported by Ted, made a beeline for the organiser of the event and explained the problem. Initially, he could not care less. "Right," said Jimmy, "in that case we have no option but to pack up and go." This was, of course, a bluff. The band was never going to give up this enormous fee that easily. It did the trick though. The promoter did not take long to realise the implication of having no jazz band for a barbecue that had specifically been advertised as a jazz event. The thought of a hundred people all demanding a refund of their £7 no doubt dominated his mind, to the exclusion of all else.

"Well, look," he said. "There is another piano in the clubhouse. But, unfortunately, our resident pianist will be playing it in the bar tonight. The only thing that I can suggest is that we swap the pianos. There is a motorised truck in the stable and if you chaps could give a hand, I'm sure we can do it." When the band pushed the wreck of a piano into the clubhouse bar, the resident cocktail-style pianist was already in full flow, playing, as Martin quickly noticed, a rather good Bechstein upright. Everybody in the bar was in black tie and Ted was receiving some disapproving looks for his scruffy appearance. This prompted him to become even more disreputable by scratching himself in the groin area. It was the event organiser who had the unenviable task of explaining to the house pianist why the pianos had to be exchanged. Not being a musician, he simply hinted that, for some technical reason, the jazz band couldn't use it.

"Apparently, they can't tune to it properly but it's all right otherwise," he lied. "I'm sure that someone of your ability won't have a problem." With that, they very quickly manhandled the two instruments on and off the truck and made a swift exit. Only Ted remained behind for a few moments to observe at first-hand how the unfortunate pianist coped with what he had just been presented with. He told the chaps later that the expression on the pianist's face, as he checked the notes from top to bottom, this being followed with the departure of yet one more hammer, was a joy to behold.

One Sunday morning, in the Rising Sun, a visibly excited Jimmy ran up the stairs. "Guess what? We can do an interval spot at Wood Green!" Wood Green Jazz Club was the top venue within London, a survivor of the pre-war rhythm clubs. It only booked the very best; bands such as Humphrey Lyttelton, Chris Barber or Alex Welsh. They ran three sessions each week: Tuesdays, Saturdays and Sundays. Jimmy, Brian and Martin often went on Sundays to hear Alex Welsh, where an eagerly anticipated highlight was drummer Lennie Hastings' rendition of 'Auf Weidersehen', in the style of Richard Tauber. It was hilarious. He stood on a table, trouser legs rolled up to give a semblance of lederhosen, a half crown screwed into one eye as a 'monocle', and sang the lyrics in cod German. There would have been an outcry if, one week, it was omitted. The jazz, though, was of the highest level, good enough to attract the likes of George Chisholm and Danny Moss to pop in during the evening, just to sit in with the band.

"You jammy bugger," said Ted. "How did you work that one?"

"Well, I just asked Art, the organiser, whether there was any chance. To be honest, I was expecting no for an answer!"

It was to be the Tuesday after next, when Sandy Brown, Europe's finest clarinet player, would be the main band, and the interval spot was to be half an hour. For the next two Sundays, the band polished, to as near perfection as they could, six of their best numbers. They even went so far as to devise little head arrangements for the opener and closer.

Came the day! Sandy Brown finished his set and announced, "Ladies and gentlemen, we are going to the bar where we may meet some of you for a drink, although not at our expense, but why not stay here because we have one of your local bands during the interval – Jimmy Prior's Jazzmen."

And off they went, Sandy's lot in the direction of the bar, Jimmy's lot getting ready to start. They went through their carefully rehearsed repertoire, almost without a hitch. The audience seemed to like what they heard. The half hour was up, but no sign of Sandy Brown. "I think we'd better carry on. What shall we play next?" asked Jimmy.

Owen said, "What about 'Old Man Mose is Dead'? I've got my starting pistol!" This was a routine that they had worked out some time ago. Owen would put his guitar down, walk to the microphone and sing the chorus, firing the pistol at each and every opportune point within the lyrics, and a few more for good measure. It was, to say the least, startling. So much so that an inquisitive Sandy Brown put his head around the door, wondering whether Wood Green Jazz Club was re-enacting the gunfight at the OK Corral. As he was already five minutes late, he ushered his band back to the stage and said some very complimentary things about the interval band. They were all pleased as punch. In the bar afterwards, and well into second pints, they wanted to keep talking about it.

"I think we all rose to the occasion," said Jimmy.

Owen, seizing the opportunity for a 'double entendre', added, "Yes, and we are just going down now." It took Martin, alone among the musicians, a little while before the penny dropped.

It wasn't all roses though. The band was booked into the Warwick Arms in New Barnet one Wednesday evening. This pub had a bit of a reputation for the odd spot of trouble; it was the local used by some of the dodgier characters in the area, most of whom had been barred from the Alex, which was just across the road. However, the pub *did* promote local jazz, and Jimmy had taken the booking as soon as it had been offered. During the first number, the landlord walked up to the stage, arms folded and stared at them until they had finished. "You didn't tell me that you used *that* trumpet player," he almost spat out. "I don't want him playing in my pub!" Everybody came off the stage and walked to a quiet area at the other end of the room.

Although the Warwick had some pretty undesirable customers, they tended to vote Tory rather than Labour. This was presumably because, although Labour was the natural party of the working classes, some of the criminal classes considered that there was no benefit in sharing things with others. A little while ago, Ted had managed to seriously upset the landlord and quite a few regulars whose political sympathies he had misread. One should not judge a book by its cover! In fact, to a man, they viewed anything left wing with contempt. So, Ted being sure that he was addressing the downtrodden workers, pulled no punches when, after a considerable amount of alcohol, he launched into a vitriolic onslaught, banging on about the need for CND thanks to the bloody warmongering, toffee-nosed government that we, as a nation, had been stupid enough to vote for. He went even further; advocating a people's revolution. He hadn't actually been barred from the pub for this, but when Ted had subsequently asked for a booking for his own band, the answer was a definite '*no*, you're a bloody commie troublemaker'.

"Look," Ted said, "how about if I drop out and let the

band carry on without me, if that's what you want?" At this point Jimmy interrupted: "I don't know, and I don't particularly care, what your beef is with Ted, but he *is* our trumpet player, and you gave me the booking for *my* band. You didn't say anything about which particular players I could or could not bring with me, so what's your problem, eh?"

The now visibly irate landlord said, "My problem is that I want all of you to clear out of my pub!"

The seven band members were standing in a semicircle facing the landlord. "OK, but we still want paying."

This was the final straw. It was known that the landlord had been a professional boxer in the past. "I'll take you all on if I have to," he said, fists clenched. The band didn't move.

Owen made things worse, deliberately. "By the way, have you got a PRS licence for that jukebox?" In the end, the band had no option but to call it a day. The landlord, incensed by Owen's veiled threat, went to the till and threw some money in Jimmy's direction. It amounted to about one third of the agreed fee.

CHAPTER 8

The seaside beckons!

Late 1961

"Martin, could you just pop into my office for a moment please?" Mr Baker called across the banking hall. The branch had just shut its doors to the public on this autumn afternoon. It was early October, and Martin had just celebrated his twentieth birthday. Mr Baker, one of the two assistant managers, asked a few desultory questions about things in general, including Martin's domestic living arrangements with his parents. "Good, good," he commented. "You see, the thing is that the registrar's department in Durrington has a large job on. It's a bonus issue, and it will take weeks of work, writing out the share certificates." Office computers were still some way off in 1961, and most clerical tasks were still performed in longhand, other than letters and statements.

A Lloyds Bank share certificate was a magnificently old-fashioned looking product, embossed with the black horse, gilded script, and produced on parchment-like paper. It would not fit into a typewriter and, in any event, the shareholders liked to see their name and number of shares written in ink, preferably in copperplate.

"They are trying to borrow about forty staff who, preferably, are unattached or, at least, don't have their own home to look after. Obviously, it will involve living away from home until maybe early next year and, it seems to me you fit the bill." Martin was not expecting this when he was called into the office. He had been racking his brains, trying to recall any of his minor errors that might have percolated upwards to Mr Baker, so he was both relieved and intrigued.

"Do you know where I will be staying, and are there any arrangements for going home occasionally, sir?"

"Oh, you needn't worry on that score. The last time we had to send someone down there, young Rogers in securities, he seemed reluctant to come back. Apparently, it was four-star hotel accommodation, free transport to and from work, free rail passes every weekend back home and, I suspect, a very good time indeed in the evenings, what with all the unattached young ladies billeted down there with the lads," Martin thought to himself, *hello, this sounds good!*

"Well thank you sir, when do I have to go?"

"Monday week. They want you to report to Hut 14, Durrington Trading Estate at eleven-thirty. There is a railway station at Durrington. Where do you live exactly? Can you get there on time, do you think?"

"Barnet actually, sir. Yes, I am fairly sure I can get there by that time."

"Jolly good, there should be a letter confirming all this to you in the internal mail, within a day or two."

Martin wasted no time telling the band what was happening and that, although he would not be around during the week, he would still be able to make any Saturday gigs, and the all-important Sunday rehearsal. Ted told him about some interesting jazz he might hear down there; he himself having spent some wild weekends in Brighton with one of his female art students. Brian, on the other hand, spoke in wistful terms about Beard's Sussex Ales and how lucky Martin was to be able to sample all the different local beers, unavailable up in north London. He was a beer connoisseur, long before CAMRA had ever been thought of. Brian was christened 'God's gift to the brewers' by Owen and, it had to said, he was no slouch when it came to downing the odd pint or four. Martin had to promise Sarah that he would not 'misbehave' when out of her sight. It was agreed that they would go to the cinema, or maybe the Royalty Ballroom, the following Saturday, when he had his first weekend back in Barnet.

Sarah had introduced Martin to the delights of the Royalty Ballroom a couple of months ago, when they were at a loose end one Friday evening and looking for something different to do. Sarah had been once before with a few girlfriends and said it had been a jolly good evening out. Martin was not bothered too much about dancing – he just managed to do the bare minimum necessary to get around the floor. Nevertheless, he liked Ted Beaumont's Band, particularly the trumpet player who, alone among the other band members, played a bit of jazz when the orchestration permitted.

The Royalty Ballroom was reached by crossing the roundabout outside Southgate Tube Station and locating a poorly surfaced, dimly lit service road leading to a cinder car park at the far end of which was the ballroom. It opened its doors three times a week to cater for young singles seeking either a good evening's ballroom dancing or, more likely, a girlfriend/boyfriend. Couples, such as Sarah and Martin, arriving together were rare, except for the few older couples who wanted to try out the complicated manoeuvres they had seen on TV's *Come Dancing*. After queuing to pay your half-crown at the cash desk and depositing your coat in the cloakroom, the double doors ahead led to the ballroom. Either side of the doors were staircases leading up to a balcony extending over three sides of the whole area. It was wide enough to accommodate tables and chairs and the bar was at the far end. Most of the males made a beeline for the bar and then the balcony rail where they had a bird's-eye view of the female talent sitting on the chairs which lined the walls downstairs. Once a suitable target had been located, and the next dance announced, they would get downstairs as quickly as they could, in the hope that no one else beat them to it. This process was repeated as often as necessary, until the man considered that he had found a potential girlfriend. Then it was 'do you fancy a drink?' and, with any luck, escorting the target upstairs to the bar area. The established protocol was that once the lady had consented to this, she was his partner for the rest of the evening. After that, who knew? Often a request for a date would be anticipated, considered and the answer already formed in her mind.

In the ballroom was a 'glitter-globe' which, as it rotated, cascaded pools of light, resembling large soap bubbles, all over the floor and the dancers. There were always spot prizes. The band would stop mid-number and the announcer would ask for the first person to come up to the stage with, for example, a wooden door key (a normal key for a wooden door), a pair of green knickers (two pound notes), the left shoe on the right foot and the right shoe on the foot that's left. This last one often resulted in the comical spectacle of male dancers hobbling around unsteadily, as they tried to swap their shoes over. The smart guys in the know did nothing at all and just presented themselves to the front of the stage. Martin's special favourite was a request for a gentleman to come forward 'with an old-fashioned centre parting in his hair'. There would be a slight pause, while several men were seen to be busy with a comb. The request would then be completed ... 'four inches wide'.

CHAPTER 9

Worthing

Late 1961

"Biggleswade! What are you doing here?" exclaimed Martin, with great delight. He had just come out of Hut 14, armed with a pack of information about the hotel he was to be staying at, meal arrangements, a map of Worthing, times of the charter bus service and last, but not least, the name of the section head that he would be working for. Biggleswade had been at Hindhead with him on the bank training course the previous year. Martin had hit it off with him right from the start. His sense of humour was dry, sarcastic and off the wall. They had written a satirical sketch together which they performed at the end of course review. This got a lot of laughs, even among the tutorial staff, who were mercilessly caricatured as blithering idiots in the sketch. Biggleswade was given his nickname by Martin in view of the fact that his real name was Royston.

"Martin, unbelievable! This is *indeed* a surprise. I assume you must be one of the lucky ones who get the four-star treatment; hotels, free meals, travel, etc.? I work in the Worthing branch, so I am just local cattle fodder. All I get out of this is one free lunch per day!"

Across the road was a pub resembling a caravan. In fact, the whole trading estate had a temporary look about it, like the prefabs Martin remembered seeing after the end of the war. So, as it was the lunch hour, Martin and Biggleswade sank a pint or two of Beard's Sussex Ales, while they had a long catch up.

That evening, Martin and nine other male clerks were deposited by the charter bus outside the Eardley Hotel on Worthing's seafront. This magnificent Edwardian building catered for a genteel clientele, some of whom were resident all year round. It boasted a vast chandeliered restaurant, two bars, a function room, a residents' lounge facing the seafront and thirty bedrooms. Martin was allocated a room on the first floor overlooking the back yard and the dustbins. Well, they weren't going to waste the front bedrooms on a load of 'students'! Nevertheless, it was vast, bigger than Martin's parents' main living room at home. In the middle of the room stood a double bed, bulky and ancient, standing about three feet off the ground. There was a wardrobe, chest of drawers and dressing table, all dark brown mahogany, and against the wall was a gas fire and next to it, a coin meter. Martin unpacked his clothes for the week, opened his cornet case and practised a little, to see whether he could still get any notes out of it. He would have bags of time between Monday and Friday for practising and was determined to return from Worthing able to play the thing properly. Perhaps he might even become Jimmy Prior's trumpet player when, as was certain to happen, Ted left to pursue his rather more catholic tastes in music. The first evening, following a four-course dinner in the hotel dining room, all ten of them went out on the town. They didn't get much further than the Connaught, a quite respectable pub along the promenade which happened to have a fruit machine and a grand piano. Before long, a few more of the new recruits joined them. The sexes had been segregated; an initiative bound to fail in its purpose. The males were at the Eardley and the Majestic; the females at the Cavendish. It was not long before Martin started talking about music; how he was learning the cornet, as well as being a pianist in a jazz band. One of the locals interrupted their conversation. "I heard you talking about jazz. There is a band over in East Worthing. I've got their card somewhere." He found it in his wallet and passed it to Martin. "Here, you can have it, I don't need it back." The card, in Gothic script, proclaimed 'The Union Place Revivalists, for Parties and Funerals'. A contact name and phone number followed.

The next day, Martin found a telephone box outside the registrar's department and made a quick call. "Hello, is that Adrian? Ah, I was given your card last night and I play piano. I am staying in Worthing for a few weeks and I wondered whether there's any jazz that might be going?"

Adrian, the trumpet-playing leader, explained that the Revivalists had no current engagements. Three of his band would soon be leaving, and he was considering calling it a day.

"Oh, that's a pity," Martin replied. "By the way, I don't suppose you know anyone who gives trumpet lessons do you?"

"I do indeed! He teaches all brass and reed instruments. His name is Peter Phillips. He lives in Preston Avenue, West Worthing. I haven't got his phone number, but he is in the book."

Back at the hotel that evening Martin found the local directory and used the payphone in the lobby. As he put the phone down he was excited with the knowledge that, in two evenings' time, he would be taking his first steps towards musical fame and fortune!

"What would you like to learn from me?" Peter Phillips asked, after Martin had introduced himself and explained that, although he had had a cornet for over a year, he had not really got very far with it as his main instrument was the piano. He further explained that he would be staying in a hotel in Worthing for several weeks, maybe months, and this would seem to be the ideal opportunity to get to grips with it, as practising at home was not too easy for various reasons.

"I would like to get a proper tone and a better range; it's jazz I am into – not really interested in orchestral playing."

Peter was in his late forties, a neat, balding man who had spent most of his adult life as a dance band saxophonist.

"Well, there are no guarantees, but I can certainly try to help you achieve this if you are able to practise for at least half an hour every day without fail. Can you do this?"

"Oh yes, I will have plenty of time in the evenings," Martin cheerfully confirmed.

During this first lesson, Peter explained how embouchures can affect the tone. He had established that Martin wanted to produce a sound like Louis Armstrong, and so he drew little diagrams of pursed lips and explained how a wider gap produced a fatter sound. This proved to be incorrect advice, which Martin never managed to reverse in later life!

He did, however, give Martin one piece of perceived wisdom for which Martin was eternally grateful. "Tone is mainly in the head," Peter explained. "Nobody knows how this works, but if you think of Louis Armstrong's tone as you play, something resembling it will eventually come. This principle applies to any tone that you might want to achieve." Only Peter Phillips, an unknown Sussex-based saxophonist, had ever said this, and Martin never read it in various trumpet tutor books that he later owned. Thanks to this, Martin was able in later life to reproduce an approximation of not only Louis Armstrong's tone but also Bix's and, much later, Chet Baker's.

The lesson continued. "This cornet of yours is in military band high pitch. Did you know this? You will never be able to play with anyone else, without an awful lot of valve-slide adjustment, and even then, it could be out of tune on certain notes."

Oh, bugger it, thought Martin, remembering how he nearly bit Jeremy Turton's hand off in his desperation to buy it.

Peter said, "Look, I could take it in part exchange for a decent trumpet if you like. I do know, for a fact, that the Salvation Army Band in Shoreham still uses high-pitch instruments, and I can pass it on to them."

Martin had not failed to notice the shelving above the picture rail which, on all four sides of the room, was stacked with instrument cases of varying sizes: the majority for alto and tenor saxophones, but a few clarinet and trumpet cases. Peter considered his stock for a few seconds and then reached up to retrieve a brown leather case.

"Here, this is a good make. It's probably about twenty or so years old, but it was a professional quality instrument in its day. This style of trumpet is not in vogue any longer, so you could have it for £25, let's say £20 because I'll allow £5 for your cornet."

The case was opened and Martin looked at a gold-lacquered, long and slim trumpet. It was, to his mind, *the* most beautiful, desirable object. Martin took it out of the green velvet-lined case and read the inscription on the bell which announced 'Buescher Truetone, Elkhart, Indiana'. The tubing of most trumpets follows a standard pattern but the designer of this model had decided, for acoustic or, more likely, stylistic reasons, to attach the main slide to the other side of the third valve. It made the trumpet look more streamlined and racy. Martin could recall seeing a photograph, from the early 1930s, of Louis Armstrong holding at arm's length and gazing admiringly at a very similar shaped instrument. This was presumably what Peter meant about it being out of vogue these days. There was a mouthpiece in the case. Peter invited Martin to have a blow. After a while Martin said, "Yes, it's a lot easier to blow than my cornet. Look, I don't have £20 right now but I *would* like to buy it if I can. Could I pay you in instalments over six weeks?" Martin was earning £500 a year, about £10 per week, but thanks to the free living provided by his employer while he was working at the registrar's department, had much more disposable income than usual. He had signed up for six lessons at five shillings a time, subject to optional extension if he was still living in Worthing after that. "Yes, that's fine by me," Peter replied. "Just don't leave the country!"

Martin got back to the Worthing seafront in record time, looked through the window of the Connaught and saw a few of his colleagues gathered around the fruit machine. He pulled up the collar of his raincoat, lit a cigarette and entered in what he fondly imagined was a nonchalant 'Humphrey Bogart' sort of manner, his new trumpet case clutched prominently in his right hand. Having ordered a drink from the bar he joined his new friends, desperately waiting for the question that never came. In the end, he was forced to say, "Do you want to see my new trumpet? I have only just got it." It turned out to be one of those unusual moments, when Martin found himself in the company of folk who weren't bothered much about music or musicians, and the display of his prized possession received no more than polite curiosity. He might just as well have been showing them his mother's hairdryer. Nevertheless, in his mind he was fast-forwarding to the prospect of playing somewhere in the Worthing area before the winter was out. He was certain that he would improve, week after week, with Peter's help. Indulging in yet another flight of fancy, he visualised the mesmorising effect his trumpet playing would have upon impressionable young ladies. *Then*, he thought, these philistines will understand what it's all about!

By the end of the first week, Martin had settled into the routines of the registrar's department and found himself in a small, congenial team headed by one of the permanent staff, Freda Bartlett. Freda was an attractive, buxom woman in her early thirties and she was the opposite of Mrs Darcey, his section head in Knightsbridge. Where Mrs Darcey was businesslike and almost without humour, Freda was not averse to a bit of mildly flirtatious ribbing, and always seemed to have the time to discuss anything and everything. She was not a clock watcher, and the day whizzed by. Martin's old mate Biggleswade was working in one of the other huts, but they both met up at the end of the working day and, more often than not, he would also turn up at the Eardley after dinner and act as a pub tour guide to the newcomers, as he had lived in Worthing all his life. He, unlike the others, was very interested in Martin's musical activities and let it be known that he had a ukulele, although he did, in all fairness, say that he wasn't very good.

On Friday night, before most of them headed for home the next morning, they decided on a pub crawl along Montague Street where there were eleven pubs in all. These ranged from basic two-bar Victorian establishments at one end of the scale to the Regency Hotel, which had a lounge bar open to non-residents – not at all suitable for a crowd of twenty-year-olds all bent on a good time! And a good time they had indeed. Biggleswade, blessed with an off-the-wall sense of the ridiculous, also had a magnetic presence that made him the natural centre of attraction. About halfway up Montague Street, already somewhat lubricated, they spilled into The Rigger, which had a single bar with a Wurlitzer jukebox in the corner. There were only four regulars drinking at the bar and the landlord seemed pleased to note the arrival of fifteen more customers.

"Is it OK to play the jukebox?" enquired one.

"Of course," said the landlord. "That's what it's there for."

Martin soon discovered that there was a smattering of Trad Jazz records – hardly surprising, as Trad was enjoying its boom period in the early sixties. He then proceeded to go through the lot of them. This did not go down too well with the four regulars, who would have much preferred to hear Chuck Berry. After Martin had selected 'Cornet Chop Suey' by Kenny Ball for the third time, the landlord suggested that it was time for someone else to have a go.

Biggleswade said that he would be happy to select a record and then proceeded to select 'Cornet Chop Suey' yet again. They didn't stay much longer in The Rigger!

On Saturday morning, the nine-twenty train from Worthing went to Brighton, where Martin boarded the fast service to London. Arriving home around lunchtime, he told his parents all about the great time he was having down in Worthing and showed them his new trumpet. They were a bit more interested than his colleagues had been, but for the wrong reason.

"How much did it cost?" asked his father. Martin explained that he would be paying for it over six weeks. This was grudgingly accepted but there were still more comments.

"You should be saving up for the future. You won't be living here for ever, will you?" was his father's advice.

"You could have used the money for a new suit for work," said his mother.

Martin, like so many of his contemporaries, wondered, for the umpteenth time, how on earth his parents' generation could have ever enjoyed themselves when they were younger.

CHAPTER 10

The poet and a debut

Late 1961

Martin was back at the Eardley Hotel the following Sunday night, having caught the last train from London. He had enjoyed an action-packed weekend, taking Sarah to the Royalty Ballroom in Southgate on Saturday night, where they danced close to the bandstand while Martin listened intently to Ted Beaumont's trumpet player, much to Sarah's irritation. Then off to the Rising Sun for the Sunday morning rehearsal; once more parading his new purchase. Ted had a blow on it and said that it would be good enough, even if it was a bit of a museum piece. He himself played a fairly new Besson and he said that he preferred the fatter sound that it made. Ted liked the word fat. He would use this adjective to describe painting, poetry, noises, beer, and even his first car. Jimmy had asked what make it was, to which Ted replied, "It's a great *fat* car, that's all I know."

On Sunday evening Martin and Sarah went to the Wood Green Jazz Club to hear Alex Welsh. Martin waited until the last minute before dashing to the Tube station. He just reached Victoria in time for the last train. Walking from Worthing Station towards the seafront at around midnight, Martin listened to the night noises on the coast; seagulls, the sound of the approaching surf, clattering of lanyards somewhere to the left. He felt the cool wind that came in gusts, the occasional sound of a car in the distance, and he noticed how few lights were on in houses and hotels. It almost seemed that he had the town to himself.

The next couple of weeks followed much the same pattern: working during the daytime at Durrington, more hotel food than any of them had ever previously imagined, early evening trumpet practice in Martin's hotel bedroom, and later on, more often than not, several pints of beer in the Connaught while some of Martin's new friends played the fruit machine for hours on end. It transpired that the only heating in the Eardley bedrooms was by coin-operated gas meter (as Martin had discovered on his first day). One of their party had found a way to open the cash box, which was only emptied by the gas board every three months. This stash of shillings became his 'float' for the fruit machine should it be needed. It is an immutable fact; the odds are always stacked against the punter and, as a result, an individual crisis was looming that didn't bode at all well. The only way out was to win the jackpot, and the only way to achieve this was by feeding yet more shillings into the fruit machine. Without this miracle, he was faced with the prospect of an unimaginable discussion with his parents after the gas board had notified the police.

Martin's trumpet lessons were paying dividends. By the third lesson he was playing duets with Peter, glad that he had learnt to read music thanks to his childhood piano teacher, Miss Baillie-Smith. He had done his daily practice routines with commendable diligence, and was now able to play a few jazz tunes, albeit quite simply and without embellishment at this early stage. Martin had also discovered that one of his colleagues played the piano. He was a bespectacled, serious-looking chap who wore the same sort of clothes as Martin's father: tweed suit, white shirt, nondescript tie and a Fair Isle pullover. This last item of wardrobe was definitely out of fashion by 1961. His name was Quentin and he professed to know nothing about jazz, as he had only trained as a classical pianist. However, most annoyingly, whenever in due course Martin and Quentin managed to have an impromptu rehearsal in the canteen at Durrington, he seemed to know exactly what he was doing with this 'alien' music that he claimed to have no familiarity with. He explained that it was fairly easy to predict how straightforward, popular tunes would progress. It was all simple stuff for someone who had Grade 8 with distinction, he added. Martin strongly suspected that this was all bullshit and that he was trying to establish some sort of superiority. Martin decided to test him by deliberately picking a tune that did not follow any kind of predictable rule.

"Here, Quentin, do you know 'Lullaby of Birdland'?"

"No, I don't know any popular jazz tunes."

So Martin sat at the piano and played just the first two bars of the melody.

"OK, Quentin, how do you think that it goes after this?" Quentin then sat down and played the next six bars exactly as George Shearing had written them. Was he a fraud or a genius? Martin had no doubts after this, although he never challenged Quentin about it.

Christmas 1961 was coming and the registrar's department was going to have a party in the canteen. Martin, Quentin and Biggleswade decided that they would play a few tunes during the evening. Biggleswade, upon being asked the question, repeated that he was not that good on the ukulele, but would try to pick it up on the night rather than have any rehearsal. Martin said that he would work out a programme of about five numbers – the only ones he had memorised on the trumpet – and perhaps they could all wear woollen ties with horizontal stripes as a uniform.

Meanwhile, another weekend had started and Martin was sitting at a window table on the Southern Electric Express from Brighton to London Victoria. Those dark green British Railways trains looked very smart, and Martin felt a little smug, thinking how he was enjoying the same kind of expensive commute as the City stockbrokers, some of whom, if appearances were anything to go by, were occupying the same carriage.

Passing a recently ploughed field, somewhere near Burgess Hill, he marvelled at the sights that only nature, at its best, can provide. The slick brown furrows positively glistened in the weak December sunlight; the rows were as parallel as lines on a ruled notepad, and there was not a bit of green in sight for acres. Even the trees were bare. He picked up his biro, rifled through his bag for some paper to write on, and began:

Mud rutted incision gleaming white and wet
In the weak sun of December
A solitary crow surveys the carnage
From a bare branch of a winter tree...

He gave up at that point. Simply could not think how to continue. Poetry was not a mainstream passion of Martin's but, on the odd occasion, when he was in the right mood, he could produce something worth reading out. He remembered that, in his last year at school, they were all asked to produce a poem for English homework. His started:

The schoolmaster wends his weary way home
He lives near the Aerodrome.

Martin could not recall how it continued, but did remember that it produced hoots of laughter from, not only the boys in his form, upper sixth science, but Mr Clarke himself.

The muse was still with him by the time the train reached Haywards Heath, so he started again:

Gaunt doorway and rickety stair
Leads to thick smoke and gin soaked air
Golden notes beyond compare
Who is this genius, and from where?
Women lusting for this Angel man,
He: modest, horn pointing down
Eyes shut, oblivious to all
Save the need to create, create, create.
Chicago and nobody sleeps,
Bix, and beauty is born.

He felt quite pleased with this and could not wait to show it to Ted Nottage, who had recently taken up with the Poetry and Jazz Movement, a new form of expression where would-be poets would read their offerings (mainly to other would-be poets) accompanied by the outpourings of unshackled jazz (supposedly sympathetically).

Later that weekend Ted expressed his professional

opinion of Martin's inspirational poem. "Pretentious bollocks," he proclaimed!

As the Jimmy Prior Band was leaving the Rising Sun, down the back stairs and through the public bar, the landlord called Jimmy over: "I've got some news for you. The brewery, Taylor Walker, is selling off the building after Christmas, so you can have the room up until then but you might want to find somewhere else for your practising as soon as you can."

"Oh, that's a bugger," said Jimmy. "What brought all this on? I thought the pub is generally quite busy."

"Oh yes, business is good here, but they have other pubs in the area and the price they are getting for this is unbelievable."

It was true, Barnet had dozens of pubs just in its town centre alone. Most of the major breweries had at least two outlets. In the days of stagecoaches, Barnet was the first stop from central London, where travellers found accommodation for the night and the horses were rested. It took many years of pub closure during the 1970s and 1980s before Barnet's High Street resembled the norm for a town of a similar size. Martin recalled one evening earlier that year when he had met up with Doug Fisher, his old schoolfriend, who now worked for ITV as a cameraman. They had started at the bottom of the hill at the Queen's Head. Then they proceeded to the Old Red Lion, the Red Lion, the Mitre, the Crown and Anchor, the Bull, the King's Head, the Star and, finally, the Rising Sun, where Martin introduced Doug to the landlord. He said, "Thish ish my old shoomate, s'Tug." They could not proceed any further as, by that time, the 'Plimsoll line' had been well and truly overtaken; in fact, the 'ship' had almost sunk. So they missed out on sampling the beers in the Albion and ten other pubs. It was a valiant effort though, almost equalling the famous Cambridge run; a challenge for the undergraduates.

After the landlord's bombshell, the band decided to stay in the pub, have a drink and exchange ideas about a new rehearsal room. Ted seized the opportunity to say that he was not sure how much longer he might be able to stay with Jimmy as things were just beginning to look up for his own band, after several months without a gig. "So," he continued, "wherever you decide to go, don't worry about me."

Geographically, the band members were scattered, from Potters Bar at one extreme, to Southgate, at the other. Ted, of course, lived just around the corner from the Rising Sun, and it was his local. Jimmy lived in East Barnet and he mentioned a cafe, at the corner of the main road and his own. "I know that it has an upstairs room with a balcony as well. Might even be able to turn it into a jazz club." Nobody else had any suggestions, so it was agreed that some of the band would meet up there next Saturday morning for a chat with the proprietor.

Martin spent Sunday evening with Sarah at the Queen's Head, at the bottom of Barnet Hill. In the saloon bar at the back of the pub they had, as was almost the norm back in the 1950s and 1960s, a resident pianist and, in this case, a drummer too. They occupied most of the small stage at the side of the bar. It was much the same sort of a set-up as in the Alex, where Martin and Sarah first met the legendary pianist Len Adams, as there seemed to be an open invitation to anyone wishing to demonstrate their prowess, or lack of it, as a budding 'Frank Sinatra'. Martin wasted no time in asking whether it would be all right for him to do a number on trumpet. The band was not aware of this, but it was to be Martin's first ever public performance on this instrument. He played 'I Can't Give You Anything but Love, Baby', one chorus trumpet, one for the pianist and then a final trumpet chorus. He did not try to do anything fancy (he would not have been able to, in truth). He just stuck to the tune. When he finished, to gratifying applause, he reflected that he had only made about half a dozen mistakes, and that he was very nearly in tune with the piano. "Well done, youngster," said the pianist through the side of his mouth that was not holding his fag in place. "Come again any time." Martin said goodbye to Sarah at High Barnet Tube Station and, in his mind, relived the performance time and time again all the way back to Worthing.

Getting off the train at around midnight a curious thing happened. Walking past the station exit was a guy clad in a duffel coat with long hair and a beard carrying a trumpet case. Martin could just see the wording on the case sticker 'The Union Place Revivalists'. He called to the guy, "Excuse me, are you Adrian?" It was indeed Adrian, the voice at the end of the telephone who had given him Peter Phillip's name as a trumpet teacher. Martin told him about the lessons and the instrument that he had bought from Peter.

"Ah yes," said Adrian. "He generally likes to make a sale. That's how I got mine!" They agreed to meet up during the week. Adrian said that the place to drink was East Worthing; where all the 'real people' lived. He added that he had little time for the 'nouveaux', most of whom pronounced the name of the place where they lived as Wahthing. A good end to a great day, thought Martin, as he bid Adrian farewell.

CHAPTER 11

The real people and a middle-aged tart

Late 1961

Christmas 1961 was now just one week away and there was a festive buzz in the air. Every evening seemed to assume a seasonal importance unlike any other time of the year; a pressing need for it to be crammed with thrills for those, like Martin, who were barely out of their teens and parental discipline. "It's a middle-aged tart," Biggleswade explained to Martin. They were making plans during Monday's lunch break for the trip to Brighton that evening.

"Eh, what?" said Martin, puzzled, in reply.

"Well, look, it says to you; 'Here I am, slightly glittering but without any depth: a Royal Pavilion that looks like a psychiatrist's nightmare; not just one, but two piers; an ice hockey stadium; a race track; the first club in Britain featuring the twist (a new dance craze); a Chinese jazz club run by someone called Uncle Bonny; a couple of dirty bookshops; a nudist beach...' Need I go on? It's also the number one choice of a town to go to for a dirty weekend."

"It's not even pretending to be respectable like Worthing, Bath or Cheltenham," he continued. "Yes, it's a middle-aged tart of a town!"

The slow train from Worthing to Brighton, passing through Shoreham-by-Sea, took half an hour. Martin checked the timetable for the last train back to Worthing and then the two of them made their way down to the Central Pier where, just by the traffic roundabout, stood the Brighton Aquarium. Here, below ground level, the Chinese jazz club operated every Monday night. Members could take one guest, otherwise you had to enrol before being admitted. This was standard practice for every jazz club Martin had visited. The membership cards were always thick cardboard, about three and a half inches by two, printed with the club's name and, sometimes, an artistic logo, leaving a dotted line for the member's name and membership number. Martin already had a couple of such in his wallet – one from Barnet and the other from Wood Green. Having both paid their half-crown combined membership and admission fee, they entered this underground dance hall and quickly found the bar. The beer was Harvey's Sussex Bitter, brewed in Lewes. Biggleswade expressed the view that the nearer the pub or bar to the brewery, the finer the ale. This completely unscientific principle was accepted without question by Martin, prompting him to take deep gulps and order a second round. Pint glasses in hand, they moved into the dance hall. The band was Mike Cotton's, an exciting young trumpet player who was, in the early 1960s, in the vanguard of all those competent (and some not quite so competent) bands following in the footsteps of the three Bs, Barber, Bilk and Ball.

Biggleswade began to expound on his theory of picking up girls.

"I have my own method," he said. "Most of us have no higher aspirations than to ask a presentable girl for a dance and to hope for the best. The one thing that we don't do is to ask the most attractive girl in the room for a dance, for fear of rejection."

"Yes," Martin agreed. "I can see that."

"Well," Biggleswade continued, "that is what I always do. I ask the prettiest one for a dance and if she says 'no' I turn around, raise my hands in the air, and shout 'Yes, rejection!'."

Martin considered this rather off the wall approach and said, "I don't know about the shouting bit. Maybe after about four pints, otherwise I wouldn't have the nerve."

"Of course," said Biggleswade. "Come and have another pint or two." During the consumption of their fourth pints, Biggleswade demonstrated his technique. He sprinted across the floor to one who must surely have been one of the loveliest girls that evening. She was observed rising to her feet and, one moment later, she was jiving with Biggleswade on the dance floor.

After the dance Biggleswade rejoined Martin looking rather smug. "Dead easy," he volunteered. Okay, thought Martin, clearly this outrageous system of Biggleswade's sometimes works. Plucking up the necessary courage, he strolled over to an equally stunning young lady and asked whether she would like to dance. She wouldn't as it so happened. Martin turned around and took a few steps towards the direction of Biggleswade.

"Rejection, rejection," he said, raising his arms and gingerly raising his voice a little.

One or two people gave him strange looks and the object of his outburst turned to the girl sitting next to her and said, "Drunk, I suppose. Good job I didn't dance with *him!*"

Another couple of pints each and another couple of rejections left both acknowledging that a) large quantities of beer do not improve the chances of winning the fair lady and

b) they would have had a much more productive evening by lowering their expectations. Another lesson learnt, thought Martin.

The following day Martin had his fifth trumpet lesson from Peter Phillips, the last one before Christmas.

"I played a number with a pianist and drummer back home in Barnet last weekend," Martin volunteered. "Also, I am going to play with a trio at the staff Christmas party on Friday."

Peter said that he was pleased for Martin and asked how it went in Barnet.

"Well, I didn't make many mistakes and I thought that I was nearly in tune with the piano."

Peter reminisced about his own early days as a beginner, and added, "Of course, in my day we always carried the sheet music with us. Playing tunes by ear was a skill that took most of us some time to develop. You are lucky to be able to do this right from the start. You will find that the next time that you play the same tune by ear you will make fewer mistakes. Believe me, I know. Now I am going to teach you how to tune up properly."

"Play me your note A." Martin duly obliged, after which Peter struck the same note on the piano. Martin's note was sharp in comparison. "Now you can adjust to that. What many musicians don't realise is that, by doing it the other way around, i.e. by playing the A on the piano first, you can blow your note in tune, particularly with a brass instrument. It's all in the head. You then think that you are in tune but you are in fact forcing your notes, upwards or downwards, to the correct pitch. This is the quickest way to ruin your lip because it is working overtime, constantly making these unnecessary adjustments. You won't find this piece of advice in any published trumpet tutor."

Martin reflected, for the second time, how lucky he was to have found Peter, or more correctly, to have been steered in his direction. At the end of the lesson Peter wished Martin a Merry Christmas and enquired whether after the next and final lesson he would still be living in Worthing. Martin confirmed that it seemed likely that there was another two months' work and he would enrol for more lessons in the new year.

The following evening Martin had arranged to meet Adrian, the leader of the Union Place Revivalists, in the Anchor, a pub in East Worthing where he had been assured the real people congregated. The dark green Southern Region station name board announced East Worthing. Martin alighted, exited the modest station, and turned left into Station Road where he found the Anchor after 200 yards. It certainly looked as if it served a different class of customer. Whereas all the central Worthing pubs had a sort of coastal charm, this one just looked the same as the terraced houses either side of it. If it wasn't for the pub sign, it might well have been mistaken for somebody's modest dwelling. Inside there was gas lighting – a great rarity, even back in the sixties. The simple bar had two handpumps: Beard's Bitter and Mild. Adrian was perched on a bar stool chatting to the landlord. The few customers turned their heads as Martin entered and Adrian bid him welcome. Martin took a cursory look around him. Two men wearing overalls were playing darts; another, shabbily dressed, was reading the *Daily Mirror* football page, smoking a roll-up and coughing intermittently. On the counter was a cracked plastic cover on top of a plate which contained miniature pork pies.

"What's your poison?" enquired Adrian. Martin said he would have a pint of bitter, which the landlord pulled up by handpump. Most of the pubs in Worthing had converted to pressurised beer, but clearly not here, where the real people lived! The landlord, a florid-faced man in his early sixties, with a bulbous drinker's nose, asked whether Martin was from around these parts. Martin explained, briefly, that he lived in Hertfordshire but was temporarily working in Durrington.

"Ah yes, you must work for Lloyds Bank then. Without them, Durrington would be a ghost town." Martin confirmed that, yes, he did indeed work for them.

Adrian gestured towards an empty table and they both moved across the room and sat down. "Well, how about that then!" said Adrian. "You, a member of the capitalist class. How does that fit in with being a jazz trumpet player?"

Martin laughed and explained that he was merely a lowly paid clerk, in all probability worse off than everybody in the bar that evening. Adrian said that he was training to be a teacher and was existing off a grant. This pub was his local and he loved it.

"Genuine working-class boozer," he explained. "You won't see any of the 'Wahthing darling' lot in here, ever! East Worthing is the only place to be, believe me."

Adrian reminded Martin of a younger version of Ted Nottage. He chatted away to him about the Barnet jazz scene and asked whether Adrian might have heard of Ted. "Rings a bit of a bell," Adrian mused. "Is he anything to do with CND?" Martin affirmed that he was one of the founder members. "That's it then. It must have been him playing the trumpet on this year's Aldermaston March. Round face, curly hair, scruffy, about five-foot-ten?"

"Yes, that's him," Martin replied. The two trumpet players moved on to a deep discussion about the difficulties of mastering the trumpet and the jazz scene down in Sussex, which was primarily centred in Brighton. Adrian talked with some passion about the Union Place Revivalists and told Martin that they were all beginners, but totally dedicated to the purity of real New Orleans jazz. When Martin explained that he was very much into Teddy Wilson, Benny Goodman, Louis Armstrong, Bunny Berigan and, above all, Bix Beiderbecke, Adrian was a little taken aback. "No, that's not the real jazz; these guys have all prostituted their art for the sake of money and fame. They have turned commercial, moved away from their roots, and their integrity." Martin considered that there was little future in trying to become a proper musician if by giving the public what it wanted, you would end up becoming a musical pariah in the eyes of Adrian. Perhaps Adrian's idea of a perfect world would be playing to yourself in your front room!

He also wondered how Adrian had assumed that someone such as Bunny Berigan was even aware of very early New Orleans jazz. He grew up in Wisconsin and played with his high school band. That's where his roots lay. He reflected that Adrian's view of jazz was not far removed from religious fervour, and was based on folklore rather than common sense. However, he had the presence of mind to change the subject.

"I am going to be playing for our staff party on Friday with a trio. It's my first ever proper gig on the trumpet.

Then, after Christmas, I might look for a pub that would let us play for an hour or so. I don't mind not being paid – I just want to play. Any ideas?"

"You could try the Lion in East Street, just off Montague Street. We used to play there last year. It's not very big, but it would be fine for a trio. If you get in there, give me a ring and I can come along with some of the others to give you some support."

Martin thanked him for this and suggested that he might like to 'sit in' for a couple of numbers should the gig materialise. After another round of drinks and a few desultory words with the *Daily Mirror* reader which, in such a short time, covered a remarkable lack of common ground, Martin bid farewell to all and sundry.

On the way back to the Eardley, Martin reflected that, although his political sympathies were firmly to the left of centre, he actually preferred gregarious company and the ambiance of a more cosmopolitan lifestyle. He remembered Ted Nottage deliberately seeking out the manual workers in Barnet pubs and monopolising their conversation, but he suspected that his only motivation for doing so was to gather useful first-hand material for future use. He did, after all, have his reputation as a scourge of the pretentious middle classes to uphold.

CHAPTER 12

Ask for Blues

Late 1961

There was a buzz in the registrar's department on Friday afternoon. Some were excused work in order to transform the canteen for the party, which was going to start at six, straight after work. Most of the staff had turned up to work that morning in their Sunday best. The women, in particular, had gone to a lot of trouble to glam up. The effect of this slowed down the productivity of most of the red-blooded male clerks, which was not particularly well received by the management, festive spirit or not!

Freda, Martin's boss, looked particularly alluring. The tight-fitting two-piece costume that she was wearing emphasised her curvaceous body to great effect. During the day, she chatted to Martin about his forthcoming musical debut. "Will you be playing any Elvis songs, Martin?" she asked. Martin explained that he only knew jazz, and he was only a novice really.

He tried, unsuccessfully, to downplay what he would be doing that evening. "You know, it's only Biggleswade, sorry *Royston*, Quentin and me just doing a little spot. It's not the main event."

"It might turn out to be, Martin," said Freda with an expression on her face that Martin could not quite decipher. "By the way, why Biggleswade?"

"Ha, yes! It's the nearest town to Royston," he explained. This was met by a look of incomprehension.

Straight after work, Martin, Biggleswade and Quentin met up in the Portakabin-style pub opposite the huts. "I reckon we will have about half to three quarters of an hour to do. Shall we start off with 'Shine', then 'I Can't Give You Anything but Love'? I can think of the rest as we go along."

"Are you going to tell any jokes?" Biggleswade asked.

Martin realised that Biggleswade's interest in music was only secondary to his need to be the centre of attention. "No, I am not, but feel free to do so yourself."

Biggleswade smiled thoughtfully, and went on, "Oh, by the way, I seem to be the only one wearing the band tie. I made a special trip to Stroud and Whittaker's to buy it last week." Neither Quentin nor, significantly, Martin had remembered this idea, first proposed by Martin himself a few weeks ago. After a couple of pints, they made their way over to the canteen, where they hoped that the proceedings had got underway. It would be terrible to be the first to arrive. All the tables had been moved to the sides, leaving a reasonable space for dancing. There were bottles of beer, Liebfraumilch, Babycham and cider for sale at the serving hatch. There were sandwiches, sausage rolls and mince pies on one of the tables, but not to be eaten until the word was given. The majority of the permanent and temporary staff were already there and were chatting to each other in that strange, unnatural way that people who normally only ever meet in a formal work environment do; enforced joviality, that sort of thing.

The general manager, who Martin had never met, tapped the microphone and made a little welcoming speech during which he thanked the forty or so temporary staff for their efforts over the last couple of months in saving the day for the department. He then announced, "I understand that we have a special treat in store. Two of our temporary staff have teamed up with one of our own and have formed a jazz trio. They will be hotting things up for us very soon."

Martin's trio played six numbers in all. The staff danced and applauded every number. Martin reflected, once again, that Quentin appeared to know exactly what he was doing on the piano. All this bullshit about playing intuitively was just that. He was even more sure of this when Quentin asked him what the next number was going to be. Anyone who plays by instinct does not need to know this, Martin thought. Biggleswade made up in enthusiasm for what he lacked in musical knowledge. Martin came to realise just why Biggleswade had not wanted to rehearse. He was a blagger! His ukulele playing was pure guesswork. Sometimes it coincided with the tune being played; at other times it didn't. It did not faze him one bit though. He jigged around while playing, grinning at the audience, occasionally kicking his right leg into the air. He was just loving it. Between numbers, as threatened, he told jokes of an esoteric nature that left many of the unenlightened puzzled. His delivery was deadpan, rather like Clement Freud, so any laughter would be dependent upon the sense of humour of the audience. Fat chance with an audience of bank clerks!

Afterwards Freda beckoned Martin over to where she was sitting. "That was great, Martin," she said. "Everybody enjoyed it. Can I get you a drink?" Martin opted for a beer, which she bought for him. "Now, Martin, tell me, do you have a girlfriend?" Martin said that he did, and that she was his first ever as such. "So, are you serious, if you don't mind me asking?" Martin had noticed, since he had been working for her, a kind of motherly interest in his well-being. She had, on one occasion, given him some shirts belonging to her husband which had become too small for him. Martin explained that he was twenty and one or two of his friends were married already; so perhaps he should be thinking about it.

Freda then, of her own volition, proceeded to offer Martin some advice. "I was married at sixteen. I had a daughter straightaway and now she is married at sixteen. So here I am, soon to be a grandmother, just thirty-three years old. I haven't had the benefit of enjoying my late teens and early twenties. I only ever had one boyfriend – my husband. Now, I'm not saying that I am not happy. No, not that. It's just a sort of question mark as to what might have been. You are a good-looking young man. Unless you are really sure about your girlfriend, don't rush into anything just yet. I know I have had a couple of Babychams, which have loosened my tongue, so you might think I am talking rubbish. Maybe I am, but I don't think so."

By now, gramophone records were being played: Bill Haley, Tommy Steele, Elvis Presley and, in deference to the older staff, currently a Victor Sylvester Ballroom Dancing LP. A waltz tune started up. "Martin, shall we have a dance?" Freda unexpectedly enquired.

"Yes, OK, Freda. I can just about do a waltz."

As they took to the dance floor Martin smelled her perfume and was only too aware that his body was in close contact with hers. Furthermore, she was clutching him more tightly than he would have expected. To his embarrassment, he began to feel a stirring in his loins which he was sure Freda would be aware of. He tried to pull away a little, but she did not relinquish her grasp, not one little bit. "It's nice to dance, isn't it, Martin?" she enquired.

"Yes," gulped Martin, "very nice."

"Do you go dancing with your girlfriend much?"

"Well, we go to the Royalty Ballroom in Southgate from time to time, but I mainly go to hear the band." He heard his own voice speaking in an unnatural higher pitch than before, as he tried, without success, to will his enthusiastic member to subside.

"You know, tonight is an excuse for us all to let our hair down. After Christmas, all will be back to normal. Don't worry about work or anything tonight, Martin," Freda suggested.

Martin's thoughts were spiralling into overdrive. Surely, she wasn't suggesting...? No, perish the thought. Mental images of the lovely Freda naked on the bed had an even more marked effect on his nether regions. As he executed a turn... left, two three, swivel... he became aware of a very slight, but definite, wriggling against the embarrassing point of contact. This could only have been Freda's doing. Mercifully the waltz came to an end. After escorting her back to her chair, Martin thanked Freda profusely, then made his excuses and rejoined Biggleswade.

"Quick, I need a drink. Let's go across the road. It's safer there."

The following morning saw Martin on his way back to Barnet for a meeting with Jimmy at the Olde Teashoppe in East Barnet. None of the other band members had turned up, so it was just the two old mates, like many times before.

"Yes, we don't use the upstairs room very often. Just for special functions," the proprietor of the cafe explained. "Come up and have a look at it."

She unlocked the door and they saw several unlaid tables, a sideboard and, most importantly, a piano. Jimmy asked Martin to check it out, and it proved to be in reasonably good playing order, and in tune.

"Yes," the proprietor continued, "if you want it on Sunday mornings that would be all right with me, as we don't open that day. You would need to collect the keys from me and lock up and return them when you leave. Ten shillings. What do you think?"

Jimmy asked, "Is there any chance that we could also use it as a jazz club and open up the balcony at the end of the room?"

"Well, maybe. But first let's see how your rehearsing goes, as far as the neighbours are concerned."

At precisely the same moment both Martin and Jimmy noticed one of the ashtrays on a table. It was clear glass and proclaimed in blue lettering: 'Ask for Blues'. Jimmy beat Martin to it by a whisker. "What a fabulous ashtray! Any chance that I can buy it from you?"

"Just take it if you want it. It's only a pub ashtray when all's said and done." The blues that the ashtray referred to was, in all probability, some brand of cigarette or maybe Rizla papers, but this was completely irrelevant to two jazz musicians, for whom the 'blues' meant something far more important.

CHAPTER 13

Friday evening raving

Late 1961/early 1962

The following day Jimmy Prior's Jazzmen had their final rehearsal in what had become their spiritual home, the Rising Sun. Jimmy told the band about the Olde Teashoppe, and proposed they meet for their first practice session early in the new year. Ted suggested that as soon as the bar opened, they might as well pay their respects to their benefactor, the outgoing landlord, in the time-honoured way of helping him to get rid of the beer in his cellar. In the bar later, Ted, in his most stentorian voice, recited to the landlord and customers a limerick that he had adapted for the occasion.

There once was a girl called Gloria
Who was shagged by Vincent du Maurier
Jack Hylton, Jack Payne,
Our Vince boy again
And the band from the Waldorf Astoria

This was met with many loud guffaws, but not from Vince, the landlord, since his wife, Maureen, had just appeared at the bottom of the stairs leading to the living quarters and had clearly heard most of this. She may even have misheard, and thought that it was her name that was being sullied. She certainly looked sour, and her mouth was firmly shut and downturned. Ted had taken some poetic licence in awarding Vince the surname du Maurier, entirely due to the fact that this was the brand of cigarette that he chain-smoked. He was also aware that he had sailed perilously close to the wind in choosing the name Gloria, which could sound rather like Maureen. And anyway, as Ted later admitted, he couldn't think of a girl's name to rhyme with Thompson. "Bloody Nottage! You're barred. At least you would be if we weren't closing for good in two days' time." Thus spoke Vince, in a tone of as much wounded pride that he could muster. "As it is, I am going to overlook this outrageous slur on my character but you can bloody well buy Maureen and me two very large drinks." Ted, slightly abashed but still smiling, was only too happy to oblige. Maureen took her drink upstairs. Vince looked up the stairs to make sure that she was out of earshot. "Bloody funny, Ted, can you write it down for me?"

A little later, Ted said: "You know, I'm going to really miss this place. I have played my trumpet, drunk your booze, scratched myself, farted, swore, and all that you delightful people have ever done is to make me welcome. Where else am I going to find a replacement? It's the end of an era."

Indeed, it was.

One more round of drinks later, Martin noticed some very animated conversation going on between Ted, Jimmy, and 'Gus', the trombone player. It seemed as if, whatever they were discussing, was for their ears only. They had moved to the back of the pub leaving Martin, Owen and Brian still propping up the bar. The drummer, Alex, had already left, after just having a half 'to be sociable' as he was not a drinker. He had not even heard the limerick. Nothing, however, was said when they all wished each other season's greetings for the forthcoming two-day public holiday. All the same, Martin had a sense of foreboding without knowing why. Perhaps they had been discussing living arrangements. Yes, that must be it. Jimmy would be leaving home after his wedding next year and Gus seemed to have itchy feet. Ted had, for some time, run a kind of open house in his four-bedroomed Victorian terraced home. All kinds of interesting people had holed up there for a bit, so Jimmy and Pam, or Gus, might be looking for a bit of temporary accommodation.

★ ★ ★

The holiday came and went. For Martin, it was Christmas Day with his parents. A fairly uneventful experience, as was generally the case, other than Martin beating his parents at whist for the first and last time. Boxing Day was a much livelier event, spent at Sarah's parents. They obviously had a family tradition, alien to the Weston family, of stocking up with bottles of nearly every spirit and liqueur known to mankind, and proceeding to sample them all over the festive season. Then nothing at all for the rest of the year.

"Have you ever tried Advocaat, Martin?" Sarah's mum enquired. She poured this into a sherry glass and demonstrated how, having swallowed as much as you can, you had to scoop up the residue with your finger and lick it off.

Fascinating, thought Martin. Try as he might he just could not envisage his own mother demonstrating such a thing. This must be why Sarah was such a liberated woman and fun to be with. Sarah had given Martin *The Pictorial History of Jazz*, a book that Martin treasured for ever. In return, Sarah received a brooch.

All too soon working life took over once more and Martin found himself, and most of the other temporary staff, in the Connaught on the first evening back in Worthing. As usual, the fruit machine was in constant use, predominantly by Frank, the 'gas meter thief'. Towards the end of the evening he beckoned over a few of his closest mates, those who were in the know about the cash problem. "I am shit scared now," he began. "We have been here over two months and I worry every day that the meter is going to be emptied and that will be the end for me. I can't tell my folks about it. I just can't. But I've got an idea. Would you bet me ten shillings each that I can't do a midnight swim?"

"Don't be silly, Frank, it would kill you in this weather," said someone. The air outside was just about zero that evening. It followed that the sea temperature would be several degrees lower.

"OK, so it must be worth a ten-bob bet for each of you. It's my funeral! Can you put the word around the others that the bet is on, without telling them the real reason why I am doing it?"

Midnight found about thirty of them standing on the beach opposite the Eardley Hotel, which had just had one or two lights left on, shining dimly behind closed curtains. The wind had got up and the sea positively roared. It was a cloudy night and so dark that the sea was almost invisible, save for the windblown spray, white and foaming. Everyone was wrapped up in coats, gloves and scarves and there was a general sense of unreality. No one was going to go for a swim in this!

Frank very quickly began to strip off. Speed was of the essence as faint heart never won fair lady! Margaret, one of the fruit machine players, said "Frank, *Frank*, please don't do this. Supposing we just lend you the money you need. You can pay us back before we all go home in a month or two."

"No, sod it, I am going to sort this out tonight. Once and for all. And if anybody sees me even approaching a fruit machine again I want you to do a rugby tackle on me, or in your case, Margaret, some other distraction perhaps!" *Well,* thought Margaret, *desperate he may be but his sense of humour has not deserted him.*

Suddenly, stripped to his underpants, he ran blindly into the freezing water. Everybody followed him to the edge, listening to his shouts of pain and a lot of thrashing noises. He could just be discerned, a white form, in the near total blackness, standing up to his waist, about ten yards out flailing his arms about him. The unseen sea was roaring all around Worthing beach. Then he was down, swimming for his life; arms and legs going nineteen to the dozen. His head went under for a moment causing a bit of concern. Then he was up, running towards the beach as fast as he possibly could in the ebb and flow of the midnight tide. Twice he fell and quickly got up again. Someone was ready for him with two large hotel bath towels and assisted him in drying off as quickly as possible. He was shivering fit to bust and found it difficult to speak clearly as his teeth were in a constant state of chatter. Towelled dry, still shivering, he pulled on a sweater, trousers and his overcoat.

"Well, that was fun," he lied. "I'm off to sit in front of my gas fire for the next hour." With that, he ran back to the hotel. He turned and said, "You can all pay me tomorrow."

"Don't forget to put a shilling in the meter tonight, Frank," someone shouted back.

Towards the end of January, Biggleswade suggested that their Friday evening drinking sessions were beginning to lose their initial allure and needed spicing up a bit. He recalled some of the student raves recounted by his elder brother, recently down from Oxford – the sort of things that are described as hooliganism when linked to the working classes, but 'high spirits' if done by undergraduates.

And so began the famous Worthing Friday night raves. The first one was by far the best. It had been decided to meet, as usual, in the residents' lounge at the Eardley after dinner. Eleven of the blokes, but none of the women, were sitting around expectantly waiting for Biggleswade, who had to come over from his parents' home. The man of the moment duly arrived, carrying clipboards. "What I think is that we should visit most of the pubs in Montague Street and ask the landlords to answer a questionnaire. The questions must all be ridiculous. It will be a hoot, getting them to answer. All up for this?" he enquired. A general air of enthusiasm pervaded the lounge. "Let's have some ideas then. I can write them down and we'll take a vote."

After a lot of discussion, the following list emerged.

1. *Do you serve Pimm's number four?*
2. *Do you stock McConachie's Green Ginger Wine?*
3. *Do you provide saucers of milk for cats?*
4. *Do you have a skittle alley?*
5. *Do you have classical music on your jukebox?*
6. *Should tax on alcohol be raised?*
7. *Do you have a spittoon?*

8. *Have you a list of cocktails?*
9. *How often do survey teams pay you a visit?*
10. *Do you allow the Salvation Army to come round with a collecting box?*

Martin suggested that they say that they were from the Milk Marketing Board, being suitably irrelevant, and this was agreed. Biggleswade suggested that they split up into two teams and he undertook to copy the questions on to the second clipboard. While he was doing this, he inserted one more question into the list that the other team, not the one that Martin and himself were going to be in, would have to read out. It said, '*Are you a Jew?*' and was number four on their list. Handing the clipboard to the other team leader he said, "Spontaneity is the way to do it. You already know what the questions are. Just read them out without any kind of preparation. Question one, question two, question three; bang, bang, bang!" Political correctness and racial sensibilities were not a feature of British life in those times but, even so, Biggleswade was sailing dangerously close to the wind with that question. His sole purpose was to have a laugh at the other team's expense, without giving any thought to the landlord's reaction, either verbally or, possibly, physically. This was going to be an irresponsible rave when all was said and done. They split into two teams of six and agreed to take opposite sides of the road. There were a lot of pubs in Montague Street and it wasn't a competition as such. There was no prize. They agreed to call it a day at ten o'clock and meet in the Connaught for a last drink.

The first pub that Martin's team came to was very busy. It was difficult to find a gap at the bar to start the drinks order. Martin waved a pound note in the air and, being on the tall side at six feet one, caught the eye of the landlord who acknowledged, by a nod in Martin's direction, that he would be served next.

"Yes, lads, what's it to be?" The six pints of Harvey's were ordered and Martin, who had volunteered to be the first, took a deep draught before asking, "Excuse me, are you the landlord?" On receiving confirmation, he continued: "Well, we are all from the Milk Marketing Board and we are conducting a pub survey. I wonder if you would mind answering a few questions for us?" The landlord, a friendly looking guy in his late thirties, said that he was happy to oblige providing he could fit it in between having to serve drinks.

And so the questions began. In answer to the first two, concerning fictitious drinks, he looked puzzled and said that, although they may exist, he had personally never heard of them. Questions three to five were simply answered "no". Question six, on taxation, produced an "are you joking?" while question seven, about a spittoon, was a surprise. "Yes," he said. "It was part of the fixtures and fittings when I took the pub over ten years ago. It's out in the backyard going rusty." So still he had not twigged that this was a piss-take! The answer to question eight was simple: "This is a pub, not a swanky hotel bar. The only cocktails I sell here are mild and bitter and gin and tonic."

Martin felt it necessary to insert words of explanation when necessary. "Yes, of course, but this survey is being used in all types of licensed premises," he improvised. Question nine confirmed that this was the first time such a thing had happened, and question ten on the Salvation Army produced the reply: "Sally Ann? How can you stop them? Mind you, nobody pays a lot of attention. They shake a tin at you and sell the War Cry. It's all harmless really and, after all, they do some good work, don't they?"

As this last remark seemed to require an answer, Biggleswade, who up to now had remained silent, chipped in: "Oh indeed, they provide a mighty service to the nation. My great grandfather was General Booth!"

This last piece of fabrication startled everyone, and at this juncture the landlord began to smell a rat. "Um, you say you are from the Milk Marketing Board. I don't quite see how this survey has anything to do with milk."

Martin now had to use all his inventive powers. "Well, it does seem strange, doesn't it? But, believe me, the questions do have a bearing on our marketing strategy. We are only management trainees, but our boss knows what he is doing. It's all to do with licensed premises," he concluded mysteriously. This was met by raised eyebrows by the landlord who just smiled and said, "My pleasure."

As they left the pub Martin said, "I didn't expect to get away with that. Whose turn at the next pub?"

And so the evening went on. The survey team were getting mixed results ranging from, in one case, cynicism after questions one and two leading to a complete lack of cooperation, to another landlord, of the 'mine genial host' type, answering all the questions with a smirk on his face, while peering intently, albeit upside down, at the handwritten questions on the clipboard. "You are all wasting my bloody time. Do you think that I was born yesterday? If you lot are from the Milk Marketing Board and if this is one of their official surveys, I'm a Dutchman!"

As they sat down, well away from the bar, in order to finish their drinks, they could hear the landlord explaining to one of his regulars: "This load of wankers come in here, having a laugh at my expense. Well, they can all fuck off when they have finished their drinks. They're all wet behind the ears anyway. Bring back National Service, I say."

As they furtively made their exit the landlord spotted Biggleswade. "Here, don't I know you? You have been in here a few times before, yes?"

"*Osmorra, halpon pruzcha. Osmorra, lyfrique*," Biggleswade replied. He was of a moderately swarthy appearance and had decided for safety's sake to assume a phoney Middle Eastern language. It didn't fool the landlord though.

"Fuck off!" was his rejoinder.

Eventually the two teams, by now considerably lubricated, met up in the Connaught. Biggleswade could not wait to see how the other team had fared, particularly with the Jewish question. "We decided not to bother with the questionnaire. The landlord of the first pub we went into said he didn't want to answer any questions, and after that we somehow didn't bother… just had a pub crawl." Biggleswade looked for all the world like a sitting MP who has just unexpectedly lost his seat at a general election. Crestfallen and speechless.

CHAPTER 14

A bitter blow

January 1962

January was always a quiet month. There had been just one rehearsal at the Olde Teashoppe. That would have been unusual under normal circumstances, but as there were no gigs in the diary, there was no pressing need for them. Ted didn't turn up, and neither did the drummer, Alex. When this rehearsal came to its unsatisfactory end, and all the gear had been taken downstairs, Martin offered Jimmy a cigarette, and observed, "I don't know, it wasn't very good was it? Makes you realise how important the trumpet and drums are."

"Yeah. To be honest, and I meant to tell you earlier, Alex is no longer with us. Ted and I have found a much better drummer, and his wife sings – something sorely needed."

It was true: only Ted and Owen attempted vocals, one of them trying and failing to sound like Louis Armstrong, and the other sounding like George Formby.

"Well, shouldn't they have been here? How else are they going to learn our repertoire?" Martin asked, slightly puzzled by all this.

"Oh, it's just one of those things. They did have a blow with Ted and me last week. Things have to happen when they have to happen sometimes and, what with you being away all week, I can't update you until later," he offered by way of an apology. Martin suspected that his old mate Jimmy was holding something back and, unusually, he was not making eye contact with Martin. "Anyway, Martin, I have got to dash. It's that bloody Sunday lunch thing with Pam's parents. You're off back to Worthing tonight?" Martin confirmed that this was the case so Jimmy said, "We could maybe meet up next Saturday lunchtime over the road in the Warwick, if you can make it, and have a proper chat about the band." This was agreed, leaving Martin more perplexed than satisfied.

He spent the whole week worrying about what might be happening in the world of the Jimmy Prior Jazzmen. The lack of gigs, the sudden departure from the Rising Sun, but, above all, his own absence from Barnet for now well over two months, were unsettling. Uncertainty was something that did not sit comfortably with Martin, who still lacked the sort of self-confidence that could junk such worries to the back of his mind. On the contrary, he kept on imagining all kinds of scenarios, none of which augured well for Martin personally.

Every Tuesday evening, he had continued with trumpet lessons, and he felt that the time must surely be coming when he would be able to play at least one number with Jimmy's band. Didn't Ted say that things were beginning to pick up for his own semi-dormant mainstream band? Yes, he did say that. Suddenly Martin felt his mood shift from worry to anticipation. Just supposing Jimmy was about to offer him the band trumpet chair? It would be bloody challenging, and Ted would be a hard act to follow, but just suppose? Then he came back down to earth with a bump. Jimmy had not even heard him play yet, and it's no use pretending that you are anywhere near the standard that the band demanded, he told himself.

After his lesson, he asked Peter, "Do you think I am good enough to join a jazz band as their regular trumpet player?" Peter, always the diplomatic one, tried to explain that perhaps Martin would not yet have the sort of endurance necessary for a two- or three-hour performance. Maybe, he suggested, Martin could just restrict himself to half a dozen numbers during the evening and let someone else cover the rest? He went on to say that, in his day, you had to absorb all the finer points of instrumental technique: working for an eternity on developing a pleasing tone, for example. Like Rome, he explained, this cannot be built in a day. He ventured to say that, from what he had heard in recent years, some jazz players couldn't care less about good tone, or even intonation, but he personally felt protective towards his pupils, and wanted to send them out into the big wide world equipped with the right skills and ready to perform. In the end, he concluded, it was clearly up to Martin but, as his opinion had been asked for, he had his reservations. Not to leave the discussion on a negative slant he went on to say that, considering the very short period of time that Martin had been coming to him, he was very pleased with his progress. "Another year should get you to where you want to be, and the great thing is that you can improvise and that is where jazz musicians score over straightforward dance band players like me."

During the latter part of the week Martin had a chat with Biggleswade and Quentin together. He explained that Adrian, the leader of the Union Place Revivalists had suggested that the Lion, off Montague Street, might be amenable to having a jazz trio. "Let's go and talk to them, yes?" That evening, they wandered into the Lion. It was, thankfully, not one of the pubs that they had visited under the guise of the Milk Marketing Board. It was a smallish, but comfortable pub that had clearly welcomed bands before. There were posters here and there including one of the Union Place Revivalists from the previous year. Martin introduced himself to the landlord and explained that they had just begun to play in public and that Adrian, pointing at the poster on the wall, had recommended the pub as a likely venue. He made the classic beginner's mistake of saying, "We don't necessarily need to be paid, we would just like to play."

At this, the landlord showed some interest. "Well, we normally have music on Saturday nights. I don't mind giving you lads a spot, and Adrian is a good nut. If he has recommended you then that's all right with me. I can give you a couple of free drinks on the night."

Martin glanced at Biggleswade and Quentin, both of whom nodded in agreement. He realised that he would have to have a weekend in Worthing, and not go home. This would bugger up his washing/ironing for the week, always diligently executed by his mother. It would also bugger up his ongoing relationship with Sarah. *Still, it can't be helped,* he thought. *Music is more important than anything else.* "OK, we'd love to do it. When could you fit us in?" he asked. A date was fixed, two weeks ahead. There was a payphone in the pub which Martin used to tell Adrian about it. He went on to say that anyone from Adrian's band would be welcome to sit in and turn it into a bit of a jam session.

Next Saturday morning, Martin and Jimmy were sitting in the Warwick Arms, the scene of the previous year's debacle concerning Ted. Jimmy began to speak, somewhat hesitantly. "I'm sorry I had to rush off last Sunday. Um, you know, Martin, we have been mates for a few years now and I have to tell you that I was very grateful for the way you stood by me when the first band all resigned. I really have never forgotten that." He swallowed a large amount of beer from his pint glass before continuing. "You probably know that Ted wants to concentrate on his own band now. He mentioned it in the Rising Sun?" Martin nodded. "Well, the thing is, he has asked me to join him on sax and clarinet. He has also asked Gus to join and the new drummer that I spoke about last week. So, I won't be continuing to run a band anymore. Actually, these days I am more into what Ted is doing; you know, small-band-mainstream, that kind of thing. I know that you like Dixieland and, I assume, want to continue doing that sort of stuff?"

Martin's head was reeling. Here was one of his good friends – no, his best friend, when all was said and done – telling him that the band they had both put together was finished. His initial response was, "In this band of Ted's, is there any chance I can be the pianist then?"

"No, he already has somebody who has been with him for some time, and anyway, it's more modern than what I think you like to do."

Martin was now beginning to grow angry. "So who is left in our band who won't be joining Ted then?"

"You, Owen and Brian."

"Look, we haven't got any gigs," Jimmy went on quickly, "and I want to move forwards musically. Ted has got a new residency at the Black Bull in Whetstone, and lots of ideas. What would you have done?"

At this point, Martin realised that he had just been presented with a done deal, and that any further argument would be pointless. He felt sad, betrayed, and angry at being excluded. But what could he do? Absolutely nothing. They left the Warwick together and promised to keep in touch. Jimmy looked uncomfortable, and Martin felt miserable. He spent the evening with Sarah at the Royalty Ballroom. He managed to tell her about the day's events without getting over-emotional, though he was having a bit of a struggle to keep his composure in check. "I am going to have a word with Pam," she said. "I'm not having this. *You* should be his pianist, after all you have done for him."

"No, listen, Sarah, Ted is to blame, if anyone is. Jimmy wanted to go along with him when he was asked. If he hadn't been asked, we would probably have carried on with a new trumpet player."

"Yes, *you!*"

"No, not me. I have had a chat with my trumpet teacher who only confirmed what I suspected. I am not good enough yet."

"Well, the pianist down at the Queen's Head liked you!"

"Yes, but I only played one number, and I only just about managed the tune, no more than that."

And so, on that significant Saturday in January 1962, a great chunk of Martin's life became disconnected without, as yet, any plan for its revival in some other form.

CHAPTER 15

A trip to Portsmouth, and the trio swings

February 1962

The following Sunday, Martin, Sarah and Brian all went to the Fishmonger's Arms, home of Wood Green Jazz Club, to hear the great Alex Welsh Band once again. Brian had volunteered to drive them all there in his Triumph Gloria.

"Has Jimmy told you the news?" enquired Brian as they drove along.

"Yes, he has," Martin said. "When exactly did he tell you?"

Brian explained that both Owen and he had been told the day after the final rehearsal. A few fruitless exchanges then took place between the two of them regarding the fickleness of musicians and the treachery of bandleaders. Brian once again recounted stories about Benny Farr, and his many questionable activities. After getting this off their chests, Brian said there were sure to be other possibilities for the three of them, including Owen. "Well, we are not exactly a band, are we?" Martin interjected.

"Ah well, you are thinking about jazz bands, aren't you? There's lots more we could do. Some of the pubs book trios ... why not piano, bass and guitar? I bet we could earn more money than a six- or seven-piece jazz band, *and* get more regular work!" This premature thought was left where it was. Nevertheless, it planted a germ of an idea.

The Welsh band was on a great high that evening. After the interval, as they often did, George Chisholm and Danny Moss turned up, just to sit in as guests. The fact that musicians of this calibre were happy to do such a thing reinforced Martin's long-held view that the Welsh band must surely be the best of its sort in the country. This turned out to be perfectly true as, in years to come, the band was asked by their managing agent to accompany one venerable American star musician after another on UK tours.

Due to various mixed factors – the bad news from Jimmy, the astonishing music, the general ambience, the presence of Sarah and Brian both in good spirits – Martin consumed much more than his usual quantity of beer. Knowing that he had a critical time window during which he had to get to Wood Green Underground Station, the first leg of his late-night journey to Worthing, he substantially increased his pint rate per hour. An embrace with Sarah, a nod to Brian then, "See you next week. Got to dash now," and he was gone, clearly in a hurry.

At Brighton, he had to be woken up by the guard. Crossing platforms for the train to Worthing he noticed that he only had two more minutes left for the connection and mentally thanked the gods for his good fortune. *Now, I must stay awake, I must stay awake*, he kept telling himself. He did everything short of placing matchsticks between his eyelids. He moved his head from side to side, tapped his feet on the floor, sang quietly to himself. Twice he succumbed, only to wake up with a start. As the train slowed down for one of the intermediate stations, Martin peered out of the grimy

window and was just about able to make out the words '...
by-sea'. *Oh good*, he thought. *This must be Shoreham, so only
three more stations.* That was unfortunately the last conscious
thought that entered his head before once again he was
woken by the guard, this time at Portsmouth, the end of the
line. It was half past midnight.

"Oh shit! Bugger, bugger bugger!" he said out loud. There
were no trains going back towards Worthing and he was well
and truly up the creek without a paddle. He sat down on
the platform seat and racked his brains for a solution. The
obvious one was to find some sort of shelter and wait for the
first morning train at 6 am, but it was freezing cold and he
was dog-tired. Not a good idea.

Then a plan formulated itself through the muddle in
his brain. Risky but worth one desperate try. One of his
colleagues in Freda's team was called Colin Frobisher and he
lived in Portsmouth. He didn't have his address or telephone
number, but Martin knew that his father was a GP. Outside
Portsmouth Railway Station, the immediate surroundings
suggested, at this time in the morning, something unsafe
and invisible. Martin was becoming anxious but, thankfully,
after 100 yards along the road he found a telephone box.
Thumbing through the directory, which was on a hinged
wall bracket, he found twenty or so Frobishers listed and,
miracle of miracles, only one with MD after his name. He
put four pennies into the slot and dialled the number. It was
answered promptly with "Dr Frobisher speaking". *Oh dear*,
thought Martin; *this is going to get me into a lot of trouble.*
"Um, I am very sorry to trouble you, but is this the right
number for Colin Frobisher, please?"

Clearly irritated: "Yes, he is my son. Who is this, and are

you aware of the time? I thought you were a patient calling me."

"I am ever so sorry, Dr Frobisher. I am a work colleague of Colin's and I would really appreciate it if I could just have a quick word. I have missed my train back to Worthing. He is the only person I know who lives in Portsmouth. Sorry, perhaps I should just hang up?"

"Just a minute... Colin, *Colin*, somebody on the phone for you!" With that, Dr Frobisher put the receiver down and disappeared. Martin could hear his receding footsteps.

After a minute, "Hello, Colin here, who's speaking?" Martin explained how he had overslept on the train and how he had found Colin's family telephone number. "Very enterprising of you!" said Colin. "Look, my dad is not in a good mood, thanks to you, so I am not going to upset him any further. What are your options?"

"I haven't really got any. I have one pound three and six in my pocket. Not enough for a hotel room even if I could find one open at this time of night. Other than that, the only other option is to walk the streets until the first train back to Worthing at six."

"Okay. You had better come here." Colin then gave the directions from the station; a twenty-minute walk. "But listen! When you get here, tap lightly on the window next to the front door. Don't ring the doorbell whatever you do. I will be waiting for you. If I don't answer it will be because my dad has not yet gone back to bed. In which case, just wait outside somewhere until I open the door."

It was a very large detached house, with a doctor's surgery to one side. Colin quietly closed the door behind him, finger against his lips, gesturing Martin into the front room. "I might get into a lot of trouble for this, but you can stay here on the settee, on one condition. Here is my alarm clock. You must be out of here by six, and you must not make any kind of a sound, particularly when closing the front door behind you. Is this crystal clear?" Martin nodded and whispered his eternal gratitude. "It's lucky for you that my parents' bedroom is at the back, on the other side of the house. So, with a bit of luck, you won't be discovered."

"What are you going to tell them, then? Surely they will want to know about the phone call?"

"Come on! You can't think that I haven't already been grilled about this? And, by the way, I have been told that they do not want one of my friends ringing in the middle of the night *ever again*. I told them that I gave you the address of the Salvation Army Hostel. Maybe I should have done just that. But at least you won't get fleas here! If the worst comes to the worst, I will say that you came here in the end because the hostel was closed for the night, I happened to be awake, and didn't want to disturb them. Remember this story well, if they happen to discover you here! I will see you at work tomorrow, hopefully." Martin began to repeat how grateful he was, but Colin cut him short with a, "Yeah, just don't do it again. My folks are very conservative and, for the moment, I have to live by their rules." He suddenly smiled: "Still, I would have done exactly the same in your shoes!"

The following day, Martin's misadventure became the subject of some considerable amusement around the office. Freda said to Martin, "If you ever get stuck at Shoreham, where I live, you must give me a ring. I'll give you the number, just in case."

Martin thought it a bit unlikely that he could be stranded

in Shoreham, when the train had still not reached Worthing, but he let it pass without comment. He had previously dismissed Freda's amorous behaviour on the dance floor as just the result of unaccustomed drinking, but now he began to wonder? Or was he reading too much into this because he wanted to? Nevertheless, there was a Mr Bartlett, so where was the problem? Martin found out sometime later that Mr Bartlett was a travelling salesman with a company car and was, in fact, often away from home!

At lunchtime, he had to buy some cigarettes. His brand of the moment was Senior Service which had only just changed its packaging to a 'flip top'. *Very smart*, thought Martin. While in the newsagent's kiosk on the Durrington trading estate, he also picked up the latest copy of the *Melody Maker*. The headline stated, in very large font, the sort usually reserved for events of cosmic importance, *Louis Armstrong's All Stars to come to Britain*. Martin's eyes nearly popped out of his head. *What!? The greatest living trumpet player is coming, and I have got to see him.* The decision was made in his head immediately, regardless of where, when or how much. He hurried to the nearest telephone box and dialled Sarah's work number at the Country Gentleman's Association. He prayed that they had a more benign attitude towards personal calls, unlike Lloyds Bank. The telephone operator put him through to Sarah's extension without so much as a murmur. "Guess what? Louis Armstrong is coming to London in April!"

Sarah's response was not exactly ecstatic: "I am trying to type up an important letter and now I've got to catch up. Is that the only reason why you rang?"

"No, and I'm sorry about your work and all that, but

we must book tickets right away. Can you get to the Festival Hall after work? I will pay you for them, but you will have to get them as soon as possible. It's bound to be a sell-out (it was). Try to get as near to the front as you can; in the middle, whatever it costs. Um, are you OK for cash? It might be as much as £10 for all I know."

Sarah said that she could afford it and would try to get the tickets after work. She then went on to say, "You're not coming home this weekend, are you? When will I see you next? You know, Martin, I don't see you that much these days and I thought that you would at least want to come back to Barnet every weekend so that we could spend just a little time together. Instead, you are playing in a pub down there. I mean, is this really, *really* important? After all, you will be coming back for good, shortly, won't you?"

Martin considered his reply for a few seconds. "It's only a one-off, but it's the first time I have got my own gig on trumpet, other than at the staff party. I'll try to make it up to you next weekend and we can talk properly about it, rather than now. I don't want to hold you up from your work."

With that they said their goodbyes, but as Martin made his way back to his desk he remembered Freda's words of wisdom at the Christmas party. Was he ready, so soon, to be tied down? Not for the first time he felt a little uneasy about the prospects of a future, already prescribed for him at the age of twenty. Most of his friends down here in Worthing seemed to have no ties and, as a result, were having a very good time. Not that *he* had been behaving as if he lived in an ivory tower; but there was a limit beyond which he would not go. There was a very attractive waitress at the Eardley Hotel whom everybody lusted after. She often came across to the Connaught after she had finished her shift and inevitably became a magnet for the attention of several hopeful males. Whenever Martin managed to monopolise her, usually only when there was a lull in the conversation, she seemed to be in some way conveying an invitation with her eyes. He often thought about her, and whether his sense of loyalty to Sarah might be being stretched to its very limit. One or two well-chosen words might be all it would take to make the move away from monogamy. He also reflected that he had significantly failed to mention Sarah's existence in his short conversations with Sally, for that was her name.

Saturday evening found Biggleswade and Martin already having drinks in the Lion, an hour before they were due to start playing. They both had a sense of eager anticipation. *This Saturday, Jazz Trio 8.30 PM,* proclaimed the chalked notice on the blackboard. Martin kept glancing at it, as if it might disappear if he didn't. He also mentally assessed the early evening clientele; trying to work out whether they had come to see him, or just out for a drink. He made himself obvious by placing his trumpet case on the piano stool, and every so often opening it up and fiddling with something. But nobody seemed to take much notice of this self-centred display. After a while Quentin turned up with a young lady who looked not dissimilar to himself. She wore horn-rimmed glasses, hair in a tight bun, a tweed skirt and a nondescript cardigan. "This is Hilary," Quentin announced.

Of course she is! thought Martin; *most appropriate.*

So, at eight thirty on the dot, the trio launched in to their first number, 'Five Foot Two'. Nobody walked out, and some of the customers started tapping their feet. Always a good sign. They finished to applause, and a bit of whistling to show approval. There was no microphone, so Martin shouted across the bar that they would be playing some jazz numbers for the next couple of hours and he expressed the hope that they would enjoy the music. "The next number will be the 'Tin Roof Blues'." He tapped in slowly, one two, one two three, and then played the lead-in notes, and the other two came in right on cue. He reflected that they sounded pretty good, but it was a very simple tune; it was in fact the first tune he had ever tried to play on the old Salvation Army cornet that he had bought from Jeremy. He shut his eyes to concentrate better and imagined he could hear a ghostly sousaphone providing a bass line to the piano and ukulele. No, this is not my imagination, he realised. He opened his eyes, but could see no one. It seemed to be coming from outside. Then as soon as it had started, it stopped. *How weird*, he thought.

After the number had ended, to another enthusiastic reception, three twenty-somethings, all sporting beards and duffel coats, walked into the bar. Martin recognised Adrian at once. The last of the trio had to bend down, in order to clear the doorframe, as he was wearing an enormous sousaphone.

"Well, Martin, we're here, as you can see. Just going to get some beers and then maybe we can join in?"

"Fabulous," Martin replied. He made a little announcement to the customers telling them that the band would any minute be doubling in size and carried on as a trio playing 'Shine'.

Introductions were effected. "This is Rufus (the sousaphone player) and this is Alan (clarinettist). Right, shall we all three join in, or maybe I should wait a bit until you need a rest on trumpet?" Martin thought that this was a very good suggestion, as he wasn't entirely sure how long his lip would last. He recalled Peter Phillips' advice about playing trumpet in a jazz band, and so maybe another couple of numbers would be enough.

Alan seemed a very serious sort of young man. "How about 'Down by The Riverside'?" he said. Martin had not bothered to consider this as suitable for his own repertoire, not even as an emergency number. He suddenly recalled the non-meeting of the minds between Adrian and himself last December and that, in all probability, Adrian's band were all of a like mind. It was going to have to be purist revivalist jazz for the time being! Off they went, Martin, Biggleswade, and possibly Quentin, into unknown, but very simple, territory. Within a few seconds, Martin found that he could not hear himself properly. Clarinets are made of wood and, as a rule, sound very pleasing. Alan's sounded as if it was made from galvanised iron, and every note seemed to be a screech of protest delivered at full volume. Rufus produced a very sonorous, but loud, parping sousaphone noise on beats one and three. When Martin attempted to play a solo, Alan didn't stop playing. Martin later learnt that this was what Alan's idol used to do, back in New Orleans. 'Down by the Riverside' came to an end, mainly as a result of Martin waving his trumpet from side to side and up and down during the last chorus. Alan said, "Oh, I thought we could have kept going for another few minutes, you know, building up the tension." Martin thought that if Alan built up any more tension on his clarinet it would shatter into little pieces.

"Come on, Adrian, I'll have a little rest for a few

numbers," said Martin, carefully putting his trumpet back into its case. Adrian tuned up to the piano the wrong way, Martin observed, not the foolproof way that Peter Phillips had taught him to do. Then Martin's band launched into a few numbers which seemed to go on for an eternity, each sounding very similar to the last. The raucous sound of Adrian, Alan and Rufus in combination, totally overwhelmed the subtleties of Quentin's piano accompaniment and Biggleswade's guesswork on the ukulele. Biggleswade, who up to this point had been relatively silent, decided to go into the joke-telling routine that he had imposed on an unsuspecting public at the Christmas party. One of the jokes concerned a stockbroker and the punchline was "Ah, but were they preference or ordinary?" This was met by mystified silence from the Saturday night regulars in the Lion. Adrian and Alan exchanged glances.

"Um, er, Biggles…, do you think we could play another number now?"

"Of course, old chap. Let's do 'Yes Sir, That's My Baby', and I will sing it!" This was not the sort of number that the New Orleans diehards would have chosen but, as they were guests, they reluctantly went along with what they considered to be commercial Dixieland rubbish.

During the interval, all three members of the Union Place Revivalists took it upon themselves to educate Quentin and Biggleswade about what 'real' jazz was all about and, in the process of doing so, disabuse them of their current views, whatever they might be. Unfortunately, they hadn't bargained for two very quirky individuals as listeners. At one stage, Quentin could be heard asking them what grades they had achieved, guessing accurately what their answers were going to be. He then went into his 'of course, any kind of popular music is child's play to someone with my background' mode, the same sort of diatribe that had so irritated Martin when he first met Quentin. Biggleswade, on the other hand, was gloriously dismissive of any concept of jazz as an art form. He managed to wind up Alan no end by inventing a personal relationship with George Formby, who, he confided, was going to take him on a tour of the music halls when he had taught him all he knew about playing the ukulele. "A sight more interesting than playing a load of boring old minstrel plantation tunes," he said, then added for good grace, "But each to his own, eh, chaps?"

Martin had kept a low profile during all this as he rightly considered that there was nothing to be gained by reopening the unfinished discussion with Adrian when he had met him in East Worthing. He silently considered the score to be Martin's trio two, Union Place Revivalists nil. The landlord had bought them all a drink and expressed the view that the evening was a success so far. He liked what he had heard and some of the customers agreed with him. "You must do it again sometime. I can't book Adrian's band anymore because they seem to have disbanded to all intents and purposes." This was true. Adrian's banjo player, trombone player and drummer had all finished their college courses and had moved away to where they could get teaching posts. Adrian had said that he couldn't work up any enthusiasm to find other like-minded players who worshipped the holy grail of New Orleans purism, and that, unlike Martin, he was not prepared to prostitute his art.

The second half of the evening followed much the same course as the first: a mixture of Martin's trio with or without the members of Adrian's band. Despite their irresolvable musical tastes, they rubbed along quite amicably and all had a last drink at the bar, again at the landlord's expense. Rufus approached Martin and said how much he had enjoyed it and, should there be a vacancy for a sousaphone in Martin's band, please bear him in mind. Martin had to explain that, owing to the nature of his daytime job, he was not expecting to be living in Worthing for very much longer, regrettable though that was. He was, that evening, unaware that he was soon going to have to make a decision that could change all that.

CHAPTER 16

The decision

March 1962

Towards the end of March, every task connected with the Lloyds Bank share issue had been completed. Certificates had been posted to the grateful shareholders, and detailed records for the corporate accounts had been finalised. It had all been done and dusted, probably with more accuracy, and certainly with more care, attention and oversight, than the soon-to-be-introduced computerisation would be able to achieve.

The temporary staff were more or less marking time, assisting the permanent employees with a range of clerical tasks. They knew that this glorious escape from reality, and in some cases responsibilities, would come to an end very soon. Biggleswade, together with others who had been seconded from local branches, had already returned to base. He still popped in to the Eardley Hotel for the now traditional Friday night drinking sessions, which sometimes included a 'rave', although never matching the level of the very first 'market survey'. The last one that they had undertaken involved them all going to the most refined licensed establishment in the area, located on the outskirts of the town. This was the favourite haunt of the landowning, hunting, shooting and fishing crowd, and the landlord kept up the pretence that he was one of them. Nothing could be further from the truth; in their eyes, he was in 'trade', was he not? The ravers decided to enter the pub, one after the other in a straight line all sporting headgear of some sort. This ranged from a deerstalker to a top hat. Once at the bar there was a ceremonial removal of hats, which were carefully placed in a line along the back of a regency settee that occupied pride of place in the room. This antique piece of furniture was the landlord's status symbol, an attempt to align himself with his favourite customers, none of whom would have ever entertained him as a guest in their own homes. It was seldom used for seating purposes.

It was with a very bad grace that he served the eight Friday ravers with pints of ale. When tongues had been sufficiently loosened, they tried to see how far they could go before the inevitable refusal to serve them any more drinks. In unnecessarily loud conversation, they alluded to the fact that all the other customers were fat, a sure sign that they did not work for a living. This went on for a while during which time the landlord could be heard muttering to a couple of his regulars. They could only catch the odd word or two – "think they are being clever" … "don't you worry, I'll sort it" … "not going to…"

Eventually he spoke.

"Right, you lot, I want all those hats taken off my settee and placed on the coat rack, which is there for a purpose. Then I'd like to know where you are going for your next drink, because it won't be here!"

Just for once it was not Biggleswade who was quick off the mark; it was John, known as Taffy, who spoke, his Welsh accent making the barb all the more delicious.

"All right, fat man. We don't like your pub, fat man.

Did you deliberately get fat to look like your customers, boyo?"

"Out!" he roared in reply, arm outstretched in the direction of the door.

"Goodbye, fat man," replied the lads, almost in unison.

All very childish, but enormously satisfying!

Letters were sent to the remaining temporary staff confirming their return date to their branch, or in some cases allocating them to a different branch. This was standard bank procedure in those days. They would not relocate you beyond what they must have decided in their wisdom was a reasonable commute. You would not actually have to up sticks and move home, but it could be something of a challenge. Martin, himself, had already been moved from Potters Bar to Knightsbridge, an overall distance of twenty-five miles. He secretly wondered whether there was a special map, locked away from prying eyes, in the bowels of the Lombard Street Head Office. On this map, Martin conjectured, would be a myriad of concentric circles covering the entire country. These would be the boundaries of commute.

There was a buzz in Martin's hut. They were all comparing notes. Some were delighted with their new branch, some not so. Some were frustrated at having to return to their original branch, some were relieved at the same prospect. Martin, however, had not received a letter. "Freda," he asked, "I have not yet received my letter; could you possibly find out whether it has been overlooked, please?"

"Ah, Martin, I do know that you will be getting a call from Mr Shoesmith."

This was the same Mr Shoesmith who had made the

little welcoming speech at the Christmas party. With a feeling of foreboding, without knowing why, Martin said, "Why, what have I done?" He was thinking that maybe he had made a cock-up on somebody's share certificate, and a complaint had been made.

Freda laughed. "Martin, you have done nothing at all. Quite the opposite. *Look*, I didn't tell you this, as I am not supposed to, but he will be offering you a permanent job here in the registrar's department. It will be for you to decide whether to accept or not. You know, we all think that you have done a really good job while working with us. It has been a pleasure to have you here, and you have fitted in very well."

Martin felt his cheeks going hot. This was unexpected praise indeed. He privately wondered how much input Freda had made into this recommendation. He considered that it may not be all to do with his work. *Blimey*, he thought, *If I move down here how long will it be before I end up in a compromising situation with Freda? I can only hold out for so long. It won't be easy to escape.*

The following morning, Freda's internal telephone rang. She picked it up, looking down. "Yes, he is… all right, I'll tell him… thank you." She looked up smiling. "Martin, you are to go to Hut 3 to see Mr Shoesmith right away." She winked conspiratorially. Martin had never been inside Hut 3 before. As befitted the status of its occupants, the decor was vastly superior to the other huts. Carpets, potted plants, pictures on the wall, a coffee table, comfortable chairs, and nameplates on the two internal doors: Mr G.W. Shoesmith, General Manager, and Mr E.S. Ridout, Assistant General Manager. Martin approached the only other occupant, the secretary, a rather severe looking lady of indeterminate years, hesitantly announced who he was and that he was here to see Mr Shoesmith. He was shown immediately into the Holy of Holies, as he had already secretly christened it.

"Ah, Mr Weston, do take a seat," invited Mr Shoesmith. "I've seen you before, haven't I?" he began. "It was at the Christmas party and you were playing one of those (here he mimed the action of playing a trombone) things, weren't you?"

"Yes, sir; it's a trumpet actually."

"A trumpet, eh? Ah yes, it was very good, a touch of the Eddie Calverts!"

Martin inwardly winced at this. He and all his jazz-minded friends considered Eddie Calvert to be the schmaltziest trumpet player who ever drew breath.

"Now, I expect you are wondering why I have asked to see you?"

"Yes sir," lied Martin.

"This share issue has been a massive task for our small department and, due to the unpredictability of the stock market, we cannot always foresee these events much in advance, and therefore we always have to transfer staff from all around the country, mainly from branches, on a temporary secondment basis. Since I have been here, we have had three such episodes. So, to make things a little easier for the future, head office has approved a modest increase in our permanent staff. We would normally recruit locally, and so we will, but we are also going to offer the opportunity to a couple of chaps who have been working with us on this last exercise, you being one of them."

He paused, in order to let the impact of what he had just said sink in. Martin adopted a suitable expression of surprise.

"As you know, Mr Weston, the bank's policy is to move staff around from branch to branch, or different head office departments, from time to time. It's all part of the development strategy. We only move people away from their home area when they either request it due to domestic reasons, or when it is a promotion. Now this would not be an immediate promotion, you understand; it is an invitation for you to consider. As you are, what?" He consulted some papers on his desk… "twenty years old, you will be on fixed-scale increments for the next ten years. So we can't offer you any additional financial incentives. I would say, however, that your work has been exemplary. Not only that, you have fitted in with your colleagues here very well. Mrs Bartlett has been singing your praises, although it would be as well not to tell her that I told you! So, all I can say to you is that, if your career continues to flourish, and when you come off the fixed scale at thirty, you should have some chance of doing much better in terms of financial rewards." He sat back, having finished the main thrust of his sales campaign.

Martin did not know whether now was the time to speak. Mr Shoesmith helped him by saying, "I realise it's a lot to think about, and probably a very big decision for you to make. So I would suggest that you mull it over and perhaps could let Mrs Bartlett know within the next few days. You will have lots of questions to consider. I'm sure that Mrs Bartlett will be able to help. If not, please come and see me again."

Martin thanked Mr Shoesmith profusely for the opportunity and explained that he lived with his parents at present and therefore he would need to talk to them over the weekend to consider the pros and cons. With that, Mr

Shoesmith stood up. Martin quickly followed suit, and Mr Shoesmith shook Martin's hand and bade him farewell. Back at his desk, Freda wanted to know how it went. Martin relayed what had been said and forestalled further debate by simply saying that his head was in a whirl right now. There were indeed many serious considerations.

Back home in Barnet he told his parents about the unexpected offer of a job in Worthing. They were both caught on the hop. "Is this a promotion?" asked Harold. Martin explained all about the Lloyds Bank annual increment pay structure and that it was completely inflexible, other than the London allowance, which he would lose by moving to Sussex. "Well, this seems a bit of a rum deal then," was Harold's opinion. He went on to say that the personnel people must surely be aware that Martin would be worse off by accepting this offer, unless they were not right in the head! As a Yorkshireman, he was always blunt and to the point.

"What do you want to do?" enquired Kathleen.

"Mum, I just don't know. I have made a lot of new friends down there; the work is more pleasant than working in a branch and not knowing what time you would be able to go home. I might be able to play jazz with a few of the chaps down there. Do you know, I just can't decide!"

There followed a discussion about how much it might cost to move into digs, how much food would cost, sending washing to a laundry, train fares back home; which, surely, he would want to continue on a regular basis, and so on. "And what about Sarah?" added Kathleen. "I thought you were both serious. You wouldn't see much of her after you had moved, would you?" Martin secretly wondered whether moving away might force that particular issue, one way or the other. All these months of freedom and irresponsibility had convinced him that there was a lot of living to be done before settling down into domesticity. Wisely, he kept these thoughts to himself.

Harold made the most telling point. "Seems to me that you would be stuck, down in Worthing, for ten years before any chance of a better deal. And that's not guaranteed either! Up here, surely there are more chances to move to another job, perhaps a different bank, if there were better prospects." This turned out, in due course, to be a most prophetic statement.

That evening he took Sarah out to the Black Horse, a pub very near to where she lived, half a mile from the town centre. He wasted no time in sharing his news with her. They were both at an age where some of their friends had left home, usually to get married, but not exclusively. They knew that within a very few years it would be almost expected of them to have moved out of their respective parental homes. That was simply the way that the world worked back then.

"If you go, Martin, I can't see how we are going to see each other much. I can't leave my job. They are very good to me, and I doubt whether I could find anything like that down in Sussex." Martin had not actually considered both of them moving to Worthing, but he gave it a bit of thought while ordering another round of drinks.

Back with his pint and her Babycham, he said: "We couldn't get away with living together. Can you imagine that happening?" This was absolutely true. Social norms were completely against two unmarried people living together. It would have been embarrassing for their parents and would have been something that other people would talk about behind their backs. What changes in society attitudes were soon to take place with the advent of the 'swinging sixties' some four years later!

"I just can't make my mind up. I have you, and all my friends here in Barnet. But I have some new friends in Worthing. The money side of things is not good. I would be definitely worse off. *Definitely!* It would be a long time before I could get a promotion. I have been thinking about buying a car, but I'm never going to manage it on the pittance I would have after paying for rent, food, and other stuff. But, on the other hand, I would really miss not being there anymore."

"Martin, it seems that you are talking yourself out of it. Having a good time is all very well, but you don't *want* to be so hard up, do you?" This was a genuine question, rather than one of the rhetorical variety.

"No, I don't. I think I'm probably going to turn it down. Dad said that, if I got fed up with the bank, there would be more jobs to look at in the London area than down there, and ten years is a hell of a long time to have to wait for more money." He related to Sarah a time when, in the Potters Bar branch, he had been serving an employee from MacFisheries who had been paying in the week's takings. On the counter was a glossy cardboard notice promoting a career in Lloyds Bank. It contained the annual salary table starting at eighteen, then the year-by-year increments up to the age of thirty. While Martin was assisting the cashier in checking the takings, this chap picked up the notice and read it. "Is this all you get?" he asked. Martin confirmed that it was indeed. "Well, in that case I'm going to stick with fishmongering," was his disdainful reply.

Around that time, Martin had composed yet another poem which he gleefully shared with Basil, one of his like-minded colleagues.

So, it's off to work the bank clerk sallies
He won't come home 'til the ledgers tally
And not even then will they leave him alone
As he burns the midnight oil at home
The Banking Diploma just has to be got
If he is ever to improve his meagre lot
He compares his rewards from the bank, his keeper
With the relative prosperity of the roadside sweeper

Sarah, visibly relaxed, believed that Martin had more or less come to a decision. "Are you looking forward to next Saturday?" she asked. That was the date that Louis Armstrong's All Stars would be appearing at the Festival Hall. Sarah had miraculously managed to obtain two tickets in the middle of the second row.

"Yeah, I just can't wait," Martin replied. Martin walked her home where they sat in her parents' back room for a while, drinking coffee and snogging. He left when Sarah's mother banged on the door. That was the signal to say that it was time for Martin to go home. Sarah's mother was well aware of what they might be up to, but was generous enough to allow them uninterrupted time together, although not quite long enough for things to progress beyond a certain point – or so she estimated!

Back at work the following Monday, Martin approached Freda. He told her without any preamble that he had decided not to accept the position in the registrar's department.

Before Freda could say anything, he quickly went on to say that he simply could not afford it. Were it not for that, he would have been happy to work down in Sussex, but, at his age, London would be a better bet for his future prospects. Freda expressed her disappointment but said how she completely understood. She did add that, in her opinion, however, it was a good thing to break the parental ties and start your own life as soon as it is possible to do so. "We all struggle to begin with," she opined. Martin acknowledged what she was saying but repeated that he had made his mind up. He went on to say, perhaps unwittingly, that he had really enjoyed the work, and that he wished that Freda had been his boss in Knightsbridge rather than the formidable Mrs Darcey. "Thank you, Martin. You know, if you change your mind I am sure that I can find you some nice cheap digs. I have a few friends who often put up students, etc. Why, I have even done it myself on one occasion."

Hello, hello! thought Martin. *What are the chances that it would be her house that appeared at the top of the list?* He still wasn't sure that it wasn't just his qualities at work that lay behind all this friendliness on Freda's part. He asked Freda whether she could relay his decision to Mr Shoesmith and, more importantly, to find out where he would be going, and when. She said that she was happy to do this, but repeated that he could change his mind at any time up to the date that he was due to leave.

Wednesday brought the notification, via the internal mail:

To Mr M.S. Weston: You are to return to Knightsbridge Branch on Monday 14th April.

Mr Baker, Assistant Manager, has also been notified of your return date. We would like to thank you for your assistance with the 1961 Bonus Share Issue.

It was signed by the general manager's secretary on his behalf.

Well that was that then: short and sweet.

"Just a week and a half to go, then," Martin said, without preamble. Freda and the other two permanent staff looked up. "Sorry, I was thinking out loud. The letter says I will be going back to my old branch on Monday week. I will miss this little hut and all you lot."

Freda called for a coffee break. "Is your old branch OK? Did you like it there?"

"Oh yes, there are a lot of people around my own age and we go out for drinks from time to time. We've got a lot of important customers too. Do you know who I once served? Shirley Bassey!"

Colin spoke up: "Well at least my parents will be able to sleep soundly, knowing that, in future, there will never be a stranded Martin, knocking on the door in the middle of the night!"

"I wouldn't bank on that," replied Martin, "I am going to see Louis Armstrong this weekend and who knows what state I will be in when I come down here Sunday night, probably over-refreshed."

Everybody looked up, including those at the next table. There was an assortment of noises representing astonishment. They clearly wanted to know more. "Yes, he is playing at the Festival Hall on Saturday. My girlfriend managed to get two tickets as soon as it was advertised. It's a complete sell-out. I just can't believe that I am going to see and hear the greatest living jazz musician in the world." Neither could they. Although none of them was into jazz, they had all heard of Louis Armstrong. Somebody started to sing 'Mack the Knife', which was one of his big hits.

"We are all envious, Martin, and you would be excused for what you call over-refreshment, afterwards. Don't forget, if you find yourself falling asleep on the train, get off at Shoreham to be safe. You have my telephone number. Better than a repeat performance at Colin's place." Freda had clearly not given up on him just yet.

So the die was cast. Martin reflected that he needed to say goodbye to a lot of friends – Peter Phillips, his trumpet teacher, Adrian, the remainder of the Friday night ravers, and, most of all, Biggleswade.

CHAPTER 17

Hello Louis, Goodbye Biggleswade

April 1962

The Northern Line starts at High Barnet where, at six o'clock, Martin and Sarah had bought two return tickets to Waterloo and were seated in a carriage waiting for the train to leave. Martin had been playing Louis Armstrong records all afternoon and was considerably enthused with anticipation. Sarah was looking forward to just visiting this acoustically perfect auditorium, built in 1951 as part of the South Bank regeneration scheme. She would have been perfectly happy with a performance by anybody. Just to be there was an exciting prospect.

They got off the Tube at Waterloo and made their way across a busy road to the vast, brutal grey concrete complex. A few years hence, this example of post-war architecture would be awarded a Grade 1 listing, but in 1962 it was still considered ugly. They found themselves in the foyer together with the other ticket holders waiting impatiently for the doors to the concert hall to be opened. Martin spotted a programme seller and went to buy one. Somewhere in the middle was a list of numbers that 'Mr Armstrong' would choose from. "Sarah, look! There's 'Cornet Chop Suey', 'Potato Head Blues', 'Strutting with Some Barbecue' … I didn't know he still played all those old Hot Five numbers anymore." In fact, he didn't.

Whoever had been responsible for the list of numbers was being extremely optimistic.

There was a sudden surge as the attendants unlocked the entrance doors. Before long the two of them were seated right in the middle of the second row; exactly in line with the centre microphone. But they still had to wait. There was a warm-up act; a very good British Trad band led by trumpeter Gerry Brown. They played well. Gerry, from time to time, would make self-deprecating comments in recognition of what was shortly to follow. At last they made their bows and exited stage right. There was a ten-minute break while the attendants repositioned microphones and generally checked that everything was set. The house lights went down, a hush descended over the audience, and five shadowy figures in evening dress could just be discerned, quietly taking their places on stage. There was a pregnant pause of maybe one minute. It seemed to Martin more like fifteen. Then the opening notes to 'When It's Sleepy Time Down South' could be heard from the rear of the stage. The band, meanwhile, was providing a quiet, well-rehearsed backing. With the advancing, unmistakeably familiar trumpet sound, the protagonist suddenly came into view as the spotlights were turned on. And there he was, now up to the microphone and singing the 1929 lyrics as he had done for over thirty years, except that he had quite recently changed the word 'darkies' to 'people'. It wasn't his idea though. Somebody in his management office suggested that he should do so, in view of changing public views on race issues. His reply was quite characteristic: "Look, Daddy, I didn't write the song, I just sing it!"

The signature tune came to an end and Louis said,

"Good evening, everybody. We are going to open up with a good old good one: 'Back Home in Indiana'." Off they went at full tilt. Martin by now was almost entering a trance-like state. He was totally overwhelmed. Sarah squeezed his hand and smiled warmly at him. She was excited too.

And so the evening went on: old favourites 'Mack the Knife', 'Muskrat Ramble', 'The Faithful Hussar', 'Blueberry Hill', 'Tin Roof Blues' and others, honed to perfection over many years, were played one after the other with just the briefest introduction from Louis between numbers. There was an interval during which Martin and Sarah just sat in their seats while many went to the bar. Another forty minutes of exquisite magic from this unparalleled legend of jazz, and then the applause for each member of the band in turn, 'Sleepy Time Down South' again, and suddenly they left the stage. "Oh no! I want it to go on forever," was the exhortation of an entranced Martin. "You couldn't ask for more!" said Sarah.

Throughout the entire evening, Louis, who was shorter and blacker than Martin had imagined, stood right in front of the two of them. Martin had watched in awe as Louis, time and time again, majestically soared up into the upper register of his Selmer trumpet, his breadth of tone undiminished by the achievement. There was a stash of crisp white handkerchiefs placed inside the back of the Steinway Grand. At the end of every number, Louis discarded one and grabbed another, having wiped his face. He did seem to sweat a lot.

As they went from the Festival Hall into the cool April air, Martin said, "We don't have to get a Tube for at least half an hour; shall we have a drink over there first?" He pointed to a large pub next to Waterloo Station. Sarah said that she was up for it, as long as they didn't miss the train. Martin managed to down three pints, the first one almost in one gulp. "I feel as if I will never calm down; I needed that! I tell you what: I am really going to concentrate on the trumpet from now on. It was unbelievable, wasn't it?" Sarah agreed that it was. They chatted about Martin's long-awaited return to Barnet next Friday and the conversation moved on to a possible holiday in a few months' time. Neither of them could realistically expect to book holidays any earlier than September, as more senior staff took priority or, in other words, June to August. Back in Barnet they said their goodnights at the Tube station and arranged to meet for a walk on Hadley Common the following morning.

Hadley Common, the name that inspired Martin's first band, Monk Hadley's Jazz Friars, was a pleasant piece of land starting exactly where the Great North Road leaves Barnet High Street. There were some impressive, old, gnarled oak trees and a derelict brewery flanked by some magnificent Georgian residences and, to the rear, a lovely little church at the top of the hill that winds down through Hadley Woods. Opposite the church was a tollhouse and gate, not in use since the 1930s. Martin and Sarah had both grown up in an age when parents had no qualms about allowing young children unrestricted play in Hadley Woods, and both knew every inch of this, the western margin of the once great Enfield Chase. Walking the common and the woods was a very pleasant thing to do on this sunny April morning. Naturally the conversation returned to the previous evening, something that would remain etched in their memories for ever. Martin told Sarah that he would be leaving for Worthing after lunch, because Sunday evening would be the last chance he had to say goodbye to a couple of friends, who would not be around during the week.

Martin arrived at Worthing station at 7.30 pm that same evening. He made his way directly to the Connaught, where he had arranged to meet Biggleswade. The front bar of the hotel was quite full already, and Martin spotted Biggleswade sitting at a table in the bay window. Having grabbed a pint, he went to join him. "Hello, Martin, there's music tonight. Did you know?" As it happened he didn't, but that was extremely welcome news. Martin wasted no time in relaying, blow by blow, the highlights of last night's concert. Biggleswade was impressed, but not overly so. It had become evident over the last few months that Biggleswade was first and foremost a fan of music hall and stand-up comedy. Jazz was some way down on his list. A pianist had arrived meanwhile and was running his fingers over the keyboard, checking the action. It was in fact a good, full-sized grand piano and clearly well looked after. After a while the pianist launched into a selection of tunes from the 'Great American Songbook'. One led seamlessly into the next. It was very tasteful cocktail music, albeit known to musicians, forever cynical, as the 'Cavalcade of Crap'. Then a smartly dressed lady of about forty was asked to sing a couple of songs. These turned out to be a sultry version of 'Stormy Weather' and an upbeat 'Bye Bye Blackbird'. As things were looking up, and moving in the right direction, Martin silently wondered whether there might be an opportunity for him to play his trumpet, which was under the table together with his bag of clothing. Then a few things happened in quick succession. The lady singer had been replaced with another, a chap entered the pub carrying an alto saxophone case, and Sally walked in, on her own.

Sally, the attractive waitress from the Eardley Hotel, despite having frequently joined the lads at the Connaught for the midweek drinking and fruit-machine playing sessions, was not liberated enough to enter a pub on her own, unless she knew that a friend would be there. She glanced around the bar, now very busy, clearly looking for someone, but without success. A flicker of recognition passed across her face as she spotted Martin. He beckoned her over to their table and made room for her. "Gosh, it's busy tonight. Have you seen Maria by any chance?" Maria was one of the other waitresses, whom she had arranged to meet that evening. Martin said he hadn't, and offered to buy her a drink. "Oh, that's very kind, Martin, but look; you are obviously here with a friend. I don't want to interrupt, but maybe I could just sit here with you until Maria turns up?" Martin introduced her to Biggleswade, whom she had not previously met, and made his way to the bar to buy her a half-pint of cider.

Biggleswade just could not resist the opportunity to ham it up. He stood up and made a slight formal bow, saying, "Dear lady, it is an honour to meet you," as he took her hand and brushed his lips across the back of it. He continued in much the same vein to a bemused Sally. "And pray, are you a native of this fair town?" he enquired. Sally told him that she did indeed live in the town and worked at the Eardley as a waitress. Having established that Biggleswade had been working at Durrington, she went on to ask whether he would be going home at the end of the week like Martin. "Oh, indeed no, dear lady. I too am a resident of Wahthing, this gem of the Sussex Riviera!"

Martin arrived with Sally's cider, much to her relief. In

all honesty, she did not know what to make of this joker Biggleswade, and wondered about his strange name too. The music was now in full swing. The pianist had called up the saxophone player to do a couple of numbers. In between trying to make scintillating conversation with Sally, for reasons that were more to do with Martin's ego than any ulterior motive, he was trying to listen to the music. Neither Sally nor Biggleswade seemed to be all that bothered about it, which made Martin's task all the more challenging; one ear on the music, the other on the conversation. He knew, in the final analysis, that he could not compete with Biggleswade when it came to being the centre of attention, but it did seem to him that Sally was less than impressed with Biggleswade's showing off.

"I am going to ask whether I can do a number," he announced to a surprised Sally.

"Do you sing then?" she asked. As nonchalantly as he could manage, Martin explained that he was a trumpet player. He considered it expedient not to add the word 'novice'. It had the effect that he had hoped for. Sally said that, oh yes, he just had to play. She wouldn't be happy unless he did, and absolutely insisted! Biggleswade joined in by saying that he played ukulele with Martin's band and, furthermore, considered himself to be an all-round entertainer. Sally was unimpressed. It was now Martin who had her undivided attention.

As soon as the saxophone player finished, Martin pushed his way through the crowd, trying to make sure that he didn't barge into any hand-held pint glasses, while desperate to reach the pianist before anyone else did. Somewhat breathlessly, he asked whether he could play a number on trumpet. The pianist's reply was, "Well, we have quite a lot to fit in before the end. Have we seen you here before?" Martin confirmed that he had never been here on a music night, although he was a pub regular.

The pianist was in the process of considering how best to say 'no' when the sax player, who had been listening to all this, said that the lad should be given a chance. He then held out his hand to Martin and said, "Stan's the name. I'll tell you what, I will play with you – should make a nice sound, trumpet and alto." Martin did two things at once: he thanked them both, whilst frantically beckoning to Biggleswade to bring his trumpet. He was asked what he was going to play and, without hesitation, said 'I Can't Give You Anything but Love, Baby', this being the number that he had played more than once before.

Biggleswade had by now arrived with the trumpet and, much to Martin's irritation, declared that he was Martin's accompanist and manager. But he had the good grace to leave it there and return to his seat. The last thing that Martin wanted was for an embarrassing bit of theatre from Biggleswade when it had all being going so well up until then. The pianist played an eight-bar improvised introduction and off they went. Martin was extremely nervous in the presence of Stan, who was a highly proficient player, somewhat in the style of Jimmy Dorsey. But Stan knew the ropes. He played soft backing phrases behind Martin's lead and, even though he could have completely blown Martin out of the water, just played a modest solo when it came to his turn. About halfway through Martin started to relax and enjoy the rare opportunity to play with top-line musicians. In fact, it made *him* play better too.

Martin eventually glanced over to the bay window, where his friends were, and was met by an admiring gaze from Sally. The number came to an end and Martin asked Stan whether he knew Peter Phillips, as they were both of a similar age. "Pete? Yes, of course, I have done many gigs with him. He's a really good tenor player. How do you know him?" Martin briefly explained about the lessons and Stan asked Martin to give old Pete his regards. When he got back to his seat, he found that Maria had now arrived and was chatting animatedly to Biggleswade. Sally kissed Martin on the cheek and asked why, after all this time in Worthing, had Martin not done this before. He said that he had, but she had not been around.

Before the end of the evening Sally and Maria left together, but not before Sally had asked whether Martin would be around that week. He said, yes, and that he would see her at the Eardley tomorrow. "Well, Martin," said Biggleswade, "I hope that you are not going to desert us down here. If you can get down from time to time, my mother has said that you can use our spare room. We can't stop the fun now, can we?" And so, after they had finished their drinks, the music had come to an end, and Martin said goodbye to Stan and the pianist, they found themselves outside on the promenade; just the two of them. "Come here, you old bugger!" said Biggleswade, a little emotional. They had a bear hug, promised to keep in touch, and said goodnight for the last time, as it happened.

Martin made his way along the promenade towards the Eardley, refreshed by the night air, salty with the spume. He reflected upon his own development; from an insecure, somewhat shy individual, to someone with a little more charisma and self-confidence. This had happened, quite quickly, over the few months that he had been in Worthing, and was all thanks to his friend Biggleswade. Sally was also very much in his thoughts. What did he really want to do, and why? He was torn between his loyalty to and love for Sarah. Loyalty was not the issue. He had been brought up to believe that cheating was wrong. But love? He was not really sure whether he knew what it was. After all, he was only twenty, and immature at that.

CHAPTER 18

Goodbye Sussex

April 1962

Martin had pretty well planned his last week in Worthing. All the remaining temporary staff were to finish at lunchtime on Friday and leave for home. His last trumpet lesson was due on Tuesday, he was meeting Adrian on Wednesday and, in all probability, there would be a last alcohol-fuelled evening on Thursday with the few who were still left from that intake of forty back in October.

Work at the registrar's department had assumed an air of unreality, for they were simply marking time. Freda found plenty to talk to Martin about. He had more or less learnt her entire life history during that week. Every so often there would be talk of how good the Sussex coast was for holidays. Had Martin ever been to Chichester, Arundel, and many other enticing places? If he did, he had to be sure to let Freda know that he was coming down!

That evening, Martin and three others were sharing a table for dinner at the Eardley, as had been their custom since almost the very first week. Sally, as she had already indicated, was doing her shift as a waitress. Martin thought that he would like to see her socially on her own, but couldn't figure out how to arrange a meeting while his colleagues were within earshot. Suddenly he had a brainwave! If anybody wanted a drink from the bar, it was charged to your room.

Order slips, which had to be signed, were provided at the tables. Martin had done this once or twice before, although most times he just took a glass of water with his meal. He removed one of these little slips from the clip next to the condiments and wrote 'bottle of light ale, room 12', and added 'see you later?'. The bottle of beer duly arrived and Sally just nodded to Martin. He winked back in return, after making sure that no one was noticing anything.

"Are you coming to the Connaught?" one of the others asked Martin. He said that he was not sure, but maybe towards the end of the evening. With that he went up to his room. He knew that they stopped serving dinner at eight-thirty during the week, and imagined that Sally might finish any time after that. Of course, because he had hardly exchanged any words with her over the past months, he had no idea whether she had to do other kitchen duties before finishing her shift. He could be left kicking his heels for hours!

He decided to repair to the lounge with a book and wait. He did not have to wait very long. Sally, still wearing her apron, emerged from the dining room. "I saw you through the swing doors. I finish at nine. Where shall we meet? ... Not here!" she added. Martin suggested the Captain's Cabin, a rather nice establishment on Sea Road.

The Captain's Cabin was a 'theme' pub, long before these became fashionable. It had a genuine ship's figurehead outside the front door – a gaudily painted, well-endowed lady projecting over the pavement below. It had 'galleon style' doors and, once inside, lots of tub-shaped seats, a pair of oars over the bar, two ships in bottles and lots of old naval prints around the walls. At ten past nine Sally came into the pub still wearing her black waitress uniform under her coat. "Sorry, I didn't have time to go home first," she offered by way of explanation. After Martin bought her a drink they, almost strangers up until then, exchanged the usual preliminaries – what they had done, where they had been, likes and dislikes, family background, etc.

Martin, somewhat hesitantly, said that he was sorry that he hadn't really spoken to her very much, all those times she had come to the Connaught, but he felt that he was out of his depth compared with (here he mentioned a few of the chaps who had already gone home). Sally just laughed and said that they had all tried it on with her, but she could hold her own. There was nothing in it. She then said that it was a pity that she had not got to know him, as he was going home at the end of the week. Not, she hastened to add, was this to be construed as any kind of an invitation but, simply, that he seemed to be unlike the macho types who always tried to chat her up, and a musician too. She said that she preferred the company of people in 'the arts'. The rapport between them increased as the evening wore on, and then it was time to go.

"Shall I see you home?"

"Yes, that would be kind of you."

As they walked the half mile or so through the residential streets Sally took Martin's arm. His brain was now going into overdrive. The big conundrum was now his and his alone to resolve. Except that he just couldn't.

The almost to be expected 'would you like to come in for a coffee?' was unashamedly met in the affirmative. A little later, in Sally's bedsit, a first kiss and then a little fumbling of the preliminary nature seemed to be met with enthusiasm. Sally suddenly said, "I'm not going to sleep with you tonight, though."

Martin was speechless. He had never imagined that any woman would consider that to be a possibility on a first date. In reality, it wasn't even a date, not in the conventional sense anyway. Martin began to feel guilty; but not enough to mention that he had a girlfriend back in Barnet. Instead he said that, of course, he had not had any intention of doing what she had just said. He found that he could not say 'sleep with you'. His strict upbringing would not allow such overtly sexual conversation with a woman he had only just met, even though Sally had made it quite clear that she was attracted to musicians.

Not knowing whether he meant it or not, Martin said that he was planning to come down to Worthing one weekend within the next month or two and Sally suggested that they write to each other. They exchanged addresses and had a long, lingering kiss on the doorstep. Sally had told Martin that she would not be working any more evening shifts that week; she was off to Redhill to visit her mum, so he knew that he might not see her again, unless things developed. But there again, his thoughts about Sarah were now in a temporary state of flux. That, he thought, would surely be resolved once Sally was a distant memory? But the see-saw of his thoughts was becoming hard to reconcile. If the pubs had still been open, he would have had another few drinks to deaden his brain cells.

The following evening, Martin went over to Peter's for his last lesson. Peter suggested that they play a few duets and then he coached Martin in how to do lip-slurs, an exercise that he insisted would strengthen the embouchure. Martin mentioned his Sunday night blow with Stan, which surprised Peter. "Do you know," he began, "Stan and I have been gigging together all around the Sussex coast for nigh on twenty-five years. We are considered to be a bit of a team. We've done all the Lallys so many times that we hardly need the music any longer!"

Martin queried the word 'Lallys'. Peter explained that, in the world of freelance dance band musicians, they were the staple diet of any library. He went on to say that Jimmy Lally had a knack of writing arrangements of any popular tune in such a clever way that they could be played by anything from a quintet up to a fifteen piece and still sound good. "How is that possible?" asked Martin. Peter opened a cupboard and pulled out a Lally arrangement. It was 'The Lady Is a Tramp'. He found the lead alto part and showed Martin how, in addition to playing the lead, all the other essential parts of the arrangement were cued in smaller script.

"So," he said, pointing to passages on the score, "imagine you haven't got a trombone player or a tenor sax, and they have a solo passage, here are the cued-in parts."

Martin asked whether they were hard to find. Peter laughed. "Every bandleader in the country has got them. The guy is a genius… must be quite rich too by now." Peter returned to the cupboard and after a bit of searching handed Martin a dog-eared copy of 'I Got Rhythm.' "I have two copies of this one. Consider this a leaving present. It's the full set: three trumpets, two trombones, four saxes, four rhythm and violin. It's got some passages for improvised solos so, who knows, you might be able to use it on a gig one day." Peter asked whether Martin was going to continue with lessons when he returned home, adding that it would be a shame not to. Martin thought that he would if he could find another teacher. He also said that he had got used to the practice routines and was definitely going to continue with them, whatever else. Then it was goodbyes, Martin's effusively expressed gratitude, a firm handshake and a final wave before a smiling Peter closed the front door. And that was that.

Saying goodbye to Adrian, who he did not know very well but nevertheless considered a friend, took place the following evening in the Lion, the scene of their joint endeavours quite recently. Adrian was already there when Martin arrived, and so was Rufus, the sousaphone player. "Ah," exclaimed the landlord, "we have a band, do we?" The reason that they were there was briefly explained, as they collected their pints and found an unoccupied table.

"Have you got any gigs up in north London?" Adrian asked. Martin told him about the demise of Jimmy Prior's Jazzmen and went on to say that three of the old band – the guitarist, bass player and himself – might possibly form a trio and look for some dance band work. At this, Adrian and Rufus looked aghast. "Come on man, you surely can't want to do that sort of thing? You are a jazz musician, and we all need to preach the message. How else will it happen without us?"

Martin had to explain that he fully understood Adrian and Rufus's dedication to spreading the word – i.e. that in their view, which he respected, New Orleans revivalism was the only pure form of jazz. But he personally had more catholic tastes as, he reminded Adrian, they had already discussed. He argued that surely there was room for a wide variety of jazz and, quite profoundly, concluded that giving the public more choice might be beneficial to all, including those of Adrian's persuasion. Audiences, he reasoned, would be more likely to cross boundaries, the more different styles that they heard.

"Well OK," Adrian acknowledged, "but, *dance bands?*"

It would be a means to an end, Martin explained. Seventy-five percent of all dance band music was in four-four time, as was jazz. "Nothing to stop us playing jazz choruses for quicksteps and foxtrots," he went on, "and we stand a better chance of getting gigs as a trio. Apart from the money side of it, we could approach venues that would not normally book a six- or seven- piece band."

The logic of all this was grudgingly accepted but then Adrian thought that he had found a trump card. "You won't get very far by just you, the only melody instrument, playing the trumpet, chorus after chorus, all evening, will you?"

"No, I wouldn't. Sorry, I should have explained that I will be on piano, which is my main instrument. I am only just beginning to play the trumpet in public."

Adrian said that he had forgotten that Martin was a pianist, and had never heard him play. Rufus wondered whether the landlord would be okay about Martin playing the piano while they were all there. Might be a nice thing to do on this, their last evening together. Martin needed no persuasion, and the landlord was more than happy. So the three of them moved across the room to the upright piano and Martin launched into his repertoire of favourite pieces: 'Honeysuckle Rose', 'Tishomingo Blues', 'All Of Me', 'Georgia On My Mind' and, finally, 'King Porter Stomp', a composition by Jelly Roll Morton which Martin had sometimes played as a solo feature with Jimmy Prior.

"I don't know why you are bothering with the trumpet,"

said Adrian. "I don't mean to be rude by the way. I quite like your trumpet playing but (he paused for the right words to formulate in his mind) your piano playing is in a different league. Not New Orleans style of course, but I can see the influence of Teddy Wilson maybe? Not that I listen to mainstream jazz," he added, rather too quickly, "but you obviously know what you are doing."

"Anyway," Martin said, acknowledging the compliment, backhanded or not, "I can do this sort of stuff all night. I will have to learn a few waltzes, Latin American and Old Time, for those that ask for it, and then I'm sure I stand a chance of the gigs I was talking about."

They ended the evening talking politics, a subject that found all three in some degree of accord, Martin and Rufus being both left of centre, Adrian being on the far left. The Prime Minister, Harold Macmillan, came in for much derision. At last! After the continuing failure to agree about music, complete harmony prevailed. They finished their pints and said their farewells, Martin promising to let them know in advance if he came down to Sussex again.

One more day and one more evening now lay ahead. Martin experienced pangs of longing for all the good times he had enjoyed since last October. He wanted to do it all over again. In this frame of mind, he found the last full day at Durrington frustrating. He just couldn't stop thinking about what he was going to be missing. Freda, sensing his mood, tried to cheer him up and told him never to forget that it was a two-way process. He, she volunteered, had brightened their lives a little, what with his music and his general enthusiasm. Once more she reminded him to be sure to get in touch should he come down again. Once more Martin reflected on the odds of him getting into a compromising situation with Freda should he do so. They would shorten considerably!

It had been arranged that the remaining twelve temporary staff would meet up in the Connaught for the last time. It had, after all, been their spiritual home for so long. It was so different from those early weeks when Biggleswade had taken over as a Worthing guide and guru, leading to some memorable nights out, where rampant irresponsibility was the order of the day. This evening the nine chaps and three women just sat at a large table and exchanged notes about what they were going to be doing next week. There was also a great deal of reminiscing about the highs and lows since October, but the fun had gone. It was almost as if the last six months had been something that they had read about in a book rather than participated in. Farewells can often be an anti-climax, and this was no exception. They didn't even get properly drunk, as they ought to have done. "See you in the morning then," they said to each other as they went back to their respective hotels and packed their cases for the last time.

Martin checked out of the Eardley, but before he was able to make his departure, one of the elderly ladies who were resident all year round beckoned him over to where she was sitting in the lounge. "I believe that you are musical?" she said. Martin nodded as she continued: "My son is playing the lead role in *The Music Man* at the Criterion Theatre in the West End. He is a real star and he has a lovely voice. Do you know the music from the show?" Martin said that he wasn't sure, so she asked him to wait a minute. She then picked up one of those old-fashioned music cases, with leather straps and a brass crossbar that had been beside her chair. She pulled out a sheaf of piano music, most being Victorian parlour ballads, and eventually found what she was looking for. A bright blue cover with a jaunty figure holding a cane in the manner of Frankie Vaughan, and in white flowing letters across the front 'Till There Was You'. She gave it to Martin. "Please have it and promise that you will learn it. It's a big hit. If you are ever in London, go to see the show. I'm sure you will enjoy it. If they let you go backstage afterwards you can tell my son that you met me in Worthing." For one moment Martin thought that she was also going to offer him a complimentary ticket; but she did not. He thanked her for the music and promised to learn it, then apologised for having to dash as the coach was waiting outside. "Yes, yes, off you go and good luck with your music, young man."

The morning at Durrington consisted of a general clearing out of desks, handing over ongoing work to a colleague on the permanent staff and saying goodbye to all and sundry. At eleven o'clock Mr Shoesmith made the rounds, shaking hands and offering a few words of wisdom. At eleven thirty the coach arrived to take them to Durrington Station. Freda, at this juncture, moved into Martin's personal space and gave him a hug. "Bye-bye, Martin. We are so sorry to see you go." Martin thought that the 'we' might be the royal variety.

Then it was the final journey home.

CHAPTER 19

Austin Royce

May 1962

The Red Lion in Barnet has an enormous bronze red lion supported on a wall bracket hovering menacingly over the pedestrians below. The pub, at the junction of the High Street and Fitzjohn Avenue where Owen lived, was where, on a Tuesday evening in May, Owen, Brian and Martin were having a brainstorming session over some pints of Friary Meux Bitter. Owen started: "I saw an advert in the *Melody Maker* from an agent, looking for solo pianists, duos and trios. There's a lot of work out there: weddings, birthday parties and the like. I reckon it's worth a shot. What do you think?"

Martin spoke at some length about the need to learn enough straight dance music, in addition to the jazz standards, to get away with it convincingly. "I need to find some waltzes, cha-chas, stuff like the Gay Gordons, the Valeta, St Bernard's Waltz, 'Knees Up Mother Brown', maybe sambas and rumbas…"

"Does anyone still do the rumba?" asked Brian, with eyebrows registering amusement.

Owen said that he had been to his aunt's fiftieth birthday recently and not only did they do rumbas, but the paso-doble as well. For good measure, he added that, naturally, we would be expected to play 'Happy Birthday to You',

'For He's a Jolly Good Fellow', 'Auld Lang Syne' and the 'National Anthem'; probably on every gig.

Martin volunteered to buy the music that they would need. He thought his first port of call might be the piano stool at his home. In there was an old *Daily Express Community Song Book* which, with a bit of luck, could contain some of what was needed. Conversation turned, inevitably, to rehearsals.

"What about the tea room that Jimmy found, just before he packed it all in?" Brian said.

"I've got a better idea," replied Owen. "This place is vast. I'd be surprised if they didn't have a function room upstairs. Let's ask."

Indeed, there was such a room, and it could be had for a very modest five shillings on a Sunday morning. Was there another time or day of the week for a band rehearsal? Clearly not; the Rising Sun had set the trend, never to be questioned. "What shall we call ourselves?" Martin asked. "I don't mind using my name if you want to." Owen also thought that his name could be up for grabs perhaps, while Brian said that he really didn't care. Talk then moved to composite names, perming two out of all the combinations of Martin Weston, Owen Meadowcroft and Brian Troughton.

Brian, bored by all this said, "Unless one of us is the bandleader and uses his name, we might as well have a completely made-up name." This required another round of drinks in order for the creative juices to flow. After a few blind alleys had been explored, to change the subject, Brian said that he was selling his beloved Triumph Gloria as he had just bought a 1949 Austin Sixteen. The great thing being that the Austin was big enough to accommodate the three of them plus instruments – his of course being a double bass.

Owen was the one with the lightbulb moment. "Hey! How about makes of motor car? Austin is a rather classy name, to start with." Owen had with him a copy of the *Barnet Press*, the local newspaper. He found a page with a bit of white space devoid of print and began to make a list. Austin, Morris, Bentley, Mercedes, Daimler, Vauxhall, Lagonda, Riley, Triumph, Healey, Sunbeam Talbot, Ford, Rolls Royce, Hillman, Humber, Standard, Jaguar. He wrote and then crossed out MG, saying that it was not a word, in itself. He substituted Guy. "They make buses and lorries," he explained. Some combinations began to emerge. Maurice Ford (from Morris), Guy Hillman, Mercedes La Gonda, Ford Talbot. Brian, trying to be the sensible one, said that he had not met many people with the Christian name Ford, and wasn't Mercedes a girl's name? He suggested that they stick with the obvious three: Austin, Guy and Morris. Owen said that, in that case, how about Maurice Ford and his Music, as it had already been suggested? Martin ventured that it sounded a bit pedestrian, just like their cars. He personally thought that Rolls sounded good. Guy Rolls, Morris Rolls, Austin Rolls? "I don't think so. Sounds like a sandwich," was Brian's opinion. Owen then came up with the winner. A name teeming with class: Austin Royce and his Music. Yes, yes, yes!

Owen then produced another surprise. "I was thinking that piano, bass and drums might be better than using a guitar. If we are going to do sambas, cha-chas, old-time dances and all that, you really need drums to get the rhythms."

Martin was quick to say, "But, Owen, we've just spent the last hour sorting out what we are going to do as a trio, with you on guitar; surely you don't mean that you're resigning before we even start? There's no question of you not being in the band. *No question!*" Brian nodded in agreement. Owen was now smiling in an enigmatic fashion, the ends of his moustache suggesting private amusement, reminiscent of Terry Thomas just before one of his classic utterances. After taking a long pull on the cheroot he was smoking, he informed them that he had been thinking about getting a drum kit. Years ago, he explained, he started out as a drummer. Martin and Brian were dumbfounded. Both privately wondered how good he would be, but both decided not to say anything. All this called for yet another round of drinks.

"Anything else we need to think about, except the obvious one – getting the gigs?" Martin asked. Owen, who seemed to be more in tune with the requirements of the dance band world than the other two, brought up the subject of a uniform. It was clearly going to be necessary to obtain dinner jackets and bow ties, two items of a gentleman's wardrobe that no self-respecting jazz musician would ever admit to owning. Martin was only glad that Ted Nottage did not, under any circumstance, frequent the Red Lion. He had long considered it to be the haunt of Tories, his natural enemy, and had he deigned to honour the premises with his custom, it would have been entirely for subversive reasons. On overhearing his mates proposing to adopt the uniform of the regimented longhair musician, he would not have been able to contain himself. To him, this would have been unexpected manna from heaven, an opportunity not to be missed. Martin could easily conjecture the well-crafted derision that Ted, the champion of the working class, would have heaped joyfully upon the three of them.

It transpired that Owen already had the full gear as, it was later discovered, he was a Mason. This was kept a closely guarded secret by most members of the organisation, only to be revealed when the masonic handshake was given and received. When it was accidentally let slip by Owen, both Martin and Brian turned up to the next rehearsal with their left trouser leg rolled up to the knee. This joke was not received well by its target.

Brian and Martin both had dark suits, which they needed for work and, for the time being, this would have to do. Martin did, however, have a plan to convert his first suit, which he now rarely wore, into a dinner jacket. It would involve a bit of tailoring on the lapels, but it might be possible. He resolved to ask Sarah whether she could do it, as she had made her own skirts from time to time, a skill that many young women learned in the austere post-war years, before many of the population had such luxuries as television sets and motor cars and the wherewithal to keep up with changing fashion.

And so 'Austin Royce and his Music' was born, as thus far had always been the case for Martin's bands, in yet one more Barnet pub. Without discussion, Brian and Martin had both tacitly accepted that should there be a need for a bandleader, it would be Owen. As time went by this proved to be a brilliant decision.

At the weekend, Martin broached the dinner jacket question to Sarah. Uncomfortable about the fact that

Martin's father had bought the suit, she insisted on being absolved of any responsibility if she made a mess of the alteration but, to Martin's relief, said that it could be done. She would cut the lapels on Martin's charcoal grey suit to the requisite curved 'shawl' configuration, then they could be overlaid with grosgrain, a robust black shiny material. The trousers would only need a thin strip of the same stuff down the central seams and 'hey presto' the dance band uniform would be Martin's!

The next bit was trickier: an explanation to his parents of what he was going to do. He decided to use a tactical ploy. "You know my mates, Owen and Brian? We are going to form a dance trio," he announced. "I will need to buy a dinner jacket. It's what they all wear."

"Don't be ridiculous," Harold said. "You work for a bank. Your future is with them. This music thing is becoming a bit of an obsession. How many of your friends actually make a living out of music? And anyway, I'm not having it!" Harold viewed anyone owning a dinner jacket with suspicion. Being a dyed-in-the-wool northerner, he considered it to be the uniform of the soft, southern privileged classes. And anyway, a musician was not a proper job. The civil service, Harold's employer, or banking, were proper jobs.

Even in his twenty-first year, Martin had to accept a degree of parental control while he still lived under their roof. He bit his tongue and refrained from saying what he wanted to say, i.e. that Henry Hall, Harold's favourite bandleader, regularly appearing on the nation's TV screens, was presumably enjoying a considerably better living than Harold. Instead, he reassured his parents that playing in bands would only be an evening and weekend occupation. They were not to worry about him leaving the bank.

Then, judging that he had regained the initiative, he played his tactical card. "Well, how about if I get my old suit converted? That would hardly cost anything. Maybe Sarah could do it. She's quite good at dressmaking you know."

"I bought that suit," replied Harold.

"Well, yes Dad, I know. But I don't wear it for work anymore. It just hangs in the wardrobe doing nothing."

Harold said that he washed his hands of the whole thing and he supposed that Martin would do exactly as he liked… as always. That seemed to be the end of that conversation, and it was as near to winning an argument with his father as Martin had ever managed.

Kathleen had said very little up to now but, as a conclusion of some sort appeared to have been reached, mentioned that she still had her father's bow tie kept safely, in its original box. He used to wear it when he sang with the Halifax Choral Society, and she thought that Martin should have it, just so long as he looked after it. Martin was transported back to 1944 in a flash. It was Jack Hellowell, his grandfather, who had first opened Martin's eyes to the joys of music by taking him to hear the Salvation Army Band, when Martin was evacuated to Halifax during the war.

CHAPTER 20

Knightsbridge

May 1962

"All right, Redgrave, you can open the doors!" barked Arnold Backhouse, chief cashier at Lloyds Bank, Knightsbridge, to the maroon-jacketed bank messenger who did not, for those of Mr Backhouse's generation, qualify for the courtesy title 'Mr'. Martin, and all those below a certain age, would not have dreamed of displaying this seeming lack of good manners, but neither Mr Redgrave nor Mr Backhouse had the slightest problem with it. It was a long-established protocol, developed from the relationship between masters and servants. Not only that, Arnold Backhouse had been a drill sergeant in the army, before going to Normandy in 1944 to win the war. Mr Redgrave had also played his part in winning the war, but neither of them acknowledged nor even spoke about each other's contribution.

Arnold, not that anyone ever called him that, apart from, presumably, his wife, was a little over five-foot five, bald, barrel-shaped, ramrod straight and exuded an air of self-importance. As befitted an ex-serviceman, his black shoes were polished to a mirror-like surface. He always wore a waistcoat into which he was now replacing his gold half hunter watch and chain. There was a perfectly good and visible clock in the banking hall but Arnold needed the staff to know that his own personal timepiece took precedence.

The opening and closing of the huge doors depended upon BMT, not GMT. His voice had that curious accent of one whose background may well have been humble but who had trained himself to sound more 'educated'. This was delivered with a rasp, probably due to forty years as a heavy smoker.

On his return from Worthing, Martin had been posted to the chief cashier's section. This consisted of seven cashiers and Martin, whose role was a ragbag of assorted tasks not fitting into one of the more clearly defined categories within the bank. He had not found his previous boss, Mrs Darcey, a lot of fun, but was beginning to wish that he was back on the foreign counter with the relatively straightforward duties that this entailed. The chief cashier's primary role was, quite literally, to oversee the cashiers' windows from a slightly elevated position in a sort of pulpit. From this perch, he could also survey the entire banking hall and, of course, bark out the order to open and shut the doors. He was never expected to perform any normal duties like serving customers at a till. No, his role was to be in charge. Nobody ever spoke their mind to Mr Backhouse. An atmosphere of apprehension, bordering on fear, was the normal experience under his regime.

The duties that he had delegated to Martin consisted of such things as sending cheques back to the payee when there were insufficient funds in the customer's account (sometimes with a letter of explanation), the calculation and payment of branch staff salaries, and entering all bank accrued 'freebies' into a ledger entitled 'Interest, Commission and Discount' (I, C and D for short), or I, ciddle and diddle as it was referred to by older staff members. The I, C and D thing never deserted Martin who, when in later life, during a conversation, should have replied 'I see' often said "I, C and D" instead, to everybody's puzzlement.

Martin was also used as a back-up to the cashiers when things got hectic. He was not trained to operate a till, but had to assist in clearing the incoming cheques. This entailed the signature recognition of a section of the bank's customers; say those with surnames from A to C for instance. Only by the process of a bank clerk recognising and approving the signature would an incoming cheque be posted to the correct account. Customers' names were not printed on cheques in 1962. Knightsbridge had a very large Arabic customer base, and the A to C ledger, which Martin often had to deal with, contained all the Ahmeds – dozens of them. Differentiating one from the other, just on the basis of scrawled signatures, taxed Martin to the limit.

A further little delight, performed on a weekly basis, was the 'calling of the ledgers'. This required two people: one to call out the latest balance on a customer's ledger sheet while the other confirmed that the same balance appeared on the customer's statement. The older bank employees had perfected a fail-safe aural system to remove any element of doubt. When enunciating the round figures 30, 40, 50, etc. one would call out thir-tie, for-tie, etc., rhyming with necktie. This ensured that there was no confusion as to whether the numbers thirteen, fourteen and so on had been called.

Martin and a couple of younger, like-minded colleagues used to delight in calling out in a loud clear voice the 'tie' appellation when there was absolutely no need to do so, as in 'twen-tie', the one round figure which could not be confused, or, even more preposterously, 'thir-tie four pounds, three shillings and two pence'. All this irked the older, more responsible staff members, but it was hardly a disciplinary offence.

When Martin had left for Worthing, one of his regrets was that he had to forgo the Friday night boozing in Tattersall's Tavern. Now he made sure that he made up for lost time. While he had been away, there had been an influx of a few more male and female clerks around the same age as Martin. So now it was necessary to bag a long table in the pub, to accommodate the larger group. This duty was allocated to whoever got there first. On the first Friday following his return, Martin regaled his colleagues with stories of the best bits from the Worthing Friday night raves. Some thought it all a bit 'student-like' but others, especially Robert Melton, one of the newcomers, were completely sold on the concept of this pseudo-intellectual irresponsibility.

"So, how about a Friday rave next week?" said Robert. There was a bit of discussion about repeating the same stunts, but Martin was firmly against that idea.

"I've done them already, and it was as much to do with the people who were involved. I don't want to be disappointed by revisiting what I have already done. By all means, do some of them if you want to, but leave me out."

Robert asked how many of them had noticed that there was a proper bar, serving pub drinks, on the platform at Liverpool Street Metropolitan Line. Nobody had. "Right then, I propose that we meet up there for drinks and maybe go on to the Edgware Road where there are some really seedy pubs. It will be a lot different from drinking here in Knightsbridge." Martin enquired in what way did this constitute a rave. Robert just said that it might turn into a rave of its own volition, to which Martin, the self-confessed expert in this field, merely shrugged his shoulders. Two of the girls, Vicky and Sue, said that they were up for it, as did four of the lads.

Another newcomer was Roger Camborne, a compulsive teller of shaggy dog stories. Having ensured that he had everyone's attention, he proceeded that evening to tell the worst joke of all time. It was called 'The Two Possibilities'.

When you are born, there are two possibilities. You will either be a girl or a boy. If you are a girl, you are laughing, but if you are a boy then there are two possibilities. When you grow up you will either get a job in Civvy Street, or you will go into the armed forces. If you get a job in Civvy Street, you are laughing, but if you go into the armed forces then there are two possibilities. You will either be sent to somewhere cushy, like Cyprus, or you will be sent to a war zone. If you are sent to somewhere cushy then you are laughing, but if you are sent to a war zone then there are two possibilities. Either you will be in a combative role or a non-combative role. If you are in a non-combative role you are laughing, but if you are in a combative role there are two possibilities. Either you will come through unscathed or you will not. It you come through unscathed you are laughing, but if not, then there are two possibilities. Either you will be wounded or you will be killed. If you are wounded, you are laughing, but if you are killed there are two possibilities. Either your body will be recovered, or it will not be recovered. If it is not recovered you are laughing, but if it is recovered there are two possibilities. Either you will be buried or cremated. If you are buried you are laughing, but if you are cremated there are two possibilities. Either your ashes will be scattered, or they will be turned into something. If they are scattered you are laughing, but if they are turned into something there are two possibilities. Either they will be used for agricultural fertiliser, or for the manufacture of bog paper. If they are used for agricultural fertiliser you are laughing, but if they are used for bog paper then there are two possibilities. Either the bog roll will be put into the ladies' toilet or the gents. If it is put into the gents, then you are laughing, but if it is put into the ladies, there are two possibilities!

Martin, at this point, suddenly remembered that he had promised to meet Sarah in the Black Horse in half an hour; and here he was, still well over an hour away from Barnet! He gulped down the remains of his pint, explained why he had to dash, and ran to the Tube station. The Black Horse, when Martin reached it some seventy minutes later, was half full and, to his relief, Sarah and another girl were sitting at a corner table. "I had given you up ages ago. By the way, this is Veronica, this is Martin." It seemed that Martin's abject apologies about having to 'just have a quick one with the new people' cut no ice. "I don't wait in pubs on my own, Martin. You should know that," was all he got by way of a reply. It seemed that when she arrived, and didn't find Martin, she had straight away retraced her steps to the door when she saw Veronica, an old schoolfriend, walk by the window. A quick knock on the window, signals of recognition, and Veronica was inside the pub.

"Ah, I see. Well, it was lucky that you both met up, wasn't it?"

"Yes, Martin, it was, but don't think this lets you off the hook!" This was said with a twinkle in her eye, maybe just for the benefit of Veronica.

The next day, both Sarah and Martin deliberately avoided any reference to the previous evening. It could have led to the sort of discussion that each had been avoiding for a few months. So best to let sleeping dogs lie. Nevertheless, they had a great evening down at the Alex, listening to the superb Len Adams. Martin, as the returning lost soul, was given a generous spot on the piano. Both Len and Ivy, his wife, wanted to hear all about Martin's six months in Worthing, so it was arranged that Sarah and Martin would go to their house for Sunday tea. Martin was not overly enthusiastic. He could think of better things to do with his weekend, but felt a sense of loyalty to the man who had turned his piano playing around.

Sunday morning saw 'Austin Royce' rehearsing in the upstairs function room of the Red Lion. Martin had found two Latin American sheet music albums, *So It's Sambas You Want* and *The Best of the Cha Cha Cha*. He had also copied out in longhand some old-time dances that he had found in the *Daily Express Community Songbook* at home. He had worked out by ear a few waltzes such as 'Now is the Hour', 'It Happened in Monterey' and, hot off the press, 'Moon River'. Owen had managed to buy a rudimentary drum kit, and Brian had brought his bass along. As all three were quite accomplished musicians, the rehearsal went along almost without a hitch. Owen, to Brian and Martin's relief, could play the drums quite well. He was certainly no Gene Krupa, but he did at least keep good time.

Some people from the bar had come up out of curiosity, hearing the faint banging of Owen's bass drum from the ceiling above. One of them was a swarthy lady of Middle Eastern appearance. She introduced herself as Maffi and then told three surprised musicians that she was a belly dancer and lived locally. She went on to say that she was looking for some gigs. Now *here* was an interesting proposition. The band had not yet appeared in public, but this was a definite carrot – self-dangling! Maybe they could do some cabaret work using Maffi? Much more lucrative. Owen seized the initiative. "Would you care to give us a little of what you can do?" Maffi said that, as long as she had some sort of Eastern rhythm on the drums, she would be happy to.

And show them she did! She hoisted up the front of her blouse and tucked it into her bra straps. Then, to the steady beat of Owen's big floor tom-tom, and nothing else, she gyrated; her belly seeming to have a will of its own as it moved in and out, up and down, side to side, in a very sexy manner. In synch, she executed slinky arm and hand movements. It was a mesmerising, crowd-pulling exhibition. Enough to elicit spontaneous applause from the few who had ventured up from the bar. "Of course," she explained, "when I am in my outfit, sequined bra and knickers and lots of tassels, it is more spectacular." The private thoughts of the three members of Austin Royce and his Music, had they been compared, would have been found to be identical and unprintable. She was a very curvaceous woman with long, flowing black hair and enormous 'come to bed' eyes.

Owen explained that they had not yet got any gigs and were at the rehearsal stage at present. He took Maffi's address and telephone number and promised to let her know if anything was in the offing where the band could use her undoubted talents. Maffi said that she might be able to arrange something too, as she had a few contacts in the entertainment world. After she had left, Martin said that the sort of gigs that might turn out to be their bread and butter, in all probability, would be weddings and birthday parties. This kind of engagement, he thought, might not be the best way to launch a belly dancer on to an unprepared audience. Nevertheless, he continued, trying to get some cabaret work was a great idea. Just, how to go about it? "Perhaps we could leave that to Maffi," Owen replied. "I am going to phone her and see whether I can go around to her place to take a few photos. I can find out what sort of contacts she has exactly, and take it from there." Brian and Martin agreed that this was an excellent idea.

That afternoon, Sarah and Martin got on a trolleybus by High Barnet Church. They got off in Whetstone, where Len Adams lived. He had a detached bungalow in a quiet street, just off the main road. His pride and joy was a fairly new Knight upright piano. In his view, of all the modern piano manufacturers, Knight produced the definitive product. It had a very good action and a deep tone. Ivy had prepared some sandwiches and cakes, which she brought in from the kitchen. Len needed no persuasion to play some of his specialities, including 'Temptation Rag', 'Canadian Capers' and, by way of contrast, 'Clair de Lune' by Debussy. There was a brief pause for refreshments before Martin was asked to play. Meanwhile, they chatted about Jimmy Prior's forthcoming wedding, and Ivy said, "I expect it will be your turn next."

Martin was caught completely off-guard and startled.

Sarah said nothing at all so, as there was a pregnant pause, Martin blurted out, "Err, ha-ha-ha, you mustn't jump the gun, Ivy."

Fortunately, nothing more was said but Len was observed kicking Ivy's ankle underneath the table. Meanwhile, in Martin's head, the wise words of Freda, regarding taking your time before settling down, came rushing back with some force; as did the vague promise that he had made to Sally (the one who had said 'I am not going to sleep with you *this time*').

They made their excuses at six-thirty and, on the way back to Barnet, Martin asked whether Sarah fancied Wood Green Jazz Club, rather than going home. She said that by the time they got there it would be around interval time so, as she had an aversion to Monday mornings, she thought that she would call it a day and wash her hair before having an early night. Martin was in no mood to argue, particularly after the guided weapon that Ivy had fired earlier, which could still belatedly explode. He certainly did not want to have any kind of discussion about marriage or the future. He sensed that neither did Sarah, but was unsure why that might be.

After a brief snog on Sarah's doorstep, Martin wandered back to the High Street fancying a pint or two. He passed the Crown and Anchor, not really wishing to drink with the 'College of Fred' students; for that was their local. He crossed the road and made his way into the Bull. This was a long, thin pub squeezed between an archway leading to a builder's yard and a newsagent's. It was dark inside – it always was, winter and summer. Customers were in short supply but, seated on a barstool with his back to Martin, was a character whose shirt had managed to escape, in part, from a very old, worn leather belt encircling an ample waist. Unmistakable: Ted Nottage! Martin tapped him on the shoulder and, as he turned around, a quantity of beer that he had been about to swallow was ejected from his mouth in surprise, most of it, fortunately, back in the direction of his pint mug.

"Martin! Jesus! What are you doing here? I thought that you had emigrated to Sussex, or some such godforsaken place! How the hell are you?" Ted had not seen Martin at all since the last rehearsal of Jimmy Prior's Jazzmen at the now defunct Rising Sun.

Martin brought him up to date with the highlights of his six months in Worthing, emphasising the way that his trumpet playing had progressed, thanks to the lessons. After some hesitation, he also acquainted him with the latest developments since he had returned home, i.e. Austin Royce and his Music. He had thought that this was going to set Ted off onto one of his mocking diatribes but, no. He seemed to be unmoved by this news, to Martin's surprise, neither scathing nor sarcastic. "Well, before I left Hereford for Barnet, one of the things I found I had to do, in order to keep my lip in, was to play in some boring old dance band consisting of several geriatrics and me. They weren't sure what to make of me though." This, Martin had no difficulty at all in believing. "Ah well, the things one has to do for one's art!"

On being told about Maffi, his eyes lit up and he asked whether, by any chance, she had a gap between her two front teeth. Martin said that he had not noticed; he had been more interested in certain other parts of her anatomy. "Make sure you have a good look then, young Martin. If she has, you will be on to a good thing. Quite a lot of Middle Eastern women have this particular dental arrangement. It's a sure sign she will fuck like a rattlesnake!" Martin made a mental note to check this out next time he saw her and asked innocently how Ted had acquired this vital piece of information. He should have known better. It was not the first time that he had played the unwitting stooge to Ted. "Oh, sweet innocent youth!" Then, in a declamatory style, sung to an impromptu tune:

"There's an old Bazaar in Cairo, where the women parade all day.
Look for the gap-toothed beauties, and send the rest away.
After the ball is over, fuck 'til the break of day'."

Martin smiled ruefully. Ted went on to say that his new band, the one that now had Jimmy and Gus as members, was doing okay, but a bit short of work. At this piece of news, Martin smiled inwardly, and felt that maybe the lack of gigs was just retribution for the way that Jimmy had left Owen, Brian and himself in the lurch. Martin asked Ted if he knew anyone who taught trumpet locally. "Yes, I do. Me!" was the surprising reply.

"Really? You *are* joking, surely? Ted, you're not going to disillusion me, and tell me that you believe in adhering to musical theory, conventional technique, or any of that stuff?" He said this, having heard Ted's totally abandoned style of trumpet playing many, many times in the past, when, on a good day, he would throw all caution, and good taste, to the wind, determined in fact to be as abandoned on his trumpet as he was in all other aspects of his life. Pretty well the exact opposite of Peter Phillips, whichever way you looked at it.

"Well, there's a lot you don't know about me, young man. I could teach you a bit. Mind you, my methods are not orthodox." Not for one moment had Martin considered that they would be! It was arranged for Martin to come over to Ted's for a 'lesson' the following Sunday afternoon, after the Austin Royce rehearsal had finished.

CHAPTER 21

Woman trouble and Austin Royce gets a break

May 1962

"Well, I don't know, Martin, you seem to have changed. There was a time when you always wanted to see me. It's not like that now, is it?" Sarah had at last spoken her mind, after weeks of bottled-up thoughts. This was her response, having been told that Martin would be going out with work colleagues on Friday, and would probably be back too late to meet her that evening. Martin was hopeless at diplomacy and mumbled something about just having come back from Worthing, needing to get to know all these new people who he was working with and, finally, the fact that he was free on Saturday, and they would do something then. Nevertheless, Sarah was not at all happy.

That Friday evening at six o'clock, Vicky, Sue, Robert, Roger, John, Derek and Martin met up in the bar at Liverpool Street Underground Station. None of them, except Robert, whose idea it had been, could believe that it would be possible to walk through a door marked 'buffet' on platform two, be confronted by a pub-style bar counter complete with handpumps and spirit optics, and pass the hours away while Tube trains came in and out of the station. The barmaid was a middle-aged lady with dyed blonde frizzy hair who called everybody 'dear'. There was draught Bass on offer which the five chaps immediately went for. Vicky and Sue had gins and tonics. It was so bizarre! It was possible to hover in the open doorway observing the homeward-bound commuters cramming themselves into the trains, which arrived about every two minutes. At one point, Roger wandered out onto the platform with his pint, but was asked by the barmaid to come back inside the door. After three rounds of drinks Robert, who was notionally in charge, said that they were all going to Hammersmith for a surprise. This was all achievable without changing trains.

Out of Hammersmith Station Robert led the way. One dingy street led to another one even more run-down and certainly, as far as the women were concerned, a bit worrying. There were boarded-up shops, street lights that were not working, litter strewn here and there and a few dodgy-looking men who, fortunately, passed without a glance in their direction. Vicky said, "Robert, I'm not sure about this. Where are we going?"

"To the most unique pub in the whole of London," was his answer.

Within another hundred yards he halted outside an unlit building. There was no pub sign, nor any clue as to the function of the place. He opened the door and beckoned them all in. Inside it was still almost dark. True, there was a 40-watt naked bulb hanging on a flex from the ceiling, which just about illuminated a staircase, leading down to the basement. Sounds of conversation from below drifted upwards as the seven bank clerks made their way down the steps. They were in London's only cider and perry house, soon to be demolished, together with all the surrounding buildings, to make way for the Hammersmith flyover. The decor was sparse: a simple bar counter behind which were six or seven cider or perry casks on a shelf. The paintwork was a uniform nicotine colour and there were patches of tar forming droplets on the ceiling; no carpet, which was just as well as the floor was littered with cigarette ends. The drinks were astonishingly cheap, and the clientele all looked as if that was about the upper limit of what they could afford. Vicky and Sue were the only women in the bar, and all the Knightsbridge 'ravers' stood out like a sore thumb.

It was a unique experience; they were all agreed upon that. Not one that they particularly relished at the time but, heigh-ho, it could at some future date, possibly when in their dotage, enable them to reminisce, 'do you know, back in 1962, I drank in a pub that was only licenced to sell cider and perry'.

During the evening, Roger told another of his shaggy dog stories. It was entitled 'Welsh Hospitality':

Evan, Megan and their daughter, Gwyneth, lived in a little mining village in Wales. One evening there was a knocking at the door and, to Evan's astonishment, it was his old mate Dai from the next valley whom he had not seen for ten years. "Megan, come here; look, it's Dai the milk come to see us." Dai said "No, boyo, it's Dai the post actually." "Oh, so it is, so it is. Come in won't you and have some food. We weren't expecting visitors, but for my old mate nothing is too good. Gwyneth, my girl, this is Dai and I want you to show him all the old-fashioned Welsh hospitality. Go and fetch him a beer from the pub." "She's grown a bit, Evan, has she not? I remember her as a little girl." "Oh yes, she's eighteen *now you know." While Gwyneth was away getting the beer, Megan prepared a meagre meal from every last scrap they had in the larder. "We'll do our best, Dai, to provide you with all the old-fashioned Welsh hospitality. You'll not go hungry here." After he had eaten and drunk the beer, Evan said, "You'll not be going home this time of the night, Dai? You can have Gwyneth's bed and she will be more than happy to sleep on the settee." "Oh, no," protested Dai, "I couldn't possibly put you out to this extent." "Look, Dai, I said nothing is too good for you, my old friend, and I meant every word of it. While you are under my roof you will get all the old-fashioned Welsh hospitality and no argument!" The following morning, Evan awoke and opened the curtains in the marital bedroom, which overlooked the back garden. There, in flagrante delicto, was his old mate Dai stuck across his daughter, Gwyneth, on the lawn. "Gwyneth, **Gwyneth**, what do you think you are doing, my girl?" he shouted. "Well, Dad, you said that we were to show him all the old-fashioned Welsh hospitality," was her hesitant reply.*

"That's just it. Arch your back girl, and keep his bollocks off the damp grass!"

The following morning, Sarah and Martin were having coffee in a little cafe next door to Barnet Jazz Club in Union Street. "I won't beat about the bush. I can't see any future for you and me and I want to end it. By the way, this isn't just about last night, I've been thinking about it for some time." Those blunt words were spoken by Sarah. Martin had been half expecting this for a while, and his own doubts about their relationship should have helped him to accept it with some sense of relief. But no, suddenly he felt upset, guilty and, illogically, wanting to plead his case for staying with Sarah. He started to say that he was sorry about his absences but really wanted to try to make a go of it, but Sarah cut him short. Her mind was made up. In truth, it had been made up for a little while but last night's episode was the final straw. She went on to say that she had already told her mum what she was intending to do, and *she* did not try to dissuade her. "You're nowhere near ready to settle down, Martin. It's all for the best, *really*. You need to get whatever it is out of your system, and don't treat your girlfriend like an afterthought. I know that none of this was intentional. I *do* know this, but you must learn to consider the other person's feelings in the future. I have only had one serious boyfriend before you, but he was considerate all the time. And none of my friends has to put up with what I have. You are not deliberately unkind, but I think you are going to have to make sacrifices in the future, or not get into a relationship that you can't really commit to."

This was the longest outburst of that kind that she had ever delivered, and it left her exhausted. Martin, once again, tried to convince her that it could be all right and repeated his sorrow at the way she felt. "All my fault," he added. Sarah smiled and took his hands in hers. "It's all right, Martin. I am not angry with you. But it really is all over. I still like you a lot, but I have to let you go. You might even thank me eventually." With that she rose to her feet and walked out of the cafe, and out of Martin's life.

Martin eventually walked back up Union Street; past the jazz club, where he and Sarah had spent so many Monday evenings, and went home. His mother, surprised to see him back so soon, asked where Sarah was. "Mum, she has finished with me," he said with an unsteady voice. "That's what she has just told me." Kathleen wanted to know why, so Martin, in his own way, explained that he had not really put her first and that Sarah didn't think Martin was ready to settle down. Kathleen said that it was probably six of one and half a dozen of the other. Martin knew that it wasn't, but said nothing.

"Well, the best thing for you to do is to 'frame yourself' (a quaint northern expression). We don't hang around feeling sorry for ourselves in *this* family." Martin decided to do just that, and went back into town to look for a blue button-down collar shirt and a knitted black tie, ready for a trip to the Royalty Ballroom that same evening.

"Ladies and gentlemen, take your partners for the interval waltz." Ted Beaumont, who was seated behind the drum kit put the microphone back on its stand and counted the band in. The tune was 'Summer Night', a particular favourite of Martin's, written by the jazz saxophonist, Benny Carter. Martin had rehearsed it with Austin Royce the previous week. He had come down from the bar area, where he had parked himself for the last hour. There were a couple of attractive girls who had caught his eye, and he noticed, with interest, that neither of them had danced more than once with the same partner. Which one to go for? One was blonde, with a bouffant hairdo and quite tall. The other had an extremely pretty, elfin-like face and brown curly hair. She was about five-foot five, and Martin thought, a little too short perhaps?

"Would you like to dance?" he enquired of the taller one.

Yes, she would. Preliminary small talk soon began. Her name was Anne and she had only recently started coming to the Royalty. She had a faint northern accent, and it turned out that her family originally came from Manchester, and she still lived with her mum and dad. Martin had already noticed that she had a nice figure and caught a whiff of her perfume. It smelled of apples. When the dance ended, and with it the start of the twenty-minute interval, Martin's offer of a drink in the bar was met with something approaching enthusiasm! *Biggleswade should be here to witness this*, thought Martin. *As easy as falling off a log.*

Anne was very happy to accept Martin's offer of a second round of drinks and stayed with him for the rest of the evening. Their conversation had been quite open, without any kind of awkwardness. She was two years older than Martin, and worked for a merchant bank. She mentioned that she lived down Cat Hill, East Barnet. This was on the same bus route that Martin had to take, so they shared the first part of the journey, during which Martin wasted no time in asking Anne whether she would like to meet him again, perhaps tomorrow? Yes, she said, that would be nice. Martin said that he just might be able to borrow his mother's car and maybe they could go for a drive to a country pub in the evening. Before getting off the bus she wrote her address and telephone number on to a page in Martin's diary. The day had dawned with a sorrowful parting and had ended with lots of promise.

Owen Meadowcroft had some news to convey at the Sunday morning rehearsal. He had been to a restaurant with his wife during the week, to celebrate their wedding anniversary. It was in Potters Bar, quite near to Lloyds Bank, where Martin had first worked. There was a small stage at the far end of the dining area and Owen asked whether there was ever any music. "Mainly just for wedding or birthday parties, and the people who book the restaurant usually sort out their own bands," was the manager's reply. Owen gave him one of the newly printed business cards that he had produced: 'Austin Royce and his Music. For all parties, weddings and other occasions'. His telephone number followed. The manager said that he would pass on the number to anyone who might enquire in the future.

"Great," said Brian. "That's a good start."

"Haven't finished yet," continued Owen. "He asked what we charged, so I told him five pounds. That's thirty bob each and a tenner towards our expenses, like Brian's petrol and the sheet music that you are buying, Martin. Anyway, the guy said that he had been thinking about a dinner dance once a month on a Saturday and," – here, Owen paused for effect – "he is going to give us a trial in June. If it goes well, we could be in for however long it continues!"

Brian bought Owen and Martin a pint of bitter each to celebrate their good fortune. Owen also went on to say that he had visited Maffi during the week and she already had some publicity photos which would be fine for promotional purposes. She also had one or two contacts in the cabaret circuit. Not the West End, more the Luton Town Hall end of the market. Nevertheless, the money was at least twice as much as the normal dance gigs. Owen said that he would write to some of these venues. He was going to try to persuade one of the typists at work to produce a letter on a roneo master. Multiple copies could then be run off on a duplicating machine. (No photocopiers back then!)

Owen asked why Martin had brought his trumpet with him, and so Martin had to explain about the 'lesson' that Ted had promised him. There was a general falling about with laughter at the prospect of Ted; suddenly the learned trumpet tutor!

When the rehearsal came to an end at noon, Martin walked to the other end of the High Street to the terraced Victorian house where Ted Nottage lived. He had never been inside before today. The phrase 'he flung the door open wide' was one that Martin had only read on the printed page before. This was literally what Ted did in response to Martin's knock. Behind Ted's ample frame, Martin could see a continuous line of paintings stacked three deep all the way along each wall of the narrow hallway. "Mind how you go. One of these might be worth something some day!" Ted led the way into the back room. There were more paintings all over the place and one caught Martin's eye straightaway. It was a portrait of Benny Farr, leader of Mr Benjamin Farr's Jazz Orpheans. But it was not a kind portrait. From the angle it was painted, the main feature was the nose, looking up the nostrils. The hair was obviously greasy, with the odd lank strand falling across his forehead. Benny was wearing a cravat and a blazer with gold buttons. There was an elaborate embroidered badge on the breast pocket. Ted said, "In all my paintings you will find a certain part of the female anatomy. Can you see it here?" Martin scrutinised the canvas for a while and shook his head. "That's because you're looking at it face on. Try turning your head to one side and look at the badge." Sure enough, at an angle of 90 degrees the object that Ted had described was painted, in some detail, as part of the pattern. Apparently, Benny had seen the portrait and had left in high dudgeon. They had not spoken to each other since.

"Right, show me what you can do." Martin played a few notes to warm up and then started to play 'Georgia on my mind'. Ted stopped him. "I don't want to hear you play a tune with mistakes. Play me a diminished chord." Martin played a low C, Eb, F#, A. "Good, now up an octave." Martin got as far as the F# but couldn't manage the A. After a few more chords, all dictated by Ted, Martin finished up with the same problem. Lack of control on the high notes.

"I know what you're doing wrong. You're forcing the bloody mouthpiece against your teeth. I can see it, as well as hear it. Look, watch me." Ted picked up his own trumpet and sailed up through the intervals reaching top C without much apparent effort. "See my lips? There's a cushion of air between my teeth and where the mouthpiece is." This seemed very much unlike anything that Martin had observed when watching Ted Beaumont's trumpet player, and others. Ted picked up a pencil and, on the wallpaper, drew a cross section through the front part of the human jaw which, in the absence of an X-ray machine, clearly defined the point that he was making. Martin noticed that there were lots of little drawings on the wallpaper. He had never been in any house remotely like this before. His wife emerged from the kitchen with two cups of tea. She was wearing a tight black skirt, black tunic top, black stockings, black hair and black eye shadow. She resembled a witch. "This is Theresa, or Terry as she likes to be called. This is Martin, whom I am going to turn into Louis Armstrong, but without him having to black up!"

"Well, can you keep the noise down? It sounds awful," was her considered response as she returned to the kitchen.

"Perhaps we should call it a day. You go home and alter your embouchure in the way I have explained. Come back when you can do it. OK?"

Martin said that he would try and, in the meantime, how much did he owe Ted for the lesson. "Nothing at all, don't be a berk. You have only been here for about twenty minutes. Anyway, I couldn't take money from a bank clerk. I wouldn't know where it had been!"

CHAPTER 22

Anne, First Car

July 1962

Martin had been going out with Anne for a few weeks. They had been to the cinema several times, most memorably to see *A Kind of Loving*, starring Alan Bates and June Ritchie; they had twice been to the Fighting Cocks, a pub in St Albans, reputed to be the oldest licenced premises in the country, and they had become regular visitors to a couple of pubs in East Barnet, near to where she lived. On the love-making scale they had reached about level seven out of ten. Given the opportunity, it would not be long before the remaining levels were conquered, but there was some restraint on Martin's part because there had been a major surprise. On their second date, she had told him that she was married but separated, and was only living with her parents because she and her husband had been renting a flat and neither of them could afford the rent on their own. This stopped Martin in his tracks. Was he equipped to deal with a situation like this? Ex-husbands would most probably be looking for grounds for divorce; the most obvious one being adultery. The thought of Martin being cited as a co-respondent in the courts horrified him. How would he ever be able to face his parents again? Ex-husbands might well turn nasty too. Anne assured him that he was not a violent man, and also unlikely to be snooping upon her. All the same, it would be sensible to be cautious in certain parts of the town. A second surprise, of an entirely different nature, was when she painted such a glowing picture of what it was like to work in a merchant bank. She had originally worked for the Westminster Bank but saw an advertisement for Sassoon and Co, got the job and found that she had moved to the 'sunlit uplands'. She worked fewer hours for quite a bit more money and less stress. Unlike the high-street banks, merchant banks did not have an age-related pay structure. They paid you what they thought you were worth. This was welcome news, and Martin decided, there and then, to start looking in the evening papers each day for any such vacancies. The third surprise concerned Anne's older brother, who worked for the post office and lived in Enfield. He possessed a Sunbeam Talbot car but, as his wife had just given birth to a daughter, could no longer afford to run it, and it would be up for sale. Martin had wanted a car of his own for quite a long time. Of course, the chief obstacle was lack of funds. Since his return from Worthing he had managed to keep £30 in a staff deposit account, saved up from the last couple of months there after having paid Peter Phillips for his trumpet. Not a lot of money for a car, unless it had depreciated considerably due to old age.

Anne said that they should go to see her brother and, at least, have a look at the car. So, on Wednesday evening they boarded the number 107 bus and got off at Ponders End, the end of the route. It was a ten-minute walk to a council estate, built in the early 1950s by the Atlee Government. Geoffrey, Anne's brother, took Martin around the rear service road to a row of lock-up garages. As they walked along, Geoffrey explained that they were just about making ends meet until the baby came along. He didn't want to sell the car but felt that he had no choice. Not only that; he would also save on no longer having to rent the garage. He unlocked the up-and-over door, and there, facing Martin, was a maroon Talbot Ten.

"Anne said it was a Sunbeam Talbot," said Martin.

"Well, she was nearly right, wasn't she? You can't expect women to be all that knowledgeable about cars, can you?"

Geoffrey started it up and drove it out of the garage onto the service road. Martin was impressed. It was an airline, pillar-less saloon, built in 1938. The profile of the back of the car was just one uninterrupted 45 per cent straight line, incorporating a flush boot. It was very streamlined, and had been marketed as a sports saloon when first made, even though it only had a modest side valve Hillman Minx engine.

"We could go for a little run if you like. Down to the roundabout and back." And so they did. Martin didn't know much about cars, but there seemed to be no expensive noises from the engine, gearbox or back axle. He checked the bottom of the doors for rust. All okay. He checked that all the lights and the windscreen wipers, trafficators and horn worked. He noticed that the seats were leather and a little worn, as were the carpet and headlining. But he loved the look of it.

"So how much are you asking for it, Geoffrey?"

"£40, if you want it. If I have to put an ad in the paper, it's going to be £50."

Martin had £30 and whatever money was left in his current account, which may or may not have been enough.

"Alright, thanks, I'll have it. But it might take me another week or two to get all the money together. Not quite sure without checking. Would that be all right with you?"

They shook hands on the deal, went back to the house and Anne knew at once, from the look on Martin's face, that he was going to buy it. On the way home Martin was unstoppable. In an excited frame of mind, he kept on talking about the car, how fantastic it was, and what they could do, not having to rely upon his mother's goodwill, and so on.

Anne said, "Yes, and, you know, it's got other possibilities, *you know!*"

Two weeks later a small group stood outside Martin's parents' house: Martin, his mum and dad, Brian and young Nick, who lived a few doors away and had recently bought a 1932 Austin Seven. They were inspecting the new purchase, just driven from Ponders End to Barnet by Martin, the proud new owner. Harold poked around the doors, sills and wheel arches, looking for rust. Kathleen sat in the passenger seat and thought it a bit on the small side and a little uncomfortable. Some time later, having read the handbook, Martin learned that the bucket seats were inflatable, and he found a valve tucked away between the back and the squab. He discovered that a bicycle pump would do the trick and, surprisingly, given that the car was twenty-four years old, there were no leaks and the seats stayed inflated and were much more comfortable. Brian had the bonnet up and was checking the fan belt, carburettor, ignition timing and the rate of charge shown on the ammeter. Brian had recently rebuilt the engine of his Austin 16 and knew as much about the workings of motor cars as anybody. Over the next few months his help would prove invaluable to Martin, whose finances would never have stretched to cover the cost of garage bills.

"Who wants a ride around the block?"

Kathleen was the only one who didn't, so the four of them climbed in – quite literally in the case of the back-seat passengers as it only had two doors. Harold, as befitted his status, sat in the front passenger seat. There was a small amount of gear crunching noises, the synchromesh being not what it was in 1938. A little later, Brian taught Martin how to double de-clutch. As they navigated corners, it did lurch a bit, due to the full load. Subsequently this was not a problem because there were never again four occupants. Harold made a comment about it being a bit like being on board ship during heavy weather. Nevertheless, he thought the car good enough, taking everything into account and what Martin had paid for it. Parental endorsement! A rare treat.

Later that day, Martin drove to where Anne lived. She had been waiting by the window, and came straight out of the front door. "Cor, yeah, fabulous! Where are we going?" was how she put it. No need for finesse! Martin hadn't really thought – just being the new owner of such a wonderful machine and able to drive it wherever and whenever he wished was all the buzz he needed right then. In the end, they drove to the Monken Holt; a pretty little countrified pub on the edge of Barnet, exactly where the shops petered out and Hadley Common began. They talked about Martin's forthcoming twenty-first birthday, *the car*, the chances of Martin leaving Lloyds Bank, *the car*, Anne's ex-husband, *the car*, the fact that Martin had not told his parents that Anne was separated, *the car*, jazz, *the car*, what Sarah had been like, *the car*, when they would next meet, ***the car*** !

As they left, Anne said that they were in the right place for a kiss and cuddle.

"Why's that?" Martin asked.

She explained that, as far as she could remember, there was a road down from the common into the beginning of Hadley Woods. Now Martin understood fully! Sure enough, as he navigated the car through the disused tollgate, there were no more street lights but his headlights lit up the gravel road ahead, which continued for a hundred yards before turning into a footpath. The headlights also lit up about a dozen cars, each parked off the road on the grass, each several yards from its nearest neighbour, and each with no lights on.

"This will do," Anne said, as they reached an unpopulated spot. Once the lights were off they could no longer make out the other cars. It was in fact pitch-black. Martin guessed that Anne must have been here before. In the confined space of the front seats, separated by the gear lever and handbrake, they attempted some kind of lovemaking. That night Anne and Martin reached level nine. Level ten was physically impossible in a Talbot 10, and would have to be put on the back burner. Anne was experienced in techniques that Martin had been unaware of until then. She taught him how best to give women what they wanted; she also demonstrated that she had an extensive knowledge of what men wanted. Everything that Martin had learned up until then was like being in the first year at school, whereas now, he was suddenly in the sixth form!

During the following week, Anne phoned Martin at home, clearly excited. Apparently, a friend of hers at work was having a party the weekend after next, and there was a possibility of staying the night. Martin checked that no one was within earshot and said that this was good timing, because if it had been *this* Saturday, he would be playing in Potters Bar with Austin Royce. He went on to say that he would probably tell his parents that he was staying with one of his workmates and would say nothing about an all-night party.

It was in Battersea. Martin decided that he didn't want to drive through the middle of London. Instead they caught a steam train from New Barnet to Kings Cross, then the Tube to Victoria, and finally a bus. It was a newish semi-detached house, built to replace a bomb-damaged Victorian property which would have been like those on either side of it. Martin mused that, if one was staggering homewards, completely blotto, there would be no difficulty in identifying where one lived – it stood out like a sore thumb. The party was in full swing when they arrived. Anne went off to find her friend, while someone thrust a bottle of light ale into Martin's hand. "Cheers," they both said. Anne came back with her friend Rosie and introduced her to Martin, "My new boyfriend." Rosie said that her parents were out, but would be back later. Nothing was mentioned about staying the night.

Martin queried this with Anne, after Rosie had left to mingle with the other guests. "I think they don't want an all-night party, but a few of us can stay. That's what she said the other week." Martin wondered how on earth it would be possible to finally reach, without any kind of restraint, level ten, while under some total stranger's parental roof. He did not have long to wonder. At twelve thirty, a car was heard pulling up outside and Rosie's parents came in.

"Rosie, a quick word, please," said her mother putting her head around the front room door.

The door was closed behind them, and after a couple of minutes Rosie re-entered and said, "I'm sorry everybody, it's time to go. Mum and Dad want some sleep." She then turned to Anne and said, "You and Martin can stay in the front room with John and me, just the four of us. But we must leave the light on. I can tell you, she is quite likely to be checking, she's like that, so it's up to you what you want to do." Anne and Martin, by this time, felt slightly cheated by a false promise which had brought them all the way from north London to south of the river. They could have stayed at home and gone to Hadley Woods again.

They decided to take their chances and thumb a lift to somewhere near home. First, they walked towards Chelsea Bridge, thumbing every car that passed. Just before the bridge a car stopped for them. "Where to?" Martin said that they needed to get to King's Cross, unless he was heading for Barnet! He wasn't, but he got them as far as the Euston Road, where he left their route. Another walk in the direction of King's Cross got them another lift before long. "Just drop us outside the station. That will be fine," Martin said. Once he had done this Anne asked what they were going to do now. Martin said that Roger Camborne, a new workmate of his, had told him that, at every London railway terminus, there was another train one, or one and a half hours later than the last one scheduled. This was provided solely to get the railway staff home. It did not appear on the timetable but, if a bona fide passenger had a ticket, they could not refuse to let you on.

It was now one thirty. They approached the station, which was in total darkness. "Don't worry, there will be a side gate or something," Martin said, hopefully. There was no unlocked gate anywhere, nor, when they peered through the latticed main gates at the front of the station, was there any evidence of a train at all. No tell-tale steam, no sounds whatsoever. "It looks like the staff train has already gone. I suppose we will have to hang around until five or six, whenever the first train leaves," Martin suggested. Anne said that it was cold, *she* was cold, and perhaps they could find an all-night cafe. They walked back to the Pentonville Road, but all the buildings were in total darkness, including the only cafe in the immediate vicinity.

On the other side of the main road, there was a short cul-de-sac. Practically all the houses seemed to have lights on. This was, as they were just about to discover, the railway travellers' last refuge, when all else had failed. Both sides of the street were lined with cheap hotels; all of which were badly in need of a makeover. Anne spoke first. "How much money have you got? I've got a couple of quid I think." Martin had a look in his wallet. He had four pounds fifty. They rang three doorbells before the fourth was answered. Yes, there was a room available and it would be three pounds fifty with breakfast. The proprietor, who had seen it all before, particularly young couples arriving in the middle of the night, made no comment about the lack of luggage or, had he bothered to look, the absence of a wedding ring. It was a double room with a basic washbasin. The curtains did not quite meet in the middle. The toilet was down the landing. But they didn't care at all about any of this. That night, with much enjoyment, level ten was satisfactorily accomplished.

CHAPTER 23

Meanwhile, 'back at the Ranche'

Late 1962

Martin celebrated his twenty-first birthday at the beginning of October, which turned out to be a muted affair. He had said that he didn't want a party – just maybe Anne and Brian along for dinner. Brian had been a regular visitor since Martin bought the car, as it was constantly in need of minor attention. So, it seemed fitting that he should be invited. Anne arrived first and presented Martin with a pewter tankard. Brian turned up with another one and said "snap". Harold had given Martin enough money for him to buy the latest Bush record player, which had an automatic record changer and separate bass and treble controls. This was a vast improvement on the old Dansette that he had bought at the age of fifteen and, after dinner, he celebrated his new acquisition by playing Louis Armstrong and Bix Beiderbecke records until his parents got fed up with the lack of variety and left them alone. In the weeks to come, Martin always took one or other of the tankards along to gigs to be used in lieu of the pint glasses. Owen asked whether he was likely to be getting a hacking jacket and deerstalker hat to go with this new 'country gentleman' image. He abandoned the idea of a personal drinking vessel shortly after this.

Back in June, Owen, Brian and Martin had successfully passed their 'audition' at Ranche's Restaurant, in Darkes Lane,

Potters Bar. They had now made five public appearances as 'Austin Royce and his Music', providing music for dining and dancing on the last Saturday of the month. It had gone well. The upright piano which belonged to Joe Ranche, the proprietor, was quite good. Not quite as good as the Neumeyer at the Weston household, but Martin was happy with it. Owen had assumed the role of spokesperson and de facto bandleader. The other two did not demur. The more they played together, the more polished the performance became. Martin was eternally grateful for his piano lessons and, even more, for having made Teddy Wilson his role model rather than any number of the more 'traddy' style pianists whom he might have latched onto when in his impressionable years. Martin discovered that the Teddy Wilson style fitted perfectly into a dance trio environment. He even found that, without much modification, it suited waltzes, Latin American, and just about everything except 'God Save the Queen'. Brian had always been a dependable bass player and Owen's drumming had improved to the point where he could confidently provide the correct rhythmic patterns for the different Latin dances and the Old Time, many of which had a 6/8 time-signature.

Whenever any customer made a request, they tended to approach Owen with the words, "Excuse me, Austin..." Eventually, Martin and Brian, somewhat to Owen's irritation, started calling him Austin. In the end, though, he came to accept it as a stage name. Perhaps he was envisaging the day when it would be up in lights outside the Lyceum Ballroom in the Strand: Austin Royce and his Mayfair Dance Orchestra. That particular fantasy would have seen him elevated from his humble position behind the drums to that of a baton-waving bandleader wearing tails and a smarmy expression. Probably exactly what he would have hoped for! Joe Ranche was happy that enough extra customers came along on the dinner dance evenings to cover the cost not only of the band but also the additional kitchen staff that he had to employ. The band was allowed one free drink and a meal after it finished playing. For the whole evening during its first gig, late in June, the band had been eyeing the dishes brought up from the kitchen by the waiters. Mouth-watering 1960s specialities such as steak Diane, coq au vin, tornados Rossini, Dover sole, followed by Black Forest gateau, marinated oranges, treacle pudding and so on. By the time they finished playing at ten-thirty they were positively salivating with anticipation.

"Three band dinners, please," Joe shouted down the staircase leading to the kitchen. "Yes, down you go. There's a table for you there." At the bottom of the stairs they were met by the head chef who gestured towards what turned out to be the staff table. It was just bare wood, stained with the blood of various joints of meat that had been parked there prior to preparation for the oven. Martin wondered whether there would be a choice. He would have quite liked the tornados Rossini but, as he said to the other two, any of the dishes would be fine. After all this time, Martin had *still* not learned the one fundamental, unwavering truth. Musicians, other than in their own estimation, are nothing special, no more so than a waiter, or even a cleaner, maybe. Three band dinners were duly produced. Ham and chips!

"Do you want any salt and vinegar?" asked the chef, a tubby man with a very round, almost circular, face. *Well,* they concluded, it wasn't his fault. He was only following Joe Ranche's instructions.

Owen quietly muttered, "Fancy going to all the trouble to cook something not on the menu. It must surely have been cheaper for them to make a bit more of one dish, and give the band the worst-looking portions?"

Owen decided to try out a joke on the chef. "How do you make a Jewish omelette?" The chef went through the list of omelettes one by one. When he reached Spanish, he said perhaps a Jewish omelette contains artichokes rather than onions? Owen adopted his Terry Thomas, inscrutable smile and explained.

"Well, first you buy two eggs…" The chef smiled, but didn't quite laugh, and improvised a further line which topped Owen's: "And then you borrow a frying pan?"

During October, Owen reminded them that they had an extra gig in November at the Potters Bar Hotel, just up the road. Maffi was to be part of their act, for the first time. This very large roadhouse provided entertainment on Tuesday, Friday and Saturday evenings. Owen had discovered it the previous month, when he had arrived at Ranche's a little too early and decided to go for a wander. The landlord, a natty Scottish gentleman, noticed that Owen was wearing a dinner jacket and struck up a conversation during which he wasted no time in advertising his own musical events. They followed a similar format to those adopted by the Alex in New Barnet and the Queens Head at the bottom of Barnet Hill, but on a grander scale. Paul De Bois, a genial, snuff-taking old soak, ran the show. On the stage was a Compton organ with three manuals and a complete row of bass foot-pedals. There was also a grand piano. Paul generally played the organ, only switching to the piano for a bit of light classical material such as 'The Dream of Olwen', or 'The Legend of the Glass Mountain'.

Dozens of would-be singers and musicians turned up on a regular basis, awaiting their turn to be called up by Paul. The music lounge, at the back of the pub, could accommodate 200 people, and it was usually half-full most evenings. Owen had revisited the pub one Tuesday evening and asked whether Austin Royce could play, one evening, during the interval. Paul agreed that this would be fine, just so long as they had – here he paused for a few seconds – "er, actually played in public before?" Owen explained that they were the resident band in Ranche's but they could play jazz as well as dance music and would love a chance to show what they could do.

"Lovely, old son," was Paul's reaction. Upon being told that they also had a belly dancer he said, "Well! I won't be having my break in the front bar *that* night. This I have got to see!"

There was to be no money for the gig, but Owen had enthused that it could open doors for them and, on that basis, was worthwhile. Maffi had gone through her routine with Owen at the Sunday rehearsals, until it was nigh on perfect. Martin had selected four jazz standards that they played well, and had little bits of rehearsed business like an unaccompanied piano solo on the bridge of 'Body and Soul'. This he had shamelessly copied from Teddy Wilson on the Benny Goodman Trio recording. They were ready to go!

Martin drove Anne to the Potters Bar Hotel. Brian picked up Owen and Maffi. The Austin 16 was a big car but, with Brian's double bass parked on one side of the back seat and its neck resting on Owen's shoulder in the front, and Owen's drum cases filling the boot and much of the available floor space, nobody had thought about Maffi having her own luggage containing her belly-dancing outfit. This had to be wedged across the rear window ledge, completely obscuring the driver's rear view. Nevertheless, they made it to the pub. A youngish lady was in full flow, as they entered:

"You don't have to say you love me, just be close at hand..."

Paul, seated at the organ but half-turned towards the audience, sported a showbiz smile, while providing exactly the right accompaniment. He had this God-given gift of being able to make a mediocre singer sound better. It was alleged that he knew every tune ever written. She finished her number to a round of applause. Paul took a pinch of snuff between his fingers and then a long pull from his pint pot, stood up and, pointing in her direction, said:

"Well, wasn't that lovely? Once again, let's hear it for Susie! And who's to be next? Mark, would you like to entertain us, old son?"

The five of them were standing by the bar at the back of the room. Maffi needed somewhere to change. The landlord said that she could use one of the upstairs rooms – he would show her up. Anne asked Martin whether this was a residential hotel, and if so…? She left the rest of the sentence unspoken. To their chagrin, it was not. As the singing hopefuls continued to demonstrate just why the pop stars of 1962 were the ones who got the recording contracts rather than them, the three chaps lugged all the gear towards the rear of the stage area, leaving Owen to assemble his drum kit alone. Then it was nine o'clock. Paul played a little flourish of a tune, signifying the end of the first set. Another pinch of snuff and then:

"Ladies and gentlemen, boys and girls, we have got something special for you during the interval. One of our local bands will be entertaining you for the next half hour. And if I were you I wouldn't miss it, from what I have been told. Sometime during their act, there will be a big surprise! Now, are you ready, boys? Yes, it's over to Austin Royce!"

As Paul walked back to the bar, they went straight into 'The Lady is a Tramp'. Yes, pretty good, Martin thought. Most of the people who were there for the first set stayed in the back bar. Some had gone around to the other bar, which had a wider range of beers and spirits. It was also somewhere where they could have a private chat for half an hour, without having to shout. Then it was 'Body and Soul' featuring Martin's laborious recreation of Teddy Wilson's solo bridge passage. So far, so good! Owen leaned across and said, "Shall we bring her on now?" Martin thought not. He reasoned that, once she was on, the band, in all probability, would become redundant. "One more number," he said. This was to be 'Tenderly', not played as waltz but in a steady 4/4 rhythm, much in the Errol Garner mode. It went really well. The audience were definitely liking what they had heard so far.

Martin and Brian left the stage. Owen donned a red fez that he had bought for the occasion, picked up his sticks and beat out an incessant rhythm on his floor tom-tom. Emerging from behind the bar area, having waited out of sight at the bottom of the stairs, Maffi advanced towards the stage. There were four distinct phases of audience reaction. First came an immediate silence born of surprise, then a few wolf whistles and cheers, then a general excited hubbub, and finally an expectant silence as she began to dance.

None of the band had seen her in her outfit before; only in black and white photographs. She was wearing a golden headband, supporting a red chiffon scarf, red and gold bra with a tasselled gold fringe, red skimpy knickers underneath a gold belt which supported three wispy transparent lengths of fabric, and high heeled shoes. The dance was a remarkable performance, which left the entire room transfixed. Paul De Bois returned from the other bar, accompanied by all the customers, after he had put the word about. All the staff left the front bar too. In fact, the only living creature not at that moment watching Maffi was the pub cat, still curled up by the fire in the front bar.

After seven minutes, Maffi gave Owen the signal for the rehearsed ending. The tempo increased rapidly. Maffi twirled around and around while gradually bending her knees, each revolution bringing her nearer the floor, like a screw being wound into a piece of wood. Finally, she was on her knees. Then, a cymbal-crash and she leapt to her feet, head upturned, arms akimbo, as if in supplication to the gods. If Paul could have added together the applause for every act that evening, save this one, it still would not have come near. It just went on and on, with the inevitable shouts for more. Owen escorted her to the stairs where she finally disappeared, to the disappointment of the audience. Paul now had to get the ball rolling again.

"Well! What can I say? *What can I say*? Now, who is going to follow that? I think it just *has* to be Diedre. Diedre, darling, can I tempt you to sing for us?"

Diedre, sport that she obviously was, got up on stage and did an exaggerated shake of her midriff before grabbing the microphone. This got quite a laugh. As she launched into

'Smoke Gets in Your Eyes', the three band members together with Anne moved to the front bar at the landlord's request.

"What are you all going to have to drink? This round's on me."

The landlord, who's name turned out to be Jim, was full of praise for the free act that Owen had provided. He said the music in itself was excellent even without the star turn. He personally liked a bit of jazz. He thought that if they could do a whole evening, with, of course, Maffi, he could offer them a paid date in the new year. He asked whether anyone sang. Well, they all sang a bit, but none of them considered themselves to be a Bing Crosby.

"Ah well, never mind but, you know, if you did bring a vocalist with you I'd cover the additional cost." Martin, in the general conversation that ensued, mentioned that he also played the trumpet and asked Jim what he would think about a regular jazz night, where musicians might come along and have a blow. Jim said his entertainment budget covered just the Tuesdays, Fridays and Saturdays but if it was *for free* maybe something could be arranged. He did emphasise that he left all musical policy matters to Paul, so Martin's best plan would be to talk to him directly. Perhaps Martin could bring his trumpet along on a Tuesday, play a number or two with Paul, and sound him out. On the way home Anne asked Martin if he would like to see her do a belly dance, maybe naked? Of *course* he would! But this kind of teasing was no use to a frustrated couple who had to rely on the chance of finding a spare bedroom at someone's party, for half an hour, and hoping that nobody tried the door. This was their current situation, other than the constraints of the front seats in the car.

CHAPTER 24

Best ever Christmas, New job

End of 1962

Martin had decided to dispense with any more trumpet lessons from Ted as, try as he might, he could not change his embouchure. But he had been diligently going through all the practice routines that Peter Phillips had drilled into him. This, he reasoned, would make him 'gig ready'. Every Tuesday evening, ever since the Potters Bar Hotel performance, he had driven over there, sometimes with Anne, but more often by himself. Paul De Bois remembered him of course and said that he was pleased that he had brought his trumpet along. "Whatever you want to play, old son, I know most of the standards."

On his first Tuesday, Martin played 'Memories of You' and 'Pennies from Heaven'. Paul said it was very good and asked whether Martin was staying for the rest of the evening. He was. "That's wonderful. I'll come and have a chat with you during the interval."

Paul was glad to have a fellow musician to tell his life story to, and Martin was a keen listener. Paul's grandparents with their five-year-old son, Paul's father, had moved from France to England at the turn of the century. Paul was born in 1920 and, when he left school, joined the army as a musician. During the war, he had been part of ENSA, the entertainments branch of the armed forces. He explained that the troops had an alternative translation of the acronym – 'every night something atrocious' – which he said was often near the mark. After his demob he played at various music halls as their resident pianist, but now he just played here and at the golf club, as he lived in Potters Bar.

"Don't you get any other work then?" Martin enquired.

"Oh yes, I get plenty of offers, but I don't have a car any more. Lost my licence! So, unless the gig is on a bus route and finishes before the last bus, I can't do them." At this point he offered Martin a pinch of snuff. Prepared to try anything once, Martin sniffed it up his right nostril. It made his eyes water and left a brown stain around his nose. "Yes, old son, lost my licence and, in all probability, will never get it back. What happened, you see, was that I was driving back from a gig rather unsteadily, due to several libations, taken purely in the course of duty, you understand?" Martin nodded. "Then I heard the bell of a police car ringing somewhere behind me so I took evasive action. Unfortunately, I found myself in a housing estate and I did not know the way out. The police car was still following. Then I finished up in a cul-de-sac. They parked themselves two inches from my rear bumper. Well, I had no option but to offer myself like a lamb for the slaughter. I got out of the car and walked to their car. 'Humble apologies, sloshed condition,' I said." He laughed ruefully at the memory.

"Anyway, I heard you play the piano with your trio just before the belly dancer came on. A bit of the Teddy Wilson, I thought." Martin nearly blushed with pride.

"You think so? He has always been my idol, you know."

"Yes, I can tell. Sometimes I have a night off. I am always on the lookout for decent keyboard players to cover for me. Might you be interested?" Martin thanked Paul for the offer but said that he didn't think he was capable of accompanying all the various singers, nor was he that familiar with the current hits, which no doubt they would want to sing.

"Well, think about it. If you come here often enough you will get an idea of what's required and, if you read, I have a vast library of song copies which Jim has stored away for me in case I ever need them."

Just before Paul had to return to the rostrum, Martin managed to broach the subject of a jazz night. He explained that he had mentioned it to Jim, and it would be an unpaid event where musicians could just come along for a blow. "I'll tell you what, old son, leave it until after Christmas and let's have a proper chat about it, eh?" He then went on to give Martin one piece of advice, regarding money. "Never, ever work below the rate. By all means work for nothing if it is a charity gig or a bit of self-indulgence, but never work for a fee below the going rate." Martin remembered this dictum ever after but, sadly, found it impossible to adhere to consistently.

Martin had introduced Anne to the delights of the Alex, New Barnet, on Fridays and Saturdays, and she hit it off with Len and Ivy. So much so that, somewhat to Martin's discomfort, Ivy always reserved two seats at her own little table which was squeezed into the small space between the bass end of the piano and the bar counter. It was not, in Martin's view, the ideal place to sit with a girlfriend. It was exactly where all eyes were focused while Len was playing. Also, it was in the same operational area where 'genial host' Tommy Taylor held forth, with all his eye-winking, wisecracking antics. This could be embarrassing, particularly when Tommy, by hand gestures, seemed to be including Anne and Martin in some suggestive piece of Max Millerism. But, on the credit side, Martin could observe Len's left hand at close quarters. With a sinking heart, he knew that he would never master – not in a million years – the facility to play stride as well as Len. Even at breakneck tempos he never missed a note.

"What are you doing for Christmas?" Ivy enquired of the two of them, one Saturday evening early in December. They explained that they would both be enduring the tradition of Christmas Day family lunches, like it or not, and independently of each other. After that, they hadn't really thought about it.

"Maybe we'll come down here on Boxing Day, if Len's playing," Martin suggested. No, it seemed that he wouldn't be.

"How would you like to come with Len and me to his sister's house in Finsbury Park? They always have a special party on Boxing Day. There will be lots of music and other entertainment. Would you like that?"

Yes, they would! So, at the end of 'Temptation Rag', the piece of music that Len was playing, Ivy said, "Len, *Len!* Anne and Martin are coming with us on Boxing Day!"

"Oh really? That's wonderful. Did Ivy tell you that there will be all sorts of interesting people there? Be prepared to be amazed. It's the social event of the year."

The following week Martin was reading the jobs section in the *Times*, on his way to work. He had only recently started to buy it. At home, they had the *Daily Mail*, which he had become acclimatised to, despite it's obvious Tory bias.

But if he was to get another job, he had to buy a newspaper which actually advertised them. Under the section reserved for stockbrokers and banking he spotted the following:

Guinness Mahon and Co are recruiting staff for a range of duties. Experience of banking or the stock market essential. Telephone Cornhill 3998 for further details.

He was aware from what Anne had told him about City-based merchant banks that this was one of them. He thought it odd that a well-known beer was in any way connected with high finance. In fact, as he was soon to learn, it wasn't. He telephoned them from a call box in the ticket office at Knightsbridge Station during his lunch hour. There was a lot of background noise. Nevertheless, he was able to make himself heard to the personnel manager's secretary and, having explained that he had worked for Lloyds Bank for the last few years, was asked to attend for an interview on Wednesday at 10 a.m. In his excitement, he gave no thought to how he was going to manage this as he was supposed to be behind his desk before nine. In the end, he had no option but to invent a dentist's appointment.

Martin walked up Lombard Street, past the headquarters of his current employer, and turned right into Cornhill. On his immediate left was Leadenhall Market, a wonderful example of Victorian architecture. Directly opposite were the imposing glass doors bearing the name Guinness Mahon & Co. in gilded script. He entered an oak-panelled, hushed lobby – almost sepulchral. Now his nerves started to jangle. He was well out of his comfort zone. This environment was in a different league to the relative homeliness of a

Lloyds Bank branch. The receptionist directed him to the lift, having told him that the personnel office was on the first floor. Once there, he was shown into a rather cramped office containing one desk, one visitor's chair, a filing cabinet and Mr Ransome, personnel manager. Martin noticed the expensive cut of his suit, an immaculately crisp white shirt and a guards' tie. Although he himself was wearing his normal business suit, he was acutely aware of the sartorial difference and felt positively shabby.

"Good morning, Mr Weston. Please take a seat. Now, yes, you are from a bank, I believe?"

During the introductory talk, where Mr Ransome demonstrated just how little Martin knew about what merchant banks did, Martin started to sweat a little. His self-confidence had already deserted him down in the lobby, and things were not improving. At the end of the brief summary of Guinness Mahon's scope of operations, and the history of the completely separate brewing and banking sides of the Guinness family, Martin was asked to say what particular skills he had acquired during his tenure with Lloyds Bank.

"Well, I have done a lot of the administration tasks, like operating the day sheet, posting onto ledgers and statements, cheque clearance, writing letters to customers and also, er, calculating staff salaries, er, reconciling the books for the daily head office returns, um, and I have worked on the foreign counter and I was sent down to our registrar's department in Worthing to work on a share issue. I was there for six months." He stopped at that point, not knowing how much actual detail he should be going into.

"Would you say that you have a good understanding of the various banking processes then?"

"Well yes, those I have been trained to do. I haven't worked on the tills and I haven't worked for the securities section, but I think that's about all."

"A lot of what we do is, what I expect you would find, only your head office does. But, having said that, we are one corporate establishment, and we do provide the usual banking services like any of the 'big five' would. Very similar, I'm sure. We have valued customers, and we like to think that we give them a more personal service than they would be able to get down the high street. A large part of our operation is devoted to the financing of major capital projects. Just one current example, which you may have read about, is the Sydney Opera House. We also deal on the stock and foreign exchange markets, both for our customers and for our own financial position. Some of our staff used to work for stockbrokers. I don't suppose that a high-street branch would have any direct involvement in these activities?"

"No, sir," Martin interjected.

"Now one of the vacancies is within our foreign exchange dealing room. Tell me a bit more about what you did on the foreign counter."

Martin explained that he had used the daily rates provided by head office to calculate the buying and selling of foreign currency, served the customers with both currency and travellers' cheques, and then, at the end of each day, did all the reconciliations and summary reports. He tried to explain the workings of the mechanical calculator used for the conversions. This was a black enamelled cylindrical device, mounted on a heavy cast-iron base. It had a logarithmic scale and a handle at either end. This raised a smile on Mr Ransome's face.

"Yes, I think we can safely leave the workings of this contraption to the mechanically minded," he said. Then he asked, "What is your current salary?"

Martin told him that it was £575 per annum.

"Well, we are looking for young chaps, like yourself, with hands-on banking experience. If you wish to come and work for us, I am prepared to offer you £700 as a starting salary. There is an annual Christmas bonus as well but, in your case, you would have to wait twelve months, as Christmas is nearly upon us." He proffered a rueful smile.

Martin gulped. Was that it? No mention of references or a medical? He was going to be taken on, entirely on the basis of this short interview! He had not been at all sure that he would have fitted the bill before Mr Ransome had spoken these last words. And he was astonished that within half an hour the process had been concluded. He remembered how long it had taken for all the red tape to be sorted out before he was offered a job with Lloyds.

"Thank you, sir, I would be happy to accept your offer."

"There is just one routine formality. Please ask the receptionist for the 'new staff personal details' questionnaire. You will need to complete this and send it back to us as soon as possible. Then, all being well, we will write to you confirming your appointment."

A final question. "How much notice do you have to give?" On being told that it was the usual one month, Mr Ransome said that his start date with Guinness Mahon would be notified to him in the letter of confirmation, taking this into account, plus a little leeway to give Martin time to hand his notice in, following which a reference from Lloyds would be asked for. Martin thanked Mr Ransome for the interview and the offer of a position. He said how much he would be looking forward to his new job. Another handshake, and he was on his way back to Knightsbridge.

The official job offer arrived in the post the following week. Martin had already shared the news with his parents, Anne, Brian, Owen and, in confidence, Robert and Roger, his work colleagues. Harold said, "*There!* Didn't I tell you that you could get a better job by staying up here, rather than moving all the way down to Worthing?" It was good to know that he had been right. Yorkshiremen are always right! Kathleen had not heard of merchant banks and needed to know that Martin was not jumping out of the frying pan and into the fire. Anne was, of course, delighted for Martin and kept telling him that he had made the right move. His workmates were green with envy when Martin told them how much he would be earning. What *he* did not yet know, and this would have made them even greener, was that the working hours were much shorter, with a four thirty finish every day, and there was an extra week's holiday and luncheon vouchers. It was a big step up for Martin.

As soon as the letter arrived, Martin asked for a word in private with Mr Backhouse (or Shithouse, as Martin had come to call him behind his back). "Um, I'm not sure what the official process is, but I need to hand in my notice."

Arnold Backhouse looked startled. "What! Did you say, 'hand in your notice'? Are you in any kind of trouble? Have you done something that the bank would disapprove of?"

There was a very long list of things that came into this category. Even growing a beard without permission would provoke the bank's wrath. Martin explained that he had been offered a better job.

"Look here, young man, a career with the bank is not one to be given up lightly. It is a job for life, offers security, a pension and good prospects. You don't want to give all that up, if you take my advice." Martin thought to himself that Arnold had risen to the giddy height of chief cashier, and was now in his final years whereas more senior staff, such as the branch manager and his assistants, were at least ten years his junior. So much for 'good prospects' in Arnold's case.

"I have been offered a job with Guinness Mahon," was all Martin said. He was met by a blank look, by way of reply. Martin correctly surmised that Arnold had no idea who they were.

"They are, as I expect you know, a merchant bank. They were looking for people with previous banking experience, and are offering a lot more money, and other benefits. Maybe there is not so much security, but I am only twenty-one and I am trying to do better for myself." He felt that perhaps he was overdoing it a bit. There was probably no need for a dialogue at all.

"Harrumph! You will need to see Mr Baker before tendering your resignation in writing to head office. You are doing well here, you know. I only hope that this is not a leap into the dark on your part. Some of these 'offers' can seem very enticing, but reality turns out to be very different."

Mr Baker, the assistant manager, was well aware of Guinness Mahon. "How did you come to hear about merchant banks?" was what he asked.

"My girlfriend works for one, and she told me what it was like compared with Westminster Bank, where she was before."

Mr Baker smiled. "Yes, actually I would have thought

that they were a bit difficult to get into, almost a closed shop. You know, what school you went to, what clubs you were a member of, the old boys network and all that?"

"Not as far as I can see, sir. They were specifically looking for people with normal branch experience."

"Ah yes. Well, I hope that all the training that we have invested in you has helped."

Not appreciating the irony of Mr Baker's comment, Martin, without meaning to sound ungrateful, steamed in with, "Oh yes, without it I wouldn't have been offered the job."

Mr Baker told him, in general terms, the form of words to use in a letter giving notice to the personnel department at head office, and wished him well.

"Looks as if we will be saying goodbye to you around the end of January, then," was his parting shot.

Martin carried on with his normal routines – work, music, going out with Anne, Friday drinks in Tattersalls until Christmas arrived. On Boxing Day, he picked up Anne from her house and drove over to Whetstone, where Len had offered to drive the four of them down to Finsbury Park and the 'party of the year'. Len had recently acquired a Ford 105E Anglia. He had been without a car for a few years, but thought it a good idea that he and Ivy should get out and about a bit more. In Finsbury Park, Len turned into a wide, treelined avenue. Five-storey Edwardian houses stretched all the way up the road, on both sides, as far as the eye could see. There must have been a lot of wealthy families about in 1903. They parked up, and rang the doorbell at his sister's house. A younger, female version of Len opened the door. The resemblance was startling.

"Happy Christmas, Connie!" Len kissed her on the

cheek. "Now, these are my young friends Anne and Martin whom I spoke about."

Connie bid them welcome, said her hellos to Ivy, and led the way upstairs. The first floor, as far as could be determined, was dominated by just one vast room. Floor to ceiling sash windows let in light from the front and back. A grand piano stood against one wall, and a few music stands were dotted around the room. There were a couple of sofas, but everyone was standing, chatting animatedly in little groups. It seemed that they all knew each other well.

"Leonard, would you show your guests where everything is, while I get on with organising the evening?"

Len took them upstairs to the kitchen and dining room. The dining room table was piled with plates of food, the sideboard with drinks. "Connie wants you to help yourself. Don't wait to be asked. Have as much as you want. It's Christmas!"

Later, Connie clapped her hands together and said, "Leonard, could you go on first, please?"

Martin and Anne had no idea what the evening had in store, other than that it was a fair bet that music would feature. Len went into his routine – some piano specialities and some songs that everybody could sing. It became apparent that among the guests there were a few 'trained' voices. Next to follow was Uncle Fred who was quite ancient. It transpired that he had been on the music halls in his younger days. He regaled them all with a couple of monologues in the manner of Stanley Holloway and a dramatic reading from Charles Dickens. Anne, who had never been bothered about anything other than current films and music, was a little bit fidgety. But then, the star turn of the evening, Len's nephew,

Clive, who was currently studying at the Royal Academy of Music played the cello to the accompaniment of Len's sister. They played 'The Dying Swan' by Saint Saens, followed by a piece of Scott Joplin ragtime. Anne was bowled over by this last piece, and was now enjoying herself. Martin was glad about that. This was certainly turning into a party to remember!

It wasn't finished yet, not by a long chalk. There were string quartets, a Marie Lloyd impression, Clive playing the piano in the style of his Uncle Len, much to Len's amusement, and then Martin was asked to play. Len had to almost drag him to the piano. How could he follow any of what he had just heard?

He said, "You know, I only play in a jazz band. That's all I can do."

Clive, who was about the same age as Martin, said, "I wish I could play jazz. Go on, I want to hear it."

Martin played three pieces that he usually played with some degree of proficiency, the final one being 'All the Things You Are', which he had recently started to make into a bit of a feature. He played the first chorus 'colla-voce' before moving into swing.

"Bravo!" someone shouted, among the warm applause.

Len came over and said, "Shift over on the stool. Let's do a duet." They had done this before, down at the Alex. Len played the bass end and Martin the treble. They played 'St. Louis Blues', not as a slow blues but as more of a stomp, like the Louis Armstrong's All Stars version.

The entertainment just went on and on. There was a barbershop quartet, conjuring tricks, more singers, Clive on his cello again, and finally Len playing a medley of wartime songs, 'Roll Out the Barrel', 'Siegfried Line', 'Tipperary', 'White Cliffs of Dover', and the finale – 'We'll Meet Again'.

On the way home Martin enthused no end about the wonderful evening he had just had. Ivy explained that all of Connie's family and friends were or had been in show business, and every year was the same.

"I told you that you would be amazed," said Len. He couldn't have been more right! Even Anne, who was really only into pop music, said that she had never had such an evening. This she did, while surreptitiously stroking Martin's bottom, in the back seat of Len's car.

CHAPTER 25

Much sitting in

Early 1963

There was almost a *smell* of change about 1963. National-
ly there was an irritation that the Tories had monopolised
things for long enough. Harold Wilson's Labour Party
looked to be more in tune with the people, especially the
younger generation, Martin being no exception. Values were
beginning to change too, and this was reflected by the spate
of 'kitchen sink' dramas and films that were in vogue. Above
all, there was *That Was the Week That Was*, a satirical programme on prime-time television every Saturday evening. It
took no prisoners, there were no sacred cows, just a lot of of-
fended politicians and other self-important persons who de-
served no better treatment anyway. Internationally, the Cold
War continued without any let up. The potential disaster
of the Cuban missile crisis had been narrowly avoided after
Khrushchev blinked first. Kennedy personally intervened to
force the University of Mississippi to admit James Meredith,
a black student. Martin Luther King was ramping up the
rhetoric. Martin had become acutely aware of the race prob-
lems both in the USA and South Africa. In his new-found
state of political awareness, he became angry about things
that he could do nothing about. He felt that the world owed
a vast debt to the American Negroes for jazz music and, while
in creative mood, started work on writing a protest song.

Generally speaking, he had a sense that his life was moving in a more certain direction. He had a new job and more money, a girlfriend (unfortunately with a husband), a car, regular work with Austin Royce, and was more determined than ever to make it on the trumpet. He had some regrets about having severed all ties with Worthing, but it was a conscious decision. He had corresponded with Sally a couple of times but, in the end, they agreed that it would be too difficult to have a long-distance relationship. He had thought long and hard about Biggleswade, but reflected that circumstances had in the past removed good friends from his orbit, and probably would again. Life goes on.

Owen proved his mettle by slowly but surely getting additional gigs for the trio. They also were looking forward to an evening at the Potters Bar Hotel in March, as proposed last year by Jim, the landlord. This would feature Maffi and a new singer, Joe. He lived across the road from Owen, and they had in the past just been on nodding terms. Then one day, noticing Owen unloading his drum kit from Brian's Austin 16, Joe walked across and had a word.

"Can I give you a hand?"

"Cheers, Joe."

"Does anyone do vocals with your band?"

"Not really – only on the jazz numbers sometimes. None of us is a proper singer. Mind you, funnily enough, we *have* been asked if we can find one for a particular gig quite soon."

Joe wondered whether Owen was aware that he once sang with a dance band? Owen wasn't! Joe came along to their next rehearsal and obviously knew what he was doing. A little bit like Matt Monro, Martin thought. He was also fond of beer, which endeared him to them as well. Perhaps a bit too fond, as he was beginning to develop a paunch. Thankfully, when on stage, his midnight blue dinner jacket covered this up.

Owen had taken him to the most recent gig at Ranche's Restaurant. There was no extra money for a singer, but the band wanted to see how things would work, as far as the punters were concerned. All went very well, and Owen suggested that they give him ten shillings from their £5 fee. There were gigs lined up in St Albans, Hemel Hempstead and Dunstable. This last one was really Maffi's, thanks to her previous contacts. The band, with Joe and Maffi, was to play for one hour as part of an evening of cabaret. They were to be paid a relative fortune – £15; £3 each!

There had also been gigs in Barnet. Martin and Brian had been wondering just how long it would be before they actually played on home territory. There was a run-down Victorian hall with a corrugated iron roof in Moxon Street, just off the High Street. It was, to put it mildly, decrepit. It had outside toilets, no heating, and had not been decorated since the 1920s. There was a funny smell inside the building, a combination of damp and vegetable soup. The chairs were mismatched and some were in the last throes of resembling a chair rather than several separate pieces of wood. Quite by accident, Owen discovered that it was still used from time to time by people who could not afford the usual hire fee for a half-decent hall. Family events such as sixtieth birthday parties seemed to be the order of the day. Owen struck up an acquaintance with the caretaker who, after being bribed by a couple of free drinks in the Mitre, was happy to pass Austin Royce's business card on to potential customers. As a rule, most brought a record player with them. After all, if you could only afford the Victory Hall – for that was its name – it was unlikely that you could indulge in the luxury of a live band. But because Owen kept the fee down to £5, or even £4/10s if pushed, a lot lower than most established dance bands would have charged, he managed to pick up the odd gig. They were all hard work though. Apart from the just about playable piano, Martin sweated his way through every single old-time dance that he knew... and then some more! The elderly guests – and they generally all were – liked Joe however, because he had a crooner's voice and sang their kind of songs.

Another Barnet-based opportunity presented itself quite unexpectedly. Terry Lightfoot, leader of one of the top Trad bands, became the licensee of the Albion, the pub next door to Barnet Jazz Club in Union Street. His schedule of gigs allowed a certain amount of leeway, and if he wasn't there as 'mine host', others could get on with the running of the pub. He had only just recorded 'There Is a Tavern in The Town' as a trad number, and here he was, in a tavern in the town. Excellent result, even if there were no weeping willow trees around for him to hang his heart on! Martin wasted no time in introducing himself to Terry, and asking whether he could play a few numbers on the piano one evening. Terry said that Martin would not only be welcome to play, but why not right there and then? After a couple of numbers, Terry, who seemed to be appreciating what he was hearing, disappeared upstairs, and returned with his clarinet. So, Martin, a twenty-one-year-old amateur musician, found himself accompanying one of the country's top clarinettists. It seemed unreal, but not quite as unreal as what had happened the previous week.

Brian and Martin had gone to Golders Green Jazz Club to hear Nat Gonella. This legendary trumpet star, a near rival to Louis Armstrong himself, had come out of retirement thanks to the work opportunities provided by the still buoyant Trad boom. He had formed his New Georgians from seasoned players who had already secured their musical pedigrees over time. Brian and Martin were both spellbound by the quality and maturity of Nat's playing. Not for nothing had he modelled himself on his hero Louis Armstrong, who, in turn, always described him as 'my boy Nat'. During the interval, Brian approached Nat, and asked whether his friend could sit in on piano for a number. Martin was kept in the dark about this until, after the first number of the second set, Nat announced that a local pianist would be joining the band for a number. He looked over to where Brian and Martin were standing, quite near the bandstand, and Brian said, "You're on, mate!"

A startled Martin was half propelled towards the stage. Nat, smiling, said, "Come on up," as the band's pianist stood up and moved away. "What do you want to play?" was the next question. Martin decided to do 'All of Me'. Off they went, and then it was Nat's turn to solo. At this point, Martin kept his accompaniment to merely vamping the chords. He was determined not to distract the great man in any way. And then Nat turned around to look at Martin, hand outstretched, palm upwards. "Your solo," was all he said. Martin, conscious of the fact that he had the backing of a first-class bass player and drummer, found it not so daunting as he had thought it would be. In fact, he played a half-decent solo. Nat then sang the vocal in his inimitable style. Never being able to pronounce the letter 'r' had become a stylistic trademark that was Nat's, and Nat's alone. Sure enough, when it got to the bit, 'eyes that cry', it became 'eyes that cwy'. From then on, Martin never failed to dine out on the fact that he had once accompanied Nat Gonella.

A work colleague at Guinness Mahon who lived in East London told Martin about a pub in Highbury that had a Monday night jazz session. It was the Alwyne Castle. He had said that it was very 'New Orleans', and Martin was sure to like it. In fact, although he said nothing to his colleague, Martin was not all that keen on the Ken Colyer/George Lewis kind of jazz. He, in his wisdom, at such a tender age, considered it to be basic and boring; not at all like the kind of stuff that his heroes did, and were still doing. It took him right back to Worthing, where he could not understand Adrian's passion for jazz musicians who could only just about play, in Martin's considered opinion. Nevertheless, Martin resolved to go there with his trumpet the very next Monday.

Getting there by public transport also involved a fairly long walk. Martin, not being quite sure of the address, set out from Highbury and Islington Station at eight o'clock and, before long, found a tobacconist shop still open. He was only going in to ask for directions, but paused to admire, in the window, an old advert for Sweet Afton cigarettes, a brand that Martin had never tried. He asked for a packet of twenty, expecting to be told that they were no longer made, but was pleasantly surprised. He now had the directions too and the pub was a fifteen-minute walk away; time to smoke a Sweet Afton en-route. He heard the closing strains of 'Over in the Gloryland' as he reached the pub, definitely a Colyer/Lewis type of number. The band was led by a trombonist, Harry King with a line-up of trumpet, clarinet, banjo, sousaphone and drums.

Martin bought himself a pint and sat down to listen. They were good at what they did, but it was not really Martin's cup of tea. The band took an interval at nine and Harry King came straightaway to Martin's table.

"Looks like an alto case?" was his introduction.

"Hello, no, it's a trumpet. I was only told about this, you know, your band playing in this pub, the other day, so I thought I would come along."

"Well, I hope you are going to have a blow with us?"

"Oh yes, please, if that's OK."

And so, after the interval, Martin found himself on stage, replacing Gavin, their regular trumpet player.

The first conundrum was what on earth to play. Martin had the choice of picking a tune that he liked, or one that he estimated they might prefer. He played the safety card, "'St. Louis Blues' OK?" Yes, it was. It went well, all things being considered. Martin forced himself to play more economically in an effort to convince this band that he was on their wavelength. He played a second number, 'Darktown Strutters', and was beginning to feel a bit smug.

This feeling was quickly shattered. Harry said, "Do you know 'Panama'?"

Martin didn't, but Gavin did, and volunteered to sit alongside Martin and play the lead.

"It's got an intro and three themes. It goes from Eb to Ab. Then there's a sort of a cascade chorus starting on high Ab, then an out chorus."

Martin considered that maybe he had been a bit too

hasty in his judgment of these guys and, more to the point, basic New Orleans jazz. He tried to play a second part to Gavin's confident lead. It worked some of the time. When it came to the cascade chorus, sensibly, he gave up and came back in for the final chorus.

"Well done, Martin," said Harry.

After the end of the gig, Harry explained that they had been there for six months and that, sometimes, Bill Brunskill came along as a guest! He waited for Martin's reaction, which was not forthcoming, as he had never heard of Bill Brunskill. He also went on to say that the band also played on Sunday *dinner times*, as he put it, in another pub in Islington. Martin would be always welcome to come along to either gig and play a few numbers. Martin, over the following weeks, did exactly that. He never met Bill Brunskill, but they did have a 'third-party disagreement'. What happened was that the band's drummer, an impressionable seventeen-year-old, posessed a booming bass drum. Martin, in his relative maturity, suggested to him that he needed to stuff newspaper in the drum to dampen the sound, which he *had* done by the next time Martin saw him. Then, a fortnight later, the booming sound returned. It appeared that the great Brunskill, upon hearing the dull thud of a dampened bass drum, asked questions. On being told the answer, he instructed the callow youth to remove the newspaper forthwith, so that "we can all hear a real New Orleans style bass drum."

Joe Williams, the new singer with Austin Royce, told Martin about another jazz venue, in Borehamwood. This was on Tuesday evenings in the golf club bar. Martin drove over there and found himself in an environment about as far away as it was possible to get from the Alwyne Castle. The bar staff wore white shirts and black bow ties. There was a proper stage with a grand piano and a drum kit in place (not the kind with a booming bass drum). There was a proper PA system. In fact, Martin was sure that Harry King and his New Orleans Band would feel uncomfortable and out of place there. After a bit, a pianist, bass player, drummer and tenor saxophonist strolled up to the stage and, after a few preliminaries, launched into 'How High the Moon'. *Ah*, thought Martin, *now this is really interesting.* It was the very first time that he had heard, in the flesh, what Harry and Adrian would have described as 'modern jazz' or, in musicians' parlance 'oobli-doobli'.

Looking around the dimly lit room, Martin noticed several instrument cases dotted around by the tables. So this was a jam session, he thought. Indeed, it was. Everyone seemed to know each other, and Martin hadn't a clue who any of them were. He had found himself in another world, a separate entity to the Traditional Jazz clique. Never the twain should meet, except by accident. He decided that he would probably not risk playing his trumpet, because he was not yet ready for this. It was all very well playing a middle-of-the-road standard in the Connaught last year, but he had the much-needed support of Stan, the alto player, on that occasion.

The evening whizzed by. There were more sax players, a guitarist, another pianist, a trumpet player and a valve trombonist. All of them came up at various times to do their bit and all of it was 'modern' – not contemporary, but stylistically from the forties rather than the twenties or thirties, Martin's comfort zone. There was an interval where

Martin found himself standing at the bar next to a tall, well-built, middle-aged man with a full head of grey wavy hair. "That a trumpet?" he said, pointing towards Martin's vacated table. Martin said that it was, but he wouldn't be playing tonight, as he wasn't really good enough.

"Oh, come on, don't be bashful, you've brought it with you, you should have a blow." After a bit more dissent from Martin, he went on to suggest that no jazz solo is ever *all* bad. There will always be *some* good notes. "What are you worried about?"

"No, the thing is, I have only really played Dixieland up to now, and I haven't been playing that long either."

"So? What's wrong with that? We all have to start somewhere, and we'll play some Dixieland then."

Who was this guy? Martin hadn't seen him playing anything in the first set.

As the interval came to an end, the pianist called across the room to this same guy: "Jimmy, baby, please come and play. *Please!*"

Jimmy, who picked up in one hand a tenor sax case that was by his feet, grabbed hold of Martin's arm with his other hand, frogmarched him back to his table, told him to get his 'horn', and got them both to the stage. To say that the rhythm section looked surprised, would be an understatement.

"Who's this?" the pianist whispered to Jimmy.

"This is a young man who is going to have a blow with me. He was a bit reluctant, but I told him there was nothing to worry about."

The pianist, having ascertained Martin's name, picked up the microphone.

"Ladies and gentlemen, it's a great privilege to welcome

the one and only Jimmy Skidmore and also, his first time here, Martin on the trumpet."

Oh my God! was Martin's immediate thought. *It's only Jimmy Skidmore, saxophone star of the Humphrey Lyttelton Band. I can't play with him, I just can't!*

He, made to leave the stage but Jimmy wasn't having any of it. He asked whether Martin knew 'Indiana', a Dixieland war horse that even the modernists sometimes played. He did, and so off they went. Jimmy led throughout the first chorus. He then called for a piano solo and, as it was coming to an end, signalled for Martin to play next. "I'll be with you all the way," he added, as a measure of comfort. Martin did his best, which fell a long way short of anything he had heard so far that evening. True to his word, Jimmy played backing phrases behind Martin's solo and gave the odd encouraging grunt of approval, from time to time. When Martin had finished, Jimmy made circular movements with his arms, inviting applause. Then it was his own turn; absolutely spellbinding. Finally, a closing chorus with them both playing freely together.

"Great, great, great!" Jimmy enthused. Of course, it wasn't, but it was a revelation to Martin that amongst all the cynics and prima donnas in the music world there was at least one gentleman. A rough diamond, but nevertheless, a man of generous spirit and kindness. There was no reason why he should have given Martin the push that he needed; perhaps someone had done the same for him when he himself was a beginner?

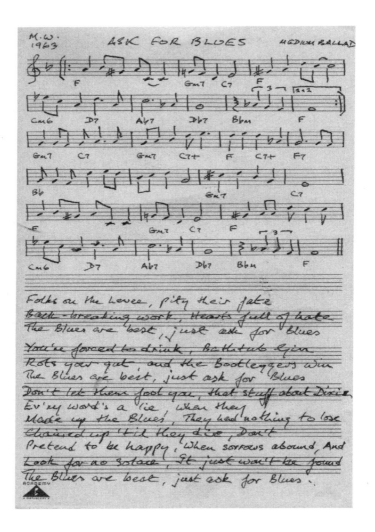

ASK FOR BLUES

M.W. 1963 · MEDIUM BALLAD

Folks on the Levee, pity their fate
Back-breaking work, Hearts full of hate
The Blues are best, just ask for Blues
You're forced to drink, Bathtub Gin
Rots your gut, and the Bootleggers win
The Blues are best, just ask for Blues
Don't let them fool you, that stuff about Dixie
Ev'ry word's a lie, when they
Made up the Blues, They had nothing to lose
Chained up 'til they die, Don't
Pretend to be happy, When sorrows abound, And
Look for no solace, It just won't be found
The Blues are best, just ask for Blues.

CHAPTER 26

'Ask for Blues': the Potters Bar premier

Spring 1963

One of the red lights on the broker's board lit up. Martin pressed the connecting button and picked up the handset. It was the guy from Sealy and Harborne.

"Morning! Scandies 14.54, 20.02, 19.33. Bye!"

These were the day's opening rates for the Swedish Krona, Norwegian Crown and Danish Krone, in that order. You had to get used to minimal information, usually gabbled at high speed. The brokers had to contact all the banks as quickly as they could. There was no chit-chat. Martin didn't even know his name!

Upon his arrival at Guinness Mahon, as a new employee he had been posted straightaway to the foreign-exchange dealing room. This was on the strength of him having served his time on the foreign counter in Lloyds, Knightsbridge. The only similarities between the work he had done there and what he was doing now were the names of the currencies. The dealing room was a high-pressure, sometimes worrying place in which to work. There were four dealers. Each had a display board in front of them containing a row of red lights, buttons and a plug-in handset. Above each light had been typed the names of the City-based foreign-exchange brokers. In addition to advising the rates throughout the day, they would make contact to enquire whether, for example, anyone wanted to take a hundred thousand dollars in two days' time, at a forward rate.

Martin was under strict instructions never to do anything at all speculative, which he thought was just as well. He certainly didn't want to be responsible for any kind of financial meltdown. His remit was to offset customers' instructions. So, he would make sure that if a customer had wished to buy currency (not for holidays, but to finance capital projects), he would manage the selling and, at the same time, buying back the same amount. The main thing was for Guinness Mahon to maintain an overall balance in US dollars, never in any other currency, including sterling. There was a telex machine in the corner which often sprang into life, chattering away. It was imperative that telexes were dealt with promptly. Exchange rates were volatile and time was of the essence. Sometimes Martin had to telex the Bank of New York to buy back dollars that were being sold. The bank's profits derived from the margins; the gap between the buying and selling rates, and the differential between a transaction made today (spot rate), and one made at a forward rate.

Often, he went to lunch with Robin, another dealer about the same age as Martin. There were a few historic coffee houses tucked away down alleyways between Cornhill and Lombard Street – the exact same places that Samuel Pepys had frequented. Of course, they didn't just sell coffee! Robin liked jazz (he was the colleague who had mentioned the Alwyne Castle), but hated the saxophone. His hero was Acker Bilk, who happened to live in Potters Bar, not far from the hotel that Martin went to at least once a week. Maybe, Martin offered, he could get Acker's autograph for Robin, if he ever bumped into him. They had plenty of discussions about Martin's musical endeavours, which frequently ended up with Robin vehemently denouncing the saxophone. This even happened when Martin recounted the chance meeting with Jimmy Skidmore, and its outcome. "Sounds like he is a really great bloke," said Robin, "but it doesn't alter the fact that he plays the instrument of the Devil." Martin took all this in good humour. He called Robin a mouldy fygge.

The opportunity to get Acker Bilk's autograph could be just around the corner, as it happened. Martin had managed to have a chat with Paul De Bois in February, and he had agreed that Martin could put on some jazz in the Potters Bar Hotel on Sunday lunchtimes. Paul agreed to be there on the first session, to help the lads out, as he put it, but was clear about not becoming the regular pianist, as it would be a bit of a conflict for him. Martin thought that it was also about playing for no money, but kept this thought to himself. Owen had come up trumps, once again. He had found a clarinet player, Brian Simmonds, who, Owen assured them, sounded just like Benny Goodman.

Came the day. The back lounge at the Potters Bar Hotel had an eerie, forlorn look about it. Martin had never seen it empty before. Even on Tuesdays, it was reasonably full – perhaps seventy or more people. On this Sunday morning, they had already set up Owen's drum kit and Brian's bass, Martin and the other Brian had been warming up their instruments, and Paul was nowhere to be seen. Other than that, a barmaid was wiping down the counter, and putting out fresh beermats on each table. Still, it was only twelve o'clock. The pub had only just opened. At twelve fifteen, Paul arrived and made a beeline for the bar. He needed an 'eye-opener'. At half past, Martin suggested that they play something. There were a few people in the front bar who might drift in, if they heard the sound of music.

Paul said that he was happy to play any standard tune, but wouldn't want to play 'those old minstrel things'. Martin was very happy to hear that. They launched into 'Who's Sorry Now', and Brian Simmonds *did*, to Martin's ears, sound a little like Goodman. Owen had been right about that. Everybody had a solo, except Owen, who made up for it by putting a four-bar tag on the end. Martin had heard bands doing this before, so knew what he had to do – play another four bars after the drum break. He also had to remember that, as the trumpet player and leader, he should make his last note obvious to one and all, in order that they all finished at the same time. This he signally failed to do, and the number came to a ragged end. "Glad to see that all these rehearsals have paid off," quipped Paul.

By now, there were six customers in the back bar, including someone with a clarinet case and someone with a guitar. Jim, the landlord, had put a handwritten poster up in both bars during the preceding week. It was good that at least a few of the customers must have read them. The band carried on. 'All of Me', 'Indiana', 'St. Louis Blues', 'Dinah', after which Paul suggested they take a refreshment break. At the bar, he proffered his snuff box to the band members. Martin declined, having been caught out before. One or two of the others accepted though and looked as if they were regretting the experience. Martin took it upon himself to have a chat to the two people who had turned up for a blow. He said they were welcome to join in after the break; which they did. The clarinet player was rather like Alan, the very loud 'New Orleans' player in Worthing, and, as such nearly drowned poor Brian out during the ensembles. The guitarist was very adept. He was able to insert extra chords, which enhanced the overall sound, making it a bit more 'modern'. Paul was very quick to follow suit. He had a remarkable ear.

Now there were about twenty people in the room. Someone came up and introduced himself as Alec Crook and asked whether he could sit in on piano. "I'd be delighted, old son," was Paul's response. "I need a refill," he added.

Alec was not quite up to Paul's standard but, there again, how many were? Nevertheless, he was competent and a willing work horse. Paul was not showing much inclination to return to the stage. It was about quarter to two, and they were looking at a two thirty finish. Martin thought that now was about the time to introduce his original composition. He had been working on a protest song for a few weeks, and now had it scored and ready to be played.

He had called it 'Ask for Blues', the slogan on the ashtray that Jimmy Prior had won from the 'Olde Teashoppe'. It could have been Martin's but for the split second when Jimmy spotted it first. *Never mind*, thought Martin. *It's my tune, and we're going to play it.*

He handed out the parts and the chord charts to those that needed them and made a little announcement.

"Well, folks, the next number is my own composition called 'Ask for Blues'. It's a sort of protest song, my little bit of support for what's going on in America right now." In fact, he hadn't thought it through all that well, because it seemed to be a commentary on both slavery and prohibition, two entirely separate events!

After the first chorus, Martin sang the lyrics:

Folks on the levee, pity their fate
Backbreaking work, hearts full of hate
The blues are best, just ask for blues
You're forced to drink bathtub gin
Rots your gut, and the bootleggers win
The blues are best, just ask for blues.
Don't let them fool you. That stuff about Dixie -
Every word's a lie
When they made up the blues, they had nothing to lose
Chained up 'til they die
Don't pretend to be happy, when sorrows abound
And look for no solace, it just won't be found
The blues are best, just ask for blues.

It seemed to go well. The tune was not a blues as such, but a standard, thirty-two bar ballad. The band played another two numbers and then called it a day. Martin announced: "That's all for this week. We are going to have a jazz session every Sunday, so please put the word around. See you next week, and thank you for coming."

This was a milestone for Martin: the very first time that he had played a whole two-hour session without any relief. His lip was fuzzy, his embouchure only just about working for the last half-hour, but he had done it! He thought he ought to send a postcard to Peter Phillips. Paul, having successfully managed to leave the entire last part of the afternoon to a willing Alec, came back from his perch at the bar and said, "I liked your tune, pretty good in fact, but those lyrics! They have actually repealed slavery and, for that matter, prohibition! Didn't anybody tell you?"

He said this with a smile, but nevertheless Martin felt slighted.

"Well, Jerome Kern wrote 'Old Man River', didn't he? And, anyway, look what's going on over there right now. Do you remember Louis Armstrong's tirade about Little Rock, a few years ago? Nothing's altered." He was getting a bit hot under the collar.

"Yes, yes, old son but, you know, 'Old Man River' was written for a musical, set in the nineteenth century."

That stopped Martin in his tracks. "No, I didn't know that."

"Look," Paul continued, "when I was in my teens, I wanted to right all the world's wrongs. I almost managed to join up to fight in the Spanish Civil War. I was just too young though. I do actually understand. You keep your lyrics as they are. Take no notice of an old fart like me. Come and have a drink."

Before joining Paul De Bois at the bar for what might turn out to be *more* than just one drink, Martin thanked Alec for helping out on piano. "I don't suppose you could do next week for us?" he asked. "Paul only wanted to do the first session, as he does a lot of other things here during the week." Alec said that he would be delighted to do next week, and any more that he could manage. That was a great relief. Martin had no intention of becoming the fall-back pianist, now that he could do a whole gig on trumpet.

The next Sunday followed more or less the same pattern, but without Paul. Alec Crook turned out to be competent, although stylistically different. He wore expensive looking clothes and high-strength horn-rimmed spectacles. Before they started playing, he told them a little about himself.

Using an inheritance, he had bought a hotel in London Colney and a Rolls Royce Silver Wraith. He no longer needed to graft for a living and was indulging himself in playing the piano or organ in various pubs and restaurants around the St Albans area.

"Pity you're not in our dance band. Your car would be exactly what we need," said Owen.

A bemused Alec queried why that should be, adding, "It's a very thirsty car, you know."

"Because we are called Austin Royce and his Music!"

Alec guffawed and continued chuckling to himself long after the moment had passed.

A tenor saxophone player turned up for a blow in addition to the guitarist who had been there the previous week. Thankfully the over-loud clarinet player was absent but, almost unbelievably, another one was there. It was just one-thirty when a group of six came though from the front bar. Martin had to do a double take. In fact, the whole band did.

Among the six, somewhat shorter than the rest, was Acker Bilk.

It was time for the interval, but Martin, who could sometimes be guilty of the sin of self-indulgence, got the band to play 'Ask for Blues' again. Then they took a break. Acker came right up to the stand.

"Yeah, very good, very good. Not heard the last number before. Sounds all right to me." Martin explained that it was his own original composition. "Yeah? I'll have to get my band to record it." Martin suspected that this was no more than idle banter (which it was). Nevertheless, he was proudly satisfied with the great man's opinion.

"Tell you what, I'll bring my clarinet along next week. Nothing too difficult mind, and only in Bb!" Acker and friends left after their drink, leaving everyone else in the room talking about him. In fact, he didn't come the following week, nor any other week for that matter. Still, Martin had a beer mat in his pocket upon which was scrawled 'To Robin, cheers Acker Bilk'.

CHAPTER 27

A leaning to port

Early April 1963

Martin was driving Anne home after another Tuesday at the Potters Bar Hotel. In addition to playing 'Georgia On My Mind' on his trumpet, Paul had invited him to play a duet with him – Martin on piano and Paul on the Compton organ. They did 'Stardust' and it felt good to have those lush organ chords behind Martin's efforts on the piano, yes, it did. Anne agreed that it sounded super. In a carefree and happy frame of mind, Martin turned left into the road where Anne lived. Suddenly, with a noise that sounded like 'sprang' the car lurched leftwards and mounted the pavement.

"Christ! What was that?" exclaimed Anne.

"I don't know, but it didn't sound good. Just a minute."

Martin reversed back onto the road. He managed to steer the car in a straight line, but the spokes on the steering wheel were now at about a seventy-five-degree angle to where they had been a few seconds ago. It was dark, which didn't help, but Martin could not see anything unusual when he got out to peer underneath the car. He drove down to the next junction and attempted to turn right. He rotated the steering wheel just as far as it could go, but the car was not playing ball. It *was* turning right, but in a very wide arc, and would certainly not have got around the corner in one go.

He backed out and went a bit further down the road

until he came to a left-hand turning. That was fine. He stopped to think.

"I wonder if I can get home by only turning left," he said.

"Well, you won't be able to do that, because you *have* to turn right into your own road," Anne replied. This was true. Theoretically he could turn left into his road but in order to do this he would have to somehow leave Barnet altogether, get onto the bypass and come off again at Stirling Corner. No, there had to be another way. He thought about all the main roads and back roads that lay ahead, between East Barnet and High Barnet. He had a rough plan in mind. First, he needed to turn the car round in Anne's road. No problem. Reverse back to the last junction and do a multiple version of a three-point turn. There was no traffic here at this time of night. Then left down Cat Hill. The junction at the bottom, where it became Brookhill Road, was a very gentle right-hand bend. Martin was confident that the car would do it on full lock. Then a left-hand bend into Station Road. All the way up to the traffic lights by the Odeon. He *had* to turn right there, to go up Barnet Hill, but the junction was quite wide. He *might* just do it. If not, he would have to mount the far pavement, hope there were no obstructions in the way, and drop down into the service road, in front of the Queen's Head, where he had made his debut on trumpet. By then, he reasoned, he could do a left onto Barnet Hill when the service road came to an end and then all would be okay until he reached Wood Street, which was a left turn. But the junction of Barnet Hill and Wood Street was at the end of the trolley bus route. They turned around here, to go back towards Finchley. Quite often, cars had to thread their way in and out of the stationary trolley buses. Martin just hoped that the last one had by now left for the depot. His final move depended upon traffic conditions. Wood Street was a fairly busy main road and, for what he had planned to do, he needed it to be traffic free in both directions for a couple of minutes. There was just one obvious flaw in the overall plan. If, for whatever reason, he was forced to steer right – say, due to unforeseen traffic conditions – he would be well and truly snookered.

He outlined his plan to Anne, who got out of the car to hold up anybody else trying to get through while Martin did a nine-point turn. "Give me a ring tomorrow!" she shouted as Martin drove off on his adventure. All went exactly to plan, although he did have to employ the dodgy and totally illegal service-road option by the Odeon. This attracted some odd looks from passing motorists, one of whom stopped and wrote something down. Martin fervently hoped that it wasn't his number plate. Also, he only narrowly avoided clipping a lamp post with his front bumper as he drove across the pavement. Mercifully, there were no trolley buses at the next junction, and he drove all the way up Wood Street, stopped on the near side of the road a calculated distance beyond the turning into his own road, which was on the other side. When he judged that it was safe to try, he reversed all the way across Wood Street, on full right-hand lock, nearly managing to back the car into Argyle Road, but not quite clearing the edge of the garden wall on the corner house. He waited, with the bonnet nearly blocking one lane, until a couple of cars had passed, then lunged forwards all the way across Wood Street again, steering the car until its rear end was in line with Argyle Road, put it into reverse, and backed up all the way until he was outside his front gate.

Brian popped round the following evening and crawled underneath the Talbot. "Hmm, you've got a broken spring. One of the leaves has sheared in half. This means that your front wheels are probably no longer parallel, because the other spring, on the driver's side, is OK. Course, you can still steer straight ahead but you will get more lock on one side than the other."

"I *know* that. I had a nightmare journey getting back last night. I think someone may have even reported me for driving over the pavement down by the Odeon."

Brian estimated that replacing a leaf in the spring would be quite expensive. "Couldn't I get a whole spring from a breakers' yard then?"

"Yes, you could, but you will never be able to fit it without a workshop and some very specialist bits of equipment," was Brian's final summation.

"Oh, well, I suppose I'll have to scrap the car then," said Martin, dejectedly.

"Tell you what," added Brian. "If you could manage to break the other spring, the steering would be parallel again."

Martin actually considered this for a few seconds: "Really?"

"What do you think!" said Brian, disdainfully.

After updating his parents, Martin telephoned Anne with the bad news. "I won't be able to pick you up anymore. Can you come over here on the bus tomorrow? We may be able to go out somewhere, just so long as I keep turning left."

Anne wondered how on earth this would be possible,

but Martin assured her that, where there's a will, there's a way. He sat down with the local street atlas for quite a considerable time. Wherever they went, there had to be a pub involved, somewhere en-route. He started making notes. *Black Horse, Green Dragon (Trotters Bottom: check RH wiggle), bypass?, Galley Lane, Arkley Hotel.*

The following evening Anne rang the doorbell. Harold answered it, somewhat surprised. "Both going out for a walk this evening then?" Martin descended the stairs, two at a time.

"No, it's all right Dad, we're going for a drive. It's left turns all the way!"

"Bless m'soul!" Harold was chuckling. "*Well,* I'll go to the foot of our stairs!" he continued. He left them to it, laughing to himself at the very idea of what his son was about to attempt. The car was facing the correct way for a left turn onto Wood Street, thanks to Martin's reversing manoeuvre the night before last. "Just you watch this. I've got it all planned. We even pass three pubs and we'll get back here facing the same way."

"Oh Martin, really? You are brilliant!"

"Oh Anne, you are so easily impressed!" as he ducked her mock punch.

So off they went: left into Wood Street, left into Stapylton Road and parked just beyond the Black Horse, often frequented in the past by Sarah and Martin. They sat down with their drinks. Martin told her that, if they managed to get as far as the St Albans Road, there was a pub called the Green Dragon where the landlord was an ex-bandleader called Billy Thorburn. He had been informed of this by Len Adams a few weeks ago, but had not yet been there. Martin actually had one of his 78s, bought years earlier at a jumble sale. The label announced *The Stars Will Remember, by Billy Thorburn, the organ, the dance band and me.* Anne wanted to know what it was like. "Very flowery. Lots of octave runs up and down the keyboard." Anne was none the wiser! Back in the car they drove along Stapylton Road without meeting another car. At its end, they turned left onto the St Albans Road and after about a mile, fields replaced the houses as they left Barnet. All on its own, a pub loomed into view. This was it.

Martin parked up outside the pub and opened the front door. There was a lobby leading to two doors. Left to the public bar, right to the saloon. Facing them, on the wall, was a faded poster: Royal Variety Performance 1951 at the Victoria Palace. There followed a list of the principal stars. Halfway down, in a modest-sized font, it announced *'Billy Thorburn'.*

"Hmm, that's pretty impressive. He must have been big, back then!" was Martin's comment.

They chose the saloon, and were met immediately by a jovial, white-haired man of medium stature standing with his back to the fireplace.

"Good evening to you both, I'll be at your service in a minute. I'm just warming my namesake in front of the fire; my name's Winterbottom."

There was absolutely no one else in the bar. Martin took in the décor at a glance: a few highly polished tables, cloth-covered chairs, a wealth of music hall and variety posters adorning the walls and a Spencer grand piano in the corner. Billy Thorburn, for it was indeed he, walked behind the bar counter and served them drinks.

"A bit quiet, so far, tonight. Weekends are our busy times. It might possibly have something to do with me playing the piano for free!"

"I have got one of your records – 'The Stars Will Remember'."

"No, really? And one so young. Was it your dad's?"

Martin explained that he bought 78s from jumble sales from time to time, and this happened to be one of them. He hastily added that he liked it very much, and that *he* also played piano.

"Oh, you play the pee-ah-no, young sir? (That was his pronunciation.) Please feel free to have a tinkle, if you so wish."

Martin was reluctant to play, knowing that he would have a critical listener, but Anne chivvied him into submission. The Spencer was in fact a baby grand. Baby grands were notorious for having the worst of both worlds – an action not as good as the average upright but occupying twice the space. About as much use as a motorcycle and sidecar combination, which has no more manoeuvrability than a car but without the weather protection. Martin did his best with 'Time on My Hands', including the Teddy Wilson intro that he had spent so long learning, but the heavy action of the piano slowed him down and made his fingers numb.

"How do you find our piano?" asked Billy, when Martin had finished. Martin gave him a politically expedient, but untrue, answer. "Well, please feel free to come any weekend evening. I can usually be persuaded to play for the price of a large Bell's," he said, with a wink. They made their departure soon afterwards. Two more miles along the St Albans Road, which mercifully was more or less straight, and then Martin slowed right down as he approached Trotters Bottom, a narrow lane on the left, which almost immediately had a right-hand bend. It wasn't much of a bend, but it needed a strategy. Martin needed to know that there were no cars coming along the lane towards the junction. Once he was sure, he turned left keeping to the right-hand side of the lane. This gave him more road surface over which to execute a minor right-handed arc. By the time he reached the right-hand bend and, by then, had crossed over to the correct side of the road, he was already halfway through the turn, and just managed the oncoming bend as the nearside wheel skirted the ditch.

"Wow, that was clever," said his admiring passenger.

"Yup, nothing to it," Martin boasted.

At the end of Trotters Bottom, there was a two-way junction: straight ahead for the Barnet bypass and left for Galley Lane. As they progressed along this very pleasant lane, flanked by the sort of houses that only stockbrokers could afford, Martin slowed down and pointed to a very large open piece of ground containing eight rugby posts. "Look, Anne, that's where I used to play rugby when I was at school. Hated every minute of it!" He carried on to the end of Galley Lane. Now all he had to do was to turn left into Wood Street, and left again into Argyle Road. Satisfied with his navigational skills, he decided to award himself a final drink before going home. He pulled up just past the bus stop and they made their way into the very large, impersonal roadhouse that was the Arkley Hotel.

Martin was conscious that there had been a lack of any kind of amorous activities that evening. He had been preoccupied with the challenge of driving a car which had a major steering defect. As Anne opened the pub door, above him, at the top of the steps, the light shone through her dress, outlining her shapely legs. Anne never wore a petticoat. Martin did not know its exact purpose, but was glad that it did not feature in Anne's wardrobe. His conclusion was that it might have been one of the very last hangovers from an earlier era, when modesty was a prerequisite for any shy, respectable young lady. A time when ankles had to be covered, corsets worn and, God knows whatever other obstacles, put in the way of red-blooded males. It was sometimes called a slip, but that was only semantics. As far as Martin could see, its function was to provide yet another layer of padding, disguising the contours of a lady's bottom. Also, when seated, the flimsy material would conveniently occupy the gap between the legs, thus frustrating prying eyes; hoping for a glimpse of thigh. Martin, on the whole, considered it to be a totally unfair, unnecessary garment. The petticoat was prone to a malfunction; it often slipped a bit, and an inch or so became visible beneath the hem of the skirt. When this happened, it was perfectly all right for anyone to call out "Charlie's dead!"

"Anne, why do people say, 'Charlie's dead?'"

"Don't you know? It's when you show a bit of petticoat!"

"Yes, I know that, *of course*, but what does it mean?"

"Absolutely no idea. What brought that on anyway?"

"I was just admiring your legs and it triggered off a chain of thought."

"Yes, I bet it did! There's something I want to talk about after you get me a drink."

Martin wondered what this would be, but didn't

have long to wait. As he returned from the bar, Anne was smoothing out a page, torn from the *Evening Standard*, that she had just fished out of her handbag. It was the small ads.

"How do you fancy a long weekend away?" She pointed to an advert in the holidays section of the page: 'Cosy little caravan with cooker and sink. Washing facilities and toilet in nearby house. Quiet location in Kent countryside. Reasonable rates. Telephone Stelling Minnis 293.'

"Yeah! Do you think we could? Fantastic idea. But I guess we will have to come up with something to tell our parents?"

"I'm not particularly worried about mine and, by the way, I still have my wedding ring, so there's no need to buy a cheap one from Woolworth's."

After a bit, they decided that Martin might say that they would be staying with Anne's uncle and aunt – she didn't actually have any, but the truth would probably never come out. As the booking of weekday holidays was something that they both had to do well in advance, they agreed that, provided the caravan was available and the cost was okay, it would be best to go down to Kent straight after work on Friday week and return late Sunday evening.

Boyed up with the excitement of it all, Martin drove right past Argyle Road without thinking. Anne reminded him that he had missed his turning. He smiled. "I have all the local knowledge, you know," as he braked and wrenched the steering wheel hard left, just about making it into Queen's Road. First left into Granville Road, left at the top, and they were back in Argyle Road, facing Wood Street, as at the start of their journey.

CHAPTER 28

The Dream of Olwen

April 1963

It was five thirty, the height of the rushhour. Martin was at Victoria Station, waiting by the entrance to the Underground on the station concourse. Anne had been successful in booking the caravan for two nights in the name of Mr and Mrs Weston. It was going to cost five pounds, which was easily affordable as Martin had received double that amount from the car breakers when they hitched up his pride and joy to the recovery vehicle, its front wheels clear of the ground. It had been a sad day, but Martin had considered that maybe a post-war car would be a better bet once he had the necessary wherewithal.

"Sorry I'm a bit late," said a flustered Anne, lugging a large suitcase up the stairs from the Underground. In it, apart from her clothes, she had the sheets, pillowcases and towels that the caravan owner had said would not be provided. She also had a bottle of milk, a loaf of bread, sugar, tea, butter, eggs and bacon. There was a shared frisson of excitement at the thought that they would be together for the next two days and nights. Martin's parents were blissfully unaware that this was going to be a 'dirty weekend' but, had they had the slightest suspicion about this, their disapproval would have been as nothing compared with them becoming aware of Anne's marital status, which Martin had been at great pains to conceal. Doing something slightly immoral and nice was exciting for all the right reasons. Martin, acting the part of the perfect gentleman, swapped cases with Anne as they made their way to the ticket office where they bought two returns to Canterbury East. They boarded the next train, at five fifty, and managed to get two seats together at a table, despite the rush-hour commuters.

As they settled down for the hour and a half journey, Martin began to tell Anne how the evening gig at the Potters Bar Hotel had gone. Owen and Joe had worked up a couple of sketches, which they had thought would go down well. There were bands on the fringe of the jazz scene by then, such as the Alberts and the Temperance Seven, who included bits of 'business' in their act. Owen was by nature a frustrated actor, and this was his chance to shine. Neither Brian nor Martin knew in advance what the other two were going to do. The music was no more than politely received until Joe started to sing. He had wisely decided to include current hits, including 'Can't Get Used to Losing You' and 'From a Jack to a King' as well as tried and tested standards such as 'All of Me'. When he sang 'Moon River' as a waltz, everyone got on to the floor. It was a moment of truth for the original trio: total justification for the decision to form a dance band rather than try to make something out of what was left of Jimmy Prior's Jazzmen.

There had been a buzz of anticipation as the moment drew closer for Maffi to make her first appearance. The plan was for her to have a spot closing the first half and another spot towards the end of the evening. Before that, Owen and Joe stood at the microphone, wearing pith helmets, and went into one of their routines. It was less than memorable.

It included such gems as Joe saying that he had news from the front: "Ladysmith has been relieved." This was followed by a loud farting noise. There was a modest ripple of laughter and Owen then came out with his punchline. "Don't take the pith out of our helmets." Martin told Anne that it was just as well that, in the end, they ran out of time for their other sketch, planned for the second set. That was the last anybody ever saw of the Joe and Owen act. Maffi followed, to great applause, whistles and catcalls. Then it was time for the interval. The second set was much the same, but without the 'comedy'. Joe was clearly an asset, as of course was Maffi, who had been overheard telling one of the customers in an outraged tone of voice that she was not a stripper. Owen asked her what that was all about, and she said that this guy had offered her some work in a Soho strip club.

By now, the train had left the suburbs and was approaching the Medway towns. Neither of them had previously visited the 'garden of England', Kent's very apt sobriquet. They watched the rolling countryside pass by: the Medway valley, the woodlands and hills beyond, orchard after orchard and, as they approached Sittingbourne, hop fields and oast houses. Every mile brought something memorable to see. The Stour Valley, as the train neared Canterbury, looked lovely. Suddenly the spire of the cathedral came into view, dominating the skyline. "We're going to have a fabulous time," opined Anne. Martin agreed.

Dusk was upon the land as they walked from Canterbury East to the bus station. The porter had given them directions. It was a bit of a trek through the historic city, which was undergoing some post-war rebuilding after a period of stagnation. A new ring road was under construction, badly needed as the A2 ran right through the narrow city centre. Eventually they found what they were looking for, assisted by the general direction that the buses seemed to be coming from or going to. At the end of the bus park was a long wooden hut announcing itself as the 'Passenger Waiting Room'. Inside were benches along each side and a buffet area at the far end. Martin looked at the timetable for the No.18 to Hythe and found that they had time for a quick cuppa.

Every so often the door would open and an employee of the East Kent Omnibus Company would call out the number and destination of the next bus due to depart. The passengers would then follow him to where it was parked. After twenty minutes he announced, "No 18 to Bossingham, Stelling Minnis, Lyminge and Hythe." It was a single-decker, and the service was not that frequent as it stopped off at a few tiny hamlets en-route. In fact, it was the last one of the day. Anne, holding a piece of paper bearing the address of the cottage, asked the conductor whether he knew the nearest stop. He didn't exactly, but said that they might as well get off at the Star in Bossingham, as it could not be that far away. It was by now totally dark, as the bus left the built-up outskirts of Canterbury and made its way along Stone Street, an old Roman road. After several miles, the bus turned left and, before long, the lights of a few houses shone brightly out of the blackness. "Star, Bossingham," announced the conductor. The bus stop and shelter were built into the pub wall. Martin considered this to be the most sensible aid to the drinking man since Heathcote-Amory reduced the price of a pint of beer in his 1960 budget.

The bus departed in the direction of Stelling Minnis, and the two lucky weekenders made a beeline for the saloon bar. Inside all was warmth and cosiness. A coal fire was burning brightly; two men were playing darts. A few people were seated at those little round pub tables with deceptively heavy cast-iron legs, ending in ball and claw feet; the kind that are in fact almost impossible to move. Martin looked at the two handpumps: Shepherd Neame bitter and mild. A keg beer too, Abbey Ale. He had not heard of this brewery, but he just loved trying out different brews. He ordered a pint of the bitter for himself, and a half for Anne. "Just got off the bus then?" enquired the landlord.

"Yes, we are down here on holiday for a couple of days."

"Ah, I thought so, by your suitcases. Mind you, we don't get many visitors in Bossingham, not even in the summer months!"

Martin asked whether he knew the whereabouts of Fieldview Cottage, and it turned out to be about 150 yards further along the road; the last house before the start of the farmers' fields.

Anne said that Mrs Pearson, the owner of Fieldview Cottage, knew that they were coming down from London after work and had said that any time up to ten o'clock would be fine. Martin looked at his watch; it was now eight forty-five. They had another two drinks and bought a screw-top quart bottle to take with them. They found the cottage without any problem, despite the lack of streetlights. Mrs Pearson answered the door and led them to the caravan, parked in the back garden. The white paint was beginning to rust, and it was quite small, with curved ends to the roof; the sort that you might see blocking a country lane as it trundled along behind a Land Rover. She showed them around, which didn't take long. There was a table and bench, a tall cupboard for clothes, a sink, a cooker and a bed, which looked halfway between a single and a double in size. "Now I shall just pop indoors and fetch you some blankets and pillows. Also, it gets a bit chilly in the evening this time of the year. Shall I bring you a paraffin heater?" They agreed that would be an excellent idea. When she returned with the heater it turned out to be the pre-war, tall cylindrical type, generally thought, by then, to be unsafe. She had thought to bring a box of matches as well. Before bidding them goodnight she pointed to a latched door next to the back door of the cottage. "That is unlocked day and night. There is a light switch, just inside. It has a toilet and washbasin. We won't be using it, so it's just for you, while you are here. Have you got any milk?" Anne said that they had brought a bottle with them. "Ah, good. But if you need another pint while you are here, I can ask the milkman for an extra one." Anne said that might be a good idea.

As soon as Mrs Pearson had left, Martin opened the quart of light ale, while Anne made up the bed. "Do you know, she said nothing about pots, pans, plates, cups, knives and forks!" he exclaimed. Then he spotted a small cupboard above the cooker. Hey presto, there they were! "Do you want to drink out of a teacup or a mug?" he asked. "There is only one of each!" They quickly consumed the Shepherd Neame light ale, not bothering to light the paraffin stove. Then, having very rapidly undressed, it was an abandoned session of lovemaking leading to total exhaustion and a deep sleep. In the morning, Anne, while stark naked, got up to make a pot of tea. Martin, in the same state, pulled the curtains back, in order to greet the day. Staring into the window and, more specifically, at Anne's backside, was the unwelcome face of a man, not six feet away. *Arrgh!* he thought, as he yanked the curtains back to where they had been. On the other side of the hedge, next to the caravan, was a public footpath!

After a breakfast of bacon, eggs and fried bread, they each had a stand-up wash, dressed for the day, and locked the caravan. "Shall we walk to the next village, Stelling Minnis?" asked Martin. It was about a mile and a half, according to the signpost, so it wouldn't take long. By then it was half past ten on Saturday morning. Although they didn't know it, they had chosen just about the sleepiest part of the Kent countryside for their holiday. There was no one about at all. There were no interesting sights to see. Just a succession of farmer's field after farmer's field, through a flat landscape. Stelling Minnis turned out to be only marginally bigger than Bossingham. The one thing it did have, apart from its pub, the Rose and Crown, was a general store. They decided to buy a few provisions, as there were no restaurants, cafes, or even a fish and chip shop anywhere nearby. "Do you fancy sausages and mash?" Anne asked. Martin certainly did; in fact, it was one of his favourite meals.

"If you keep on offering me things like this, I will have to marry you," he jested. Anne went unusually quiet – not even a smile or, better still, a laugh.

As there were no competing attractions, they checked out the pub. It was bigger than the Star, but not so homely. There was a piano, however. After some more Shepherd Neame bitter, Martin asked whether he could play it, and got a 'yes' for an answer. There were no more than six other people drinking in the pub at that time, but they seemed to like Martin's efforts. After a couple of numbers, he closed the lid; thinking that he shouldn't outstay his welcome.

"No, don't stop. Do you know any Beatles numbers?" one of them asked.

"I'm sorry, I know that I should, but I've not learned them yet."

"Well, just play a bit more of what you were doing. We liked it. Would you and your young lady like a drink?"

And so, as Martin continued to play, the drinks kept coming, at the expense of the Rose and Crown's customers.

"Hey, Martin, if you can keep on doing this all the time, perhaps I would be a fool not to marry you!" Now *that* was a joke, without a doubt.

When the pub shut its doors at two thirty, they had decided to spend the afternoon in Hythe. They didn't have to wait too long for the bus, and when it arrived, lo and behold it had the same conductor on board. He asked whether they had found the address they were looking for without any trouble. They got chatting in between stops. He told them that they would find plenty to do in Hythe, and had they heard about the Romney, Hythe and Dymchurch Railway? As they hadn't, he explained that it was built in the 1920s as a regular commuter line along the coast, but in miniature scale. During the war, it was commissioned by the War Office. They mounted machine guns onto flat trucks, and used the railway to patrol that vulnerable part of the coastline. Now, it was mainly a tourist attraction, but it did stop at Maddison's Holiday Camp, which was very handy for the campers.

They said goodbye to the conductor, as they alighted at Red Lion Square in the centre of Hythe. Far from finding plenty to do, they walked the length of the high street, looking in shop windows and noting the several pubs, all of which were closed until they reopened at six. At its end, they walked the short distance to the beach and sat down for a while, admiring the view. There was a large tanker on the horizon, slowly making its way westwards. Martin picked up a handful of pebbles and demonstrated how to skim them over the water. He managed to get one to bounce five times, so quit while he was ahead. Anne had a go, but all her efforts were in vain. Martin told her that this was the way that the bouncing bomb worked. She had not seen *The Dam Busters*, unlike most of Martin's male friends. Although an avid cinema goer, for Anne there always had to be some romantic interest; *The Dam Busters* had none at all!

"Hey, look, how about that miniature railway? The conductor said that the station was quite near where we got off." Now that was a good idea. Hythe Station was an unexpected surprise. It really was just like a normal railway in every detail, except size. Nothing like other miniature railways that Martin had seen as a boy, when holidaying with his parents in Blackpool or Scarborough; this one had closed carriages, for a start. *This* one had exact scale-model steam locomotives, looking for all the world as if they had been plucked straight from British Railways and shrunk. In fact, it operated on a fifteen-inch gauge track – far bigger than any recreational miniature railway. It was three thirty by now, and they knew that if they didn't catch the five o'clock bus back to Bossingham, they would have a two- hour wait for the next (and last) one. So there was just about enough time for a one-hour return trip to New Romney. That was a pity, because Martin would have liked to travel the whole length of the fourteen miles of track between Hythe and Dungeness, a strange, wilderness-like place, they had been told.

They were fascinated by the journey. The view from the

carriage alternated between glimpses of the sea, and close inspection of residential back gardens. The train stopped at Dymchurch, St Mary's Bay and New Romney, where they alighted, walked across the track, and got on the return train, which was letting off a significant amount of surplus steam as they passed it. "That saves me having to take my coat to the cleaners!" was Anne's instant joke.

On the way back, having the carriage to themselves, Martin found himself worrying about Anne's guarded reaction to the subject of marriage earlier in the day, even though it was in jest. It was time to speak.

"Anne, what caused you to separate from your husband? Did he leave you, or was it the other way around?" She looked a bit startled; clearly not expecting this sort of a question, right out of the blue.

"I left him actually. We weren't getting on. There was nothing in common, and I didn't want to stay trapped."

"Oh, so there wasn't something, some big thing, that could bring on a divorce then?"

"Well, if he had left me, I could claim 'desertion' as a reason, but I'll just have to wait it out, I suppose."

"Couldn't he divorce you for desertion then?" asked the innocent Martin.

"No, he won't be doing that. He wants me back but, as far as I'm concerned, he can go jump in the lake!"

Martin felt very uneasy. The whole thing wasn't as cut and dried as he had imagined: a husband wanting his wife back, probably jealous that she may be seeing someone else; Anne leaving for what seemed to Martin to be the flimsiest of reasons. Hardly a good omen for a new long-term relationship. What to do?

Anne spoke again: "I do really like you a lot, Martin. Don't fret about my marriage. Lots of people make mistakes that they regret. They don't *all* do anything about it, even if they might want to. Can we talk about something else now, please?"

Anne managed to cook a presentable sausage and mash using the primitive cooker in the caravan, and it was now time to go to the Star for the evening. You got 3d back on an empty beer bottle, so Martin brought it with him. Once in the pub, the landlord wanted to know how they had enjoyed the day, what were their first impressions of Kent, and would they please have a drink on the house. Anne whispered, "We're doing all right for free drinks today. Pity there's no piano." The dartboard was free, so Martin challenged Anne to a game of 301 which he lost, much to his chagrin.

"Best of three then," he said. He proceeded to lose the next one, making Anne the winner. Some of the regulars had been watching with interest. One of them asked whether Anne would play a game with him, if they had finished? She said that she was up for it, so long as her 'husband' didn't mind.

Two or three people had been coming in and out of a door, leading off the main bar. Martin decided to investigate. In it he found some jigsaw puzzles, a rocking horse, a few children's toys and a record player. It was the pub games and children's room. Beside the record player were a pile of 45s and EPs. They were, in the main, hits from a good few years back: Tommy Steele, Cliff Richard, Doris Day, Jimmy Young, etc. There was one, however, that caught Martin's eye. The George Melanchrino Orchestra playing the *Warsaw Concerto*, *The Legend of the Glass Mountain*, and *The Dream of Olwen*. This last piece was a favourite of Len Adams, who could usually be persuaded to play it in the Alex. Martin had never heard the orchestral version before, so he put it on the turntable. He was hooked; it was marvellous. He played it again, then the other two tracks. What a superb record, he thought. Someone else came in, and found a record of their choice. Martin gave up his temporary ownership of the record player for the moment and returned to the bar.

Since he had been away indulging himself, a small crowd had gathered around the darts playing area. It seemed that Anne had been holding her own on the dartboard, despite being the only woman player. But her sporting prowess was not the only attraction. Martin couldn't help noticing that all eyes were upon Anne's well-proportioned bosom. It bounced, every time she threw a dart. *Well*, he thought, *they're not getting any of it, but I am!* At the end of the current match, which she narrowly lost, Martin bought her a refill.

"Where did you learn to play like that?"

"In a former life," was all she said, with an air of mystery.

"You'll never guess. There's a record of *Dream of Olwen* in the back room. You know, Len often plays it. You must come and hear it."

She followed him through, to some orchestrated groans of disappointment from the darts crowd. After three more playings, she agreed with Martin that it was a great record. Praise indeed, from one who only, as a rule, liked the latest chart-toppers.

"When I get home, I am bloody well going to learn it, no matter how long it takes me."

They went back to the darts players, and he lost her

for the rest of the evening. He was not too bothered – he was able to sample all the beers, draught and bottled, while perched on a barstool.

Time to go, and another quart bottle of pale ale was duly purchased. In the dark, he was a little unsteady on his feet. He blamed this upon the monopolisation of his darts-playing 'wife', leaving him with no option but to carry on drinking. Back in the caravan, he decided to light the paraffin heater. After that, he immediately became aware that he had an urgent need for the toilet. Forgetting about the heater, upon his return he walked straight into it, and it fell over. It was one of those heart-stopping moments when time seemed to stand still. They were both frozen to the spot, waiting for the inevitable 'whoosh' of incandescent paraffin flames, wondering whether they would escape with their lives and, if so, whether Mrs Pearson had a fire extinguisher. And then, nothing. It had simply gone out. They both experienced the euphoria of total and utter relief. Martin sat on the bed and, with a shaking hand, opened the beer.

They greeted the morning sated by the night's passion and not really wanting to get out of bed, so they just lay there, curtains slightly parted at the window, admiring the view and listening to the variety of birdsong. Eventually, having used up all the remaining bacon and eggs for a very late breakfast, and having stripped down the bed, they began to pack. All towels and clothes for the wash wrapped up in the sheets, and back into Anne's suitcase. Everything else in Martin's. It shared the load a bit. Then a bit of a tidy-up and time to say goodbye to Mrs Pearson.

"Thanks very much for the stay. It has been very nice. It was £5, wasn't it?" as Martin held out five £1 notes.

Mrs Pearson wrote out a receipt. It was made out to Mr and Mrs Weston. Anne told her that she had left the remaining tea, sugar, butter and bread in the cupboard in case it was of any use to anyone.

"Well, safe journey back to London and don't forget, if you know anyone who fancies a nice, quiet caravan holiday, perhaps you could recommend us."

It was approaching midday as they walked up the road towards the Star.

"The bus goes at one, so let's go and have a last drink."

The landlord greeted them like real friends.

"What time are you off then?" he enquired, drawing off the stale beer left in the pipes from the previous evening. Having been told that they had an hour to spare, he asked them whether they fancied a look at the cellar as he had to rig up another barrel. This was a novelty. "Just mind how you go down the steps." Neither of them had been down into a pub cellar before. The first thing that assailed their senses was the smell of damp. The rough brick walls were moist to the touch. The next was the beery smell. Martin inhaled deeply. Large wooden barrels were supported on cradles, as was the pressurised Abbey Ale. This, the landlord explained, was the way forward. "Before long there won' t be any more handpump beer. It's a bit of an art, getting it just right. You can't learn cellar-craft overnight, but the keg stuff is dead simple. Hardly needs any training at all!"

They had a drink before the bus was due, and the landlord, who had finally announced, "The name's Fred by the way," regretted that they were not locals because he said he could really do with Anne in his darts team. Martin asked whether he could play the Melanchrino record just once more?

"Of course you can. Leave the door open so we can all hear it." He played it twice, in the end.

"Why don't you have it? You're the only one, as far as I know, who has ever been interested in it. I think it was left by one of our customers a long time ago." Martin was over the moon at this and managed, with some difficulty, to buy Fred a drink. He had a modest half of mild. Then it was time for goodbye, and the bus journey to Canterbury.

Martin mused out loud, "I wonder how Owen and the lads are getting on?"

"Oh yes, it's normally your jazz session on Sundays. Will they manage without you?"

"I should think so. Brian, you know, not my mate the bass player; the new one who plays clarinet? He can more than hold his own. I wish I had half his talent!"

They had talked about having a look around the city but, in the end, agreed that it wasn't such a good idea, what with having to lug suitcases wherever they went. "A little trolley, the size of a suitcase, would be a good idea. I wonder whether anybody makes anything like that?" They didn't. In fact, it would be another thirty years before anyone thought to put wheels onto suitcases. As the train made its way out of Kent and into the suburbs of London, the changing view from the carriage window mirrored their changing mood. The feeling of still being on holiday evaporated mile by mile until by the time they approached Victoria Station, it had vanished completely. During the journey, Anne removed her wedding ring and put it back into her handbag.

CHAPTER 29

Let's twist again

Summer 1963

"It was Rachael, actually. She knew!" Martin was banging in a tent peg, making sure the guy rope was taught. It was the start of a spur-of-the-moment holiday, using the week that Martin had already booked off work, expecting to have been spending it with Anne. A few days earlier, Brian, who had been trying to cheer up his old mate, suggested a drive out to the Prince of Wales at Bentley Heath, to join in with the darts crowd. It was more of a social occasion than a serious contest. They did play some conventional 301 but, in the main, other dartboard games such as 'knockout', 'cricket', 'killer', etc. It was all good fun, accompanied by reasonable quantities of McMullen's Bitter. One of the gang was from Derbyshire. He had recently moved down from Chesterfield with his job. "Never been to Derbyshire then?" he asked, with a hint of surprise in his voice. "Well! There's the Dales, the Peak District, the caverns at Castleton. Oh, and lots more. God's own county, you know!" He painted a tempting prospect. Brian turned to Martin:

"Why not? Fancy a camping holiday then?"

The Chesterfield man continued: "And if you go to Matlock, you'll spend all your days there. Aye! Take the cable car up to the Heights of Abraham. Fantastic views!"

Brian had all the camping gear and, at the moment, the

only car. They had found a campsite in Cromford, just a mile or two outside Matlock Bath.

Martin continued: "After she stopped answering my telephone calls, I went to the Cherry Tree at the top of Totteridge Hill. You know Rachael, friend of Anne's?" Brian nodded. "Well, I knew she was one of their barmaids." Martin was unburdening himself to Brian at long last. Up until then he had not wanted to talk about Anne. "Well, she told me that I was just one of a long line of boyfriends. She went for anything in trousers, but none of them lasted long."

"Sounds as if you're better off out of it, mate." Brian was trying to say something positive, for the sake of his friend.

"It's easy for you to say that, but I went a bit off the rails for a few weeks. You know I did. She was a cracker though, don't you think?"

"Oh yeah, I'd say! But she *was* still married, wasn't she?"

"I know. I never told my mum and dad. I never thought about how the whole thing was going to pan out. But I didn't expect the sudden lack of communication. She never actually said that it was over."

He was still sore about Anne; hence the overuse of the word 'never'; an appropriate word under the circumstances. Never, *ever* was there any prospect of the sort of future that Martin might have hoped for.

It hadn't been long after their holiday in Bossingham. It started with Anne cancelling the odd date, which then became a more frequent event. Then, at the Royalty, a stranger to Martin came up to her and whispered something, which made Anne giggle. She was reticent about whom he was, and what he had just said, when Martin asked her.

Apparently it was just one of a group of friends whom she knew from a couple of years back. Finally, she stopped answering the phone. It was always her mother at the other end, who promised to tell Anne that Martin had rung. Martin wrote her a long letter, full of sorrow and bitterness. There was no reply.

"Could you sort out the groundsheet, please?" Brian asked. It was clear to him that a line should now be drawn under any prolonged agonising over Martin's failed love life. There would, no doubt, be ample opportunities for Martin to revisit this theme, later in the week. But he, Brian, had driven all the way from Barnet that day, and was now determined to have a good time. Just for the moment, he had done enough of the 'friend in need' bit. Tent sorted, it was back in the Austin 16, and off to sample the high spots of Matlock Bath. It seemed that there must have been some sort of event going on judging by the decorative streamers draped from lamp post to lamp post. It wasn't easy to park either, but having eventually found a convenient side street, they entered the first town centre pub that they came to. It was rather like walking into Thomas Telford's workshop. Everywhere was cast iron. The bannister rails, the brackets supporting the bar canopy, the ornamental lights, the tables, the chair legs, the shelving behind the bar, the mirror frames. "Good to be in the Black Country," Brian observed. They ordered a couple of pints of Offillers Ale, and spent some time looking at the faded sepia photographs of an earlier Matlock, which adorned the walls. "Might as well have some music?" Brian suggested.

"Aye, just for a bit, like," was the landlord's answer to Martin's request to play the piano. He had recently been working on an old waltz: 'Am I Wasting my Time'. His version began, as the composer intended, in three-four time. Then followed a bit of an improvised bridge in, what he fondly imagined, was the 'Teddy Wilson' style, leading to a four-four swing version. As a finale, he changed the key from F to G. They seemed to like it.

"That's the style, lad," said one of the customers. Martin played a couple more numbers, including a non-vocal version of 'Ask for Blues' then, as it was seven o'clock and the allure of unvisited drinking establishments was getting stronger, called it a day. "You'll be back some time, I hope?" were the landlord's welcome parting words, as they left for the next pub.

Leaving the second pub, which had no piano, Martin became aware of indistinct heavenly voices. "Am I drunk already, or can you hear it?"

"It's coming from somewhere up there," Brian said, pointing above the town centre rooftops. A narrow, winding street, with a gradient that would have been a challenge for most family saloons, ascended from the rear of the pub. Up and up they walked, all the time the voices getting nearer and more distinct. After two hairpin bends, much like those on the Amalfi Road in Italy, a pub with a front patio surrounded by substantial railings loomed into view. It was perched on a rock ledge, high above Matlock Bath, a sort of Alpine Schloss in the middle of Derbyshire. The beers on tap were from Wards, another new brewery for Brian to tick off the list. Outside, the view downwards was quite spectacular. They were about 200 yards directly above the high street which, as they had suspected, had now been taken over by a carnival procession. They had the best possible view of the

Matlock Festival, a modest but proud event. There was a river just on the far side of the main road which, possibly in Victorian times, had been enlarged to accommodate a man-made island, reached by a footbridge. In the centre was a cast-iron bandstand, and a brass band was in the process of setting up their music stands. "Ah-ha!" said Brian. "This will be the festival's 'pièce de résistance', I'll be bound!"

Martin popped inside to order another two pints as the Matlock Silver Band opened with a Sousa March. The sound quality, over water and from a long way below, was quite magical. Matlock Bath is situated in a valley, and the surrounding hills acted as an echo chamber. A small crowd had congregated on the far side of the road below and applauded each number. Then, unexpectedly and totally out of character, they played their own version of 'Let's Twist Again'. It was as compelling as it was bizarre. The arrangement faithfully followed the melody line of the Chubby Checker original but without any trace of its syncopated rhythms.

"Aye, lad, we play things properly oop north. None o' this new-fangled top o' t'pops roobish," mimicked Brian. It was one of those cherished moments to be stored away for retelling at a later date.

Martin turned to Brian. "D 'you know what, mate? Bloody women! I think I *am* going to enjoy this holiday."

"That's the style, lad!" Brian had already picked up the Derbyshire lingo.

It was getting near to ten by the time they left the town. Just before the left-hand junction to Cromford, Brian pulled in to the car park of the Wayside Tavern, soon to become their regular last port of call before turning in for the night.

This one served Home Ales, yet another untried brew. Brian was having a field day! They took the precaution of buying two screw-top quart bottles of Robin Hood IPA to take back to the campsite. By the end of the week there was a great deal of empties in the boot of the Austin. Brian had brought a portable radio with a shortwave band and, once they were tucked into their sleeping bags, tuned in to AFN, which could always be relied upon for its jazz content. And there, in the middle of a Derbyshire field, swigging light ale from a bottle, they were captivated by the magical sounds of Louis Armstrong's All Stars. Total bliss!

During the week, they sampled the beers of every single pub in Matlock Bath and Matlock, its bigger sister. Martin played the piano in the five establishments that were so equipped and, as a result, both of them received several free drinks. They ate in restaurants and tried in vain to find one that served mashed or boiled potatoes with the meal. It was always the ubiquitous chips, never any variation. Brian did ask one of the waiters whether they could do boiled potatoes for them, it being a 'southern delicacy'. "Nay, lad, I'd have to boil oop a pan just for the two of you, like." They did too, as recommended by the Chesterfield darts player, go up to the Heights of Abraham by cable car, and down into the famous caverns of Castleton.

On the way home to Barnet, having first obtained a considerable amount of cash back from the dozens of empty Robin Hood IPA bottles, Martin operated Brian's portable radio, moving it around with the bends in the road, to maintain a signal. It was Saturday morning, time for *Jack Jackson's Record Roundup*. Before the war, Jackson had been the 'hot' trumpet player with Jack Hylton, rivalling Nat

Gonella, with Lew Stone. Now, as a disc jockey, he could be relied upon to bring a superior degree of musical taste to his weekly selections than most of his well-known competitors. But it was not just the music that persuaded the BBC to give him this prime Saturday morning slot. Between the records were some very clever bits of tape splicing. He would invent a running script, with himself as the main character and, more often than not, Tony Hancock as his stooge. He blatantly used cuttings from the very popular *Hancock's Half-Hour* radio programme; presumably with the permission of Galton and Simpson, the scriptwriters. At the end of the broadcast, Martin turned the radio off and the discussion inevitably turned back to gigs. As they approached the outskirts of Barnet, Brian wondered what had been going on in their own little musical world, while they had been away. He didn't have to wait long to find out.

CHAPTER 30

Quo Vadis?

Summer 1963

Owen greeted them with the news that they had been half expecting. The Sunday morning jazz session at the Potters Bar Hotel had come to an end. Landlord Jim had been sorry. He personally liked the music, but the audience had been sparse and he couldn't justify continuing to employ the extra staff in the back bar. From Owen's point of view, it was a blessing in disguise. There had been at least two Sundays where there had been no point in even starting. Musicians, prepared to play just for fun, seemed to be in short supply. Paul De Bois may have been right: "never play below the MU rate." Other times, Martin, much against his inclination, had been forced to play the piano. It was either that or abandon the session. Owen went on to say that Joe Ranche wanted the monthly restaurant gig to carry on as long as enough customers kept on coming. Small comfort to Martin, who only really wanted to play the trumpet, not the bloody piano. Ah, but there *was* a glimmer of hope, it seemed. Alec Crook, the hotel and Rolls Royce owner, and occasional pianist, had been negotiating with a pub in St Albans, hoping to be employed as their resident organist. He confided to Owen that, once he had got his feet under the table, there might be a good chance for a 'bit of jazz'. However, he warned that it was a small stage in a modest-sized bar. "A couple, or maybe three of you. No more than that," he had suggested. Martin was given to understand that he would be definitely asked to play trumpet should this come to pass. Owen said nothing to Brian though.

Meanwhile, Austin Royce and his Music were picking up the odd gig, but without the benefit of their star attraction. Maffi had moved back to London in the hope of bigger and better things, but not before fulfilling her final booking with Austin Royce, at Dunstable. It seemed that Owen had been more than a little unprepared for the venue. None of the band, nor even Maffi, who had obtained the gig, had ever been there before so, in all fairness, could not have been expected to know what was in store. When they arrived, they found themselves in something resembling an aircraft hangar. There must have been well over fifteen hundred noisy people standing around the dance area. There seemed to be no seats. Forcing their way to the stage at the other end, which could have easily housed the London Philharmonic Orchestra, was a problem. There just weren't many gaps between the clusters of bodies, and there was a distinct lack of acknowlegement that the musicians whom they had paid to hear were endeavouring to get through, lugging various drum cases, a double bass, microphone stand, etc., and would have appreciated a bit of cooperation. Only one comment was made, during this physical struggle: "'Ere, mate, watch where you're going!" Despite everything, they reached the other end of the hall, out of breath and with a sweat on. The stage manager asked them to leave their gear in the wings, as they were to be the second act, due on stage in about one hour's time.

"Have you got your own PA?" he enquired. Well, they

had: it was a 30-watt amplifier and a single speaker with one microphone for Joe's vocals. "Is that it?" he gasped, incredulously. "You'll never be heard with this lot," gesturing towards the assembled masses.

In desperation, he managed to persuade the main act, a rock and roll band, to leave their own PA on stage, as they would have to return for the last hour anyway. That was a relief. The Austin Royce ensemble stayed for just five minutes of Vince Berry and the Thunderclaps, then decamped to the nearest pub, nursing their eardrums. At last, the moment arrived: the best-paid gig they had ever had! Even with individual microphones for the piano and bass and yet another one for Joe, they were fighting a losing battle with the audience from the very beginning, whichever way you looked at it. Whereas the incessant heavy rock beat of Vince Berry had satisfied the audience's basic musical expectations and primal requirements, the polished swing rhythms of Austin Royce had just about the opposite effect. It provoked audible discontent. Whereas the lurid multicoloured jackets sported by the Thunderclaps splashed reflected light from the spotlights, Austin Royce's dinner-jacketed band evoked the sepulchral appearance of pall-bearers.

One or two of Joe's vocals were fairly well received, unlike the backing, what with its total absence of amplified guitars and the wrong style of drumming. Rock drumming places a heavy, unsubtle emphasis on the first and third beats of the bar. Owen's drumming, based on the styles of popular music that pre-dated rock, emphasised the second and fourth, or even beats. The audience, weaned exclusively on rock and roll, were quite literally caught on the wrong foot. Ballroom dancing was for squares, or their parents, and so they made no attempt to dance to something that one couldn't jive to. Instead, completely ignoring the band, they chatted animatedly with each other; hundreds of voices at once. When the decibels generated by the audience eventually drowned out the band, the stage manager shouted at Owen from the wings: "For God's sake bring on the girl. *Now!*"

Maffi just about saved the day. Most of the male audience moved up to the front of the ballroom for a closer look, anticipating something that was never going to happen. The women stayed firmly at the back. If looks could tell, their collective view would have been that Maffi was no better than she should be, a brazen hussy. All 'Dunstable girls' to a tee, their education sadly lacked an appreciation of oriental culture. No, they had decided that this was just pure depravity. The set came to an end without Martin, Joe or Brian taking any further part in the proceedings. They dismantled their equipment to enthusiastic cheers from the audience, not for what had just taken place, but for the return of Vince Berry, who could be seen retuning his guitar at the back of the stage. The stage manager paid out the money but told Owen that he should not expect any return bookings unless he got up to date, changed his act and got some proper PA equipment. Owen, having first pocketed the money and never one to take criticism lying down, replied: "Don't worry, we wouldn't come back to this dump in a million years!"

One Saturday morning, early in July, Martin, for no particular reason, found himself brooding about his unfulfilled ambitions. He made himself a cup of Nescafé and retired to the main living room, where the family grand piano lived. 'Moonglow' came to mind. There was another melody which fitted the harmonies perfectly: 'The Theme from Picnic'. After bit of desultory fiddling around with the two tunes, committing the second one to memory for future use, he slammed the lid down. Just what was the matter? He sat down by the window and took stock of his life. There were five main strands: music, girlfriends, friends, personal transport and his job.

He had proved to himself that he could play a whole session on the trumpet, even though he might flag a bit towards the end. That would surely improve, the more he played? He was established as a pianist who could play both jazz and dance music. But every time he played the piano, he wished that it was the trumpet. He had no current girlfriend, despite a few trips to the Royalty, after being dumped by Anne. Worse than that, all his musical friends were either already married, or soon to be. He was running out of single free spirits to socialise with. He had no car and had to rely upon public transport or Brian's Austin 16. But as Brian was himself getting hitched in August, that option would soon disappear as domestic bliss inevitably replaced drinking with mates. He did not even have the benefit of his mother's car any longer, as it had been recently sold. Kathleen had rarely used it, so when the time came for yet another year's renewal of the road tax and insurance, Harold had decided to dispense with it. Martin's job at Guinness Mahon was a good one by most people's standards, but he saw others working in the creative media, or even teaching, and envied them. Perhaps he was becoming too much of a 'glass half-empty' individual? He wanted everything to be better than it currently was.

He mentally drew up a short-term 'to do' list. Ignoring

for the time being the job and lack of car situations, which could wait their turn, he would redouble his efforts to become a trumpet player first and foremost and a pianist in a secondary role. It would mean many visits to pubs where live music was performed, with a view to getting noticed and then, hopefully, booked. To get another girlfriend, he would go to the Royalty that very evening. It was undoubtedly his best chance of meeting someone to go out with. It had sometimes worked in the past. As an afterthought, he realised that he had got out of the habit of socialising after work. The Friday evening drinking sessions, so much a part of his working week at Knightsbridge, were a thing of the past. Why not contact Robert Melton next week? Why not invite Robin, his one friend at Guinness Mahon too? It might be fun; no, it *would* be fun. He would personally make sure of this.

At 6 pm, he put on his new Italian style suit, tailor-made by Burtons, a cream-coloured shirt and a horizontally striped knitted tie. "Just off to Southgate," he called down the hallway to Kathleen, "should be back before midnight." One hour later, the doors had only just opened and he found himself in the queue, shuffling along the cinder path towards the cash desk and cloakroom. There was a very tall girl about twenty people ahead. He couldn't help noticing her because she was surrounded by shorter people and her yellow hat rose above the crowd, like a sunflower amongst the geraniums. As soon as he was inside, and had obtained a pint of beer from the bar upstairs, he surveyed the evening's talent show. *Hmm, quite a few prospects tonight*, he mused to himself. It wasn't long before he spotted the tall girl when she stood up to dance with a shorter man. He had only seen her back view when in the queue. Now he could see that she was quite attractive – not in a pretty, girly way, more what might have been described as elegant, with finely chiselled features. A sort of classic *Vogue* magazine face. She was wearing an expensive-looking twin-set and flattish heels. For tall girls, the wearing of high heels might put them at a disadvantage. Not many men were looking for an 'Amazon'.

From his vantage point, he watched her progress around the dance floor, noting that she sat down and thanked her dance partner, who then walked away. "Aha!" Martin sprinted downstairs before the next dance was announced. He was not the only one moving in her direction, but he just reached her before anyone else did. Blast! It was a slow foxtrot, a dance that he couldn't do. But it was now or never. She rose to her feet. Martin noticed, with relief, that she was about one inch shorter than he was; she would be about five eleven with her shoes on. Martin decided to do a modified version of the waltz, inserting one extra step after the 'one two three' pattern. Marlene, as she was called, cottoned on to what Martin was doing. "If you don't mind me mentioning it, you seem to have your own steps for the foxtrot. I'm doing my best to follow, but they're different from what I know." Martin apologised, and had to admit that he didn't really know the correct steps but (and here there was no option but for him to be a bit forward), said that he wanted to dance with her and there seemed to be a queue forming!

Next up was a quickstep. Marlene allowed Martin the privilege of another dance. It was only fair, after all, that he be given another chance to accompany her around the floor, without both of them constantly trying to avoid feet clashing. They exchanged the usual introductory details while dancing. Enough for Marlene to want to sit down for a while in the bar area and continue the conversation. She was a year younger than Martin and lived with her parents in Little Berkhamsted, which she imagined Martin had not heard of. "Well, as a matter of fact, I *have* been there, just once while I was still at school. The father of one of my friends took us both for a ride out into the countryside one evening and we ended up at the Beehive. Is that anywhere near where you live?" Yes, it transpired that it was. Martin went into a brief explanation about foreign exchange dealing, and merchant banking in general. He did this in a desultory way, as if to imply 'this is not at all interesting; I am only doing this until something more creative comes along'. Marlene, on the other hand, had an outdoor, adventurous sort of a job. She worked for the Ministry of Agriculture, monitoring diseased farm animals across the whole of Hertfordshire. The Min of Ag had provided her with her own transport, a small Ford Thames Van. She had to deal with such things as fowl pest and swine fever, almost on a daily basis; sometimes treating the herd, sometimes reporting back to the department that the entire stock would have to be exterminated. She explained that she did not have to do the actual deed herself, much to her relief. Martin went on to tell her about his musical activities. This he did with a lot more enthusiasm in his tone of voice than when describing his work.

Marlene said that she was an amateur painter in her spare moments and usually carried her easel and canvases in the back of the van. She liked to paint landscapes, and there were plenty of great views around Hertfordshire. She would often start a picture while eating her lunchtime sandwiches and finish it off at home or, if the sun was in the same position, revisit the scene. Without seeming to be overly enthusiastic, unlike Martin's first encounter with the eager Anne, she agreed to meet Martin during the coming week. Martin explained about his lack of transport. She found the 'only turning left' episode highly amusing, and volunteered to drive over to Barnet. No, Martin wasn't having any of it. He would get to Little Berkhamsted by bus. Marlene explained where the nearest bus stop would be and at the end of the evening they left the Royalty separately, even though she offered to drive Martin to the main road, where he could catch his bus home.

The working environment at Guinness Mahon was much more relaxed than Martin had previously experienced. There was pressure, yes, and a level of responsibility entrusted in the dealers, Martin and three others that, if mismanaged, could conceivably bring the bank to its knees. They never thought about this, nor was it ever discussed. But they knew, beyond a shadow of a doubt, that at the end of every day's trading, there had to be more US Dollars on deposit than any other currency. That way, the bank was protected against any untoward shift in exchange rates. The dollar was all-powerful and inviolate. Richard Burrows, the head dealer was a friendly man, not given to any kind of emotional outburst. If he needed to correct the way one of his staff was working, he did it in the manner of one colleague to another. He always got the right result, simply by helping rather than chastising. He was in his mid-forties, tall, slim, bespectacled and single. As a way of keeping in his good books, the brokers would sometimes send tickets for Test matches or Wimbledon, etc. He was not a social climber, nor was he about to be influenced by these freebies, so he accepted them, but not for himself. Instead he passed these little treats on to his staff, in strict rotation, knowing that they were in no position to develop unhealthy preferences for one broker or the other while he was keeping a watchful eye on things.

"Martin, m'boy, would you like to go to The Oval on Friday? Marshall's have sent a ticket for the Vauxhall Stand." Martin most certainly would! He loved cricket, even though he had never made it into the school team This was despite his father making sure that he was born in Halifax, rather than Barnet, a paternal decision that was mainly due to the war, but partly because it would have qualified his son to play for Yorkshire when the time came. Martin had never been to a Test match. He had only ever seen televised snippets. He was elated at the prospect. Just so long as he put in a full morning's work, he would be free to leave at lunchtime. He had already arranged to meet up with Robert Melton at Lloyds, Knightsbridge that same evening, and Robin, his dealer friend, was going to come along too as, Martin had promised him, it would be a 'good laugh'. All slotting in nicely, he thought. But before all that, though, he was going to meet with Marlene on Thursday evening and had been thinking of little else since last Saturday.

It was a single-decker London Country Bus, number 328. An hourly service to Hertford, calling at Bentley Corner, Potters Bar, Northaw, Newgate Street, and Epping Green. The stop for Little Berkhamsted was about three quarters of a mile from the actual village, along Church Road. It was a glorious August evening, still hot at seven o'clock. Martin had asked the driver to let him know when his stop was coming up, although he needn't have bothered because he, Martin, had been counting off the stops past Potters Bar. It was a request stop, and he was the only one to get off. There was nothing in sight but fields and one solitary telephone box, but the moment he stepped onto the grass verge, his heart leapt. There she was, looking very attractive, wearing a floral print cotton dress and a big smile. "Hello, I wasn't expecting to be met. Look, I have got the directions you gave me." He fished a piece of paper out of his pocket, as if to prove it.

"It's such a lovely evening, I thought it would be nice for us to have a little stroll. I guessed which bus you would be on. They're only once an hour," was Marlene's reply. He considered taking her hand, but thought better of it. It was their first date, after all. They might not get on – the next hour or so would tell.

They chatted about this and that while walking up the hill towards Marlene's village. Among other things, she confirmed what Martin had already guessed: that she was named after Marlene Dietrich. Film-going parents had a lot to answer for. She gave Martin a conducted tour of the high street; two shops, a church and a pub. This was the Beehive, where Doug and Martin had sat outside drinking shandies a long time ago. He told Marlene about his days as the leader of a skiffle group, and how that became his entry point into the world of jazz. He told her about Doug, and how he had lost touch with some of his old friends, but time marches on and all that. They went to the Beehive, although Marlene said that she wasn't much of a drinker. A little more of her life story emerged. Very interested in classical music, particularly violin concertos. Liked to holiday in Europe.

Had just one serious boyfriend in the past. Was studying for a biology degree at evening classes. Yes, a very different sort of girlfriend than Anne. Couldn't be more so, but maybe that's what Martin needed at this juncture of his life, when everything seemed to be in a state of flux.

There wasn't a great deal of time. Martin's last bus left at nine forty-five. Marlene asked whether he minded walking to the bus stop on his own, as she didn't fancy returning, by herself, in the dark, and her van was parked some distance away. Well, of course he didn't mind. It was a full moon, and a cloudless night, so he would be able to see enough of the road. Marlene smiled, and reached into her handbag for something. It was a torch. "You can borrow this, I didn't expect you to bring your own. Round here we all have torches. One day they might install streetlights in the lane. There's enough people who use that bus, after all." Martin considered how thoughtful she was. And just suppose they hadn't got on? In all probability, she would still have lent him the torch. Well, it certainly seemed as if she must want to meet up again. Martin wasted no time with the invitation. Marlene thought it might be a better idea to meet in Potters Bar. That way, Martin could easily get home by either train or bus. As they said goodbye, standing close to each other, Martin kissed her on the cheek, and she reciprocated.

CHAPTER 31

Reunion

August 1963

"Bloody fantastic! Just got there in time to see Trueman get nineteen, batting at number eight. Hall and Griffith were lethal; soon polished off the tail-enders. Then, West Indies went in to bat; Conrad Hunte got eighty, Trueman couldn't get him, although he bowled like a demon. I just can't get over it; there they were, in the flesh! Barrington, Dexter, Sharpe, Sobers, Frank Worrell and …? Look, here's the scorecard: all legends, only seen them on television up 'til now. Didn't cost me a penny either; well, only the beer!" It was 6pm in Tattersalls Tavern. Martin was recounting as much as he could remember of the afternoon's play at the Oval to Vicky, Sue, Robert, Roger, Norman; all his former work colleagues. Robin from Guinness Mahon had just joined them, and was scrutinising Martin's scorecard with a lot of interest, for he would be going on Monday. Robert addressed the Lloyds contingent: "Where did we all go wrong?"

Martin offered an explanation, "Well, you know, you've either got it or you haven't!"

This prompted a barrage of beer mats to be thrown in his direction. Robin, having only just been introduced, tried to play devil's advocate:

"The whole thing is run by the Guinness family.

There's absolutely no one on the board who isn't either called Guinness, or married to one of them. Sooner or later Martin and I will have come to the end of the road as far as promotion is concerned. At least you don't have that problem."

Robert said that he would be more than happy to have that problem if it meant shorter hours, longer holidays, luncheon vouchers, tickets to the Oval.

"Yes, bugger the long term. I want it now," Roger added.

They decided on a pub crawl along the King's Road, Chelsea. There were some classic drinking establishments, brimming with Edwardian fixtures and fittings; monopolised by the trendy set, with their loud, confident Chelsea accents and opinions. The opportunities for baiting the 'Hooray Henrys' were rife, but the raving spirit seemed to have deserted them. Maybe they just couldn't be bothered that evening or, horror of horrors, maybe they were maturing and no longer had the enthusiasm for pranks. Reaching the curiously named World's End Tavern, Martin couldn't help noticing the piano. He nearly bumped into it, just inside the doorway, facing the window. The pub, on a bend in the road, appeared to be at the very boundary between Chelsea and Fulham. To the well-heeled Chelsea residents, it must have seemed indeed like the border post at the end of their cosy little world.

None of his friends had heard Martin play the piano before. They had not known what to expect, but it was not long before he was getting quite a few brownie points, particularly, he noted with interest, from Vicky. After half an hour of non-stop jazz piano, Martin sat down with the others. Roger had just bought a round and was bursting to tell them his latest joke. It was entitled 'The long-distance lorry driver': *There was this long-distance lorry driver who was constantly randy. He never picked anyone up unless they were female, below thirty and looked as if they were 'up for it'. He had been fortunate that day. A fit-looking university student from Cambridge had thumbed a lift back to London. She asked to be dropped off anywhere near Bloomsbury. The lorry driver, being a bit cunning, found a quiet side street not far from the British Museum and parked against the kerb. After a prolonged snog, he asked "How about a shag then?" She said, no, anybody could see them in the cab if they were passing by. "Oh no, not in the cab. If we get underneath the lorry, we'll be invisible. Trust me." So, underneath, they got. Now, not only was he a long-distance lorry driver, but considered himself to be a long-distance shagger. It was, to him, a matter of personal pride that he kept going for at least twenty minutes. Oblivious to everything while approaching the point of no return, he felt a tap on his shoulder. He craned his head round, and was confronted by a pair of well-polished boots with blue serge turn-ups and knife-edged creases rising above. It spoke. "Excuse me, sir, but just what do you think you are doing?"*

Quick as a flash, the lorry driver replied, "I am mending my lorry, officer."

"You are not mending your lorry, sir. There are three reasons for this: 1. Your feet are the wrong way up, 2. One hundred people don't usually watch someone mending his lorry, 3. Someone stole your lorry ten minutes ago!"

It was now eight thirty, and some had to go home, so they retraced their steps back up the King's Road. Passing the Six Bells, a pub which they had briefly visited earlier that evening, the sound of live jazz could be heard from an upstairs window. Martin thought he should investigate. Did anyone else want to come in? No, they were at various levels of need for catching a Tube homewards, and didn't have the extra hour or so to spare. *This is a million miles away from how things used to be*, thought Martin.

"I wouldn't mind coming in," said Vicky.

"Good! Well, cheers everyone, have a nice weekend. Oh sorry, I forgot that most of you have to work tomorrow morning!" He ducked, as mock punches were directed at him.

Upstairs, the jazz club, a properly organised thing with membership cards and so forth, was in full swing. The band was Wally Fawkes and his Troglodytes. "Blimey, we're really lucky," Martin explained to Vicky. "Wally Fawkes used to play clarinet with Humph. He's already a legend!"

The jazz was of the middle of the road, 'mainstream' variety which Martin was beginning to prefer to 'trad'. During the evening, Vicky updated Martin with all the latest news from Knightsbridge. Arnold Backhouse had moved down to Somerset, leaving a lot of euphoric cashiers in his wake. The relief at having been freed from this tyrant was overwhelming. Not for nothing had his nickname been Shithouse. One of the securities clerks had married the telephonist, much to everyone's surprise. A new general clerk, called Nigel, had taken a shine to Vicky, but she was not interested and had to keep on telling him so. Very time-consuming. At ten fifteen, they both needed to catch tubes; Martin to Barnet, Vicky to Clapham Common. As they ambled back along the King's Road towards Sloane Square Underground Station, Martin, out of a sense of pure devilment, said, "I really don't fancy going home just yet.

Why don't we have a few more bevvies and stay up here somewhere?" Vicky had been clutching Martin's arm. She jerked to a standstill, nearly pulling Martin off-balance.

"*Mr Weston*, I hope you are not propositioning me? I'll have you know that I am not that sort of a girl!" Martin actually had reason to believe that she was, by all accounts, and furthermore, she was grinning from ear-to-ear, like a Cheshire cat.

"No, no! Er, yes? Perhaps maybe?" was Martin's reply – hedging all bets. Two more side streets to cross before the square. At the second, looking both ways for oncoming traffic, Martin spotted the illuminated sign of a budget hotel. He steered Vicky leftwards down the road, receiving no protest whatsoever.

"Ooh! I didn't think you meant it," she said.

They went through the front door to the reception desk.

"No, no!" Vicky cried as she changed direction, letting go of Martin's arm. The receptionist seemed amused as Martin swiftly followed her outside.

"Sorry," was all he managed to say.

"Have you got a girlfriend, at all?"

"Nothing serious," he replied, quite truthfully. As they reached the station Vicky said that maybe they could keep in touch, *just for old time's sake.* They exchanged telephone numbers, and went their separate ways.

On his way back to Barnet, Martin reflected on his cavalier attitude towards the fairer sex. Was there such a thing as faithful love, or did it only exist in books and films? One person for ever, that sort of thing. Time and time again he had been prepared to be polygamous, whenever the opportunity arose.

The following evening, Martin took himself off to the Potters Bar Hotel. This was a single bus ride away, and they came back reasonably late. He had toyed with the idea of going to the Alex, but wanted to play the trumpet, if only for a couple of numbers. Paul was delighted to see him, as always. "Martin, old son, to what do we owe this pleasure? Don't think I have ever seen you here on a Saturday before." It was much busier than the Tuesday or Friday sessions, and Martin wondered whether, in view of this, he would still be okay for a blow? "Don't you worry about that, old son, it's guaranteed." Martin knew that this had no bearing on his prowess as a trumpet player, it was just Paul's way of making everyone feel special. It was this quality that had ensured his longevity at the hotel.

"Can I go on in the first half, please? I can't stay too late as I haven't got a car any longer." After playing 'All of Me' and 'The Very Thought of You', Martin returned to the bar to order a pint for Paul in readiness for the end of the first set.

"Well, I hear that the Sunday jazz has finished. That's a pity. Have you found anywhere else to play?"

"Possibly. Owen said there might be a chance of something in St Albans. I don't know though. I can only get there if Brian gives me a lift. But even that's doubtful. He's talking about moving to Cambridge. Did you know he is getting married this month? Another thing; I have met someone, a new girlfriend, and I have to rely on her for lifts. It's the wrong way around, isn't it? I must start looking for another car. Maybe my Christmas bonus will cover it."

Paul listened half-heartedly to Martin's tale of woe. "I've been more years than I can remember without a car. It's not the end of the world. Why don't you look at pubs within your area? Get yourself known to all the local musicians or whatever. Join a band. *Form* a band even!" Martin reflected that this was exactly what he intended to do, but it was good to have someone of Paul's stature confirming the way ahead. "Anyway," Paul continued, offering a pinch of snuff, which was sensibly refused, "you know, I hope, that you can always come here and do a couple of numbers on trumpet. If you come on all three days I'm here, you will have played six numbers every week. Almost half a normal gig!" They both laughed.

CHAPTER 32

Getting to grips

October 1963

Marlene and Martin had assumed the role of a couple to the outside world. Celibacy was not something that he had been planning on, but he found her company agreeable and also, he had to admit, her intellect and appreciation of the arts. When opportunities for lovemaking presented themselves, Marlene would go just so far and no further. During a somewhat awkward conversation she confided that she was not going to go 'all the way' before marriage. Martin thought that even 'halfway' might have been something. Well, that was that then! Another feature of their relationship, novel within Martin's experience, was her dislike of pubs such as the Alex and the Potters Bar Hotel. She was not a drinker, yet didn't mind the odd evening in a country inn; the kind where the customers were well-heeled and polite. Yes, she was about as opposite to Anne as could be imagined. Anne liked the Beatles, Marlene Beethoven. Anne booze in general, Marlene only Babycham. Anne partying all night, Marlene a nice walk in the countryside. Anne sex, Marlene restraint.

For Martin, the upside of this very different sort of relationship was that he could revisit all the pubs where he might get a sit-in without having to check with Marlene. She was aware of Martin's determination to play the trumpet.

Had he been forced to give up that ambition, she reasoned, he might become resentful and no fun to be with. So, in a funny sort of way, he had more personal freedom. He had his own little list of potential opportunities: Monday, the Alwyne Castle, Tuesday, the Potters or Elstree Golf Club, Friday, the Potters or the Queens Head, Saturday, Black Bull or the Potters, Sundays, possibly St Albans. He had been to the Alex and explained to Len what he was doing just in case they thought that he had deserted them. Len told him to get on with it and not to bother about 'us old fogeys'.

"Just let us know when you're on the wireless," he added. Then, "By the way, Ivy and I thought that your new young lady was very nice. An improvement on the last one, we thought. More sophisticated, is that the right word? Classy, anyway."

Martin thanked him for the compliment but thought it best to say nothing about Marlene's dislike of the Alex. Len and Ivy had changed their opinion about Anne, once Martin had told them about the way things came to an end.

Martin had not been to the Queen's Head since his public debut on the trumpet. They remembered him.

"You came in here, what? A year ago, at least, wasn't it?" This was from Ted, the drummer. In fact, it was more like two years, while Martin was commuting to Worthing.

After playing 'When You're Smiling' and 'Georgia', Ted said: "Why not stay on stage for a bit? We've got a couple of singers coming up. Feel free to join in." Now this *was* a challenge. All very well thinking on your feet as a pianist, which he had had to do in the past with Austin Royce, but this was a different proposition. He would have to find the right notes. Any fumbling would be obvious.

"Well, OK. Thank you. If I just sit here, and play what I know, would that be all right with you? You know, I might not know some of the tunes, or whatever." They were fine with this.

As the first singer tackled 'Take These Chains From my Heart' in the key of G, Martin kept out of the way for most of it. His second number was 'I'm Confessin'. Wonder of wonders, Martin knew it – not as a result of having heard the recent Frank Ifield recording, but because it was a track on a Louis Armstrong LP that Marlene had bought him for his birthday earlier in the month. He was able, not only to play a chorus of his own, but to construct what he hoped were sympathetic backing phrases behind the singer. He had worked out that the trick was to not get in the way, just stay in the background; long notes rather than jazz licks. It was all right, and Martin felt a genuine sense of achievement. Over the last year or so, his repertoire had expanded beyond the strict boundaries of jazz, and he was happy with this too. Not for him the dyed-in-the-wool purism of Adrian and the Union Place Revivalists. After a further ten minutes or so, he decided to quit while he was ahead, but not before Ted had given him the green light: a definite and genuine invitation to come every week and have a sit in.

On the following Monday, Martin made the trek over to the Alwyne Castle. Harry King welcomed him back after his considerable absence. He sat in and was asked whether he could play 'Maryland, My Maryland', which, coincidentally, he had only just learned off a Bunk Johnson EP. Although Bunk was one of the original pioneers of jazz, unlike the guys that people like Adrian worshipped, he had been a schooled musician and, later, became a teacher himself. In Martin's book, this was the badge of acceptability. 'Maryland' was not an easy number for a novice trumpet player. It kept going for a long time before the trumpeter could rest his chops, but Martin just about managed. Gavin, the regular trumpet player was complimentary about Martin's efforts, and asked for his telephone number. "I'm going on holiday soon. We normally have Bill Brunskill to cover for me when I can't do it, but do you fancy it?" Did he fancy it? Was the Pope a Catholic?

He had heard about a trio, playing at the Black Bull in Whetstone on Saturday evenings, and decided to investigate. There was a large back room, almost as big as the one in the Potters Bar Hotel, but the audience here was only about a quarter of its size. However, there were a few enthusiastic regular attendees, all sitting near the front and clapping enthusiastically, and this made up for the lack of numbers to some extent. The trio were all West Indians, led by Cyril on the tenor saxophone. Musically, it was a bit of a mixed bag. Martin had always expected, in his naivety, that any black person would be able to swing like Coleman Hawkins or whoever. This clearly was not the case with Cyril. It was a lacklustre performance. Nevertheless, Martin asked for a sit in, which was granted, without any hesitation. "We don't ever get other musicians coming along to hear us – just sometimes the odd singer. Yes, you are most welcome."

"What would you like to do?"

"How about 'I Can't Give You Anything but Love?'"

"Oh, yes, man, what key?"

"F?"

"Well, we do it in Bb." Martin said that he would try to

play it in their key. All part of his self-imposed development programme. Actually, it didn't go too badly. Next up was 'The Lady is a Tramp'. "What key?" asked Cyril.

"C?"

"Well, we do it in F."

And it went on in the same vein. Every single tune was in the wrong key! In later years, Martin was eternally grateful for this extra hard work, making his musical brain work overtime. In the end, it made him twice the musician he would otherwise have been. There was an exchange of telephone numbers at the end of the gig.

"Well, I can't be that bad then. That's three offers on the trot," Martin concluded.

At the beginning of the following week, Marlene asked Martin whether he would like to go to Norwich for the weekend. She had recently attended a ministry conference in a three-star hotel; just on the London side of the city. They had had a riotous time, it would seem, and she thought that it might be nice for Martin and herself to soak up the culture that Norfolk had to offer. Martin had to ask for a day's holiday on the forthcoming Friday. This turned out to be no problem at all. Out of Martin's three weeks' annual leave, one of the weeks could be split up into shorter periods, at the bank's discretion. They drove up in Marlene's van, stopping by the obelisk on the A11, in the middle of Thetford Forest, for a packed lunch. Arriving at the hotel at the same time as a coachload of tourists, they were eventually allocated their rooms. Marlene in thirty-five, Martin in thirty-nine. He cast his mind back to those licentious days with Anne, not so very long ago; when they were both frantic for sex, and reflected on how things had changed. Marlene had made the booking and he had guessed that it would be separate rooms, even though nothing had been said.

They had dinner in the hotel. Maybe it was the expression on the manager's face. Maybe it was his unhurried footstep. Something undefinable grabbed everybody's attention, without them knowing precisely why. As all eyes turned towards the manager, the dining room fell silent.

"Ladies and gentlemen, could I please interrupt your meal for just one moment? I have just heard on the radio that President Kennedy has been shot. We don't know any more than this at present, but I will update you if I can."

Saturday found them exploring Norwich on foot. Marlene was keen to visit the art gallery, where she told Martin about the Norwich School of Painters. He had been a great fan of Monet, ever since taking his art O level and being introduced to impressionism by the art master. He found the dark, foreboding Norfolk landscapes by Crome and Cotman very much to his liking. Then it was a trip to the coast in the van. After driving through Great Yarmouth and northwards along the flat Norfolk coastline, they found themselves in California-on-Sea by lunchtime. They wondered which came first and concluded that as the Pilgrim Fathers came from Boston, Lincolnshire, not very far away, it must have been this one-eyed place that had given its name to its counterpart in the USA, the state that was renowned for all the frivolous good things in life.

"Cecil B DeMille should have come here for the beach scene in *From Here to Eternity*!" Martin commented.

Marlene, demonstrating that she possessed at least as good a sense of irony as Martin, said, "Actually, I believe it was Fred Zinnemann, but, yes, what a great shot it might have been, panning up from the couple on the beach to that!"

'That' was a single-storey pub, more like a prefab: very much like the one in Durrington where Martin and Biggleswade had enjoyed many a lunchtime pint. Martin ordered some drinks and found himself drawn in to the single topic of conversation in the bar that day – the assassination of Kennedy and the arrest of the gunman. He made his own contribution: "I heard on the radio that Lyndon Johnson was sworn in as president while on board an aircraft. They must be desperate people, the Americans; 'gotta have a prez' immediately!"

After lunch, they made their way to Filby Broad. Captivated by the view across the water, Marlene asked whether Martin minded her doing a quick watercolour? Martin smoked a couple of cigarettes as he watched her skilful interpretation of the view take shape.

"I must say, you're very good."

Marlene was keen to play down her talent. "You think so? Actually, I have been thinking of taking a course so that I can really get to grips with it. Anyway, that's enough for now. I can finish it off at home."

Dinner in the hotel was a bit of an ordeal. All the coach party were already seated in the restaurant when they arrived. That put them at the back of the queue, as far as the waiters were concerned. The talk was mainly about Kennedy which, by now, Martin found tedious. By the time they were served after-dinner drinks in the bar, it was already quite late. They kissed goodnight in the corridor and went to their respective rooms. In the morning, there was a knocking on Martin's door. It was Marlene, in her dressing gown. She came in and sat on the side of the bed. Martin's thoughts moved immediately in an obvious direction. They had a kiss and cuddle before she rose to her feet, and left to get dressed. And that was it! Martin was now convinced that, unless he married Marlene, there would be no further progress on the physical front. He kept that thought in his head from that day onwards.

Brian telephoned on Tuesday. "I'm going to Welwyn Garden tonight to see Kenny Ball. Want to come along?" They got to the Cherry Tree by seven thirty, half an hour before the doors to the adjoining ballroom were due to be opened; reserved that evening for the jazz club. In the bar, Kenny and his band were playing darts. Brian knew John Bennet, the trombone player, and introduced Martin. "Come on, time to go to work!" Kenny announced. "All hands to the pump; grab a drum case or two."

John said that if Brian and Martin lent a hand, they would no doubt get in for free! This proved to be absolutely correct. Once inside, they had a rare treat. Before the public were let in, there was just time for a quick rehearsal. Kenny took the band through a new number that he wanted to do. It was 'My Mother's Eyes'. He had in mind a sort of shuffle rhythm in the style of Louis Prima. They had a couple of run-throughs before Kenny was satisfied. It was not long before this became a big hit when it was released on Pye Records. In later years, Martin was able to recall how he was there at the start. On the way home, Brian confirmed that he would be moving to Cambridge before the end of the year. They had found a nice little semi on the outskirts of town, and it was only now a matter of the formalities.

CHAPTER 33

Vadis?

December 1963

It was partly due to Brian's departure from Barnet, partly due to Martin not being too bothered about playing the piano, but mainly due to Owen's bombshell. His wife was pregnant, and they knew that it would be totally impractical to look after a baby in their rented bed-sit. "We have applied for a council house in the St Albans area. It appears that the waiting list in Barnet is as long as Rastus's hose!" This was a reference to a risqué song that Owen used to sing with Jimmy Prior's Jazzmen. It was called 'Deep Sea Diver' and among the double-entendre laden lyrics was the line '*and I can reach the bottom 'cause my hose is so long*'.

Neither Owen nor Joe possessed cars. Brian's move to Cambridge had for the time being given Austin Royce and his Music a transport problem. The very product that inspired the name of the band was the one vital ingredient that was missing! As a consequence, it was by mutual consent that the band stopped playing for the Ranche Restaurant dinner dances. Joe Ranche was sorry to see them go, but they had had a good run, for all that. The budget-priced gigs at the Victory Hall were still trickling in. Martin had decided that, when Owen moved away, he would take it upon himself to inform the caretaker that they would not be looking for another drummer, and so close that door too.

They all knew, anyway, that Martin had set his sights on becoming a trumpet player. Not just a pianist who from time to time sat in on trumpet with various bands for the odd number or two, but as a main event. There was one bright side to Owen becoming a St Albans resident. Alec Crook had managed to get his feet under the table at the White Hart. He was now ensconced as their resident organist and, good as his word, had persuaded the landlord that a Sunday morning jazz session would make a nice change from the normal musical repertoire of current and not-so-current popular songs. No date had yet been set for the first session but, what with Owen soon to be in situ, it couldn't be far off.

Meanwhile, Martin had been enjoying his now regular guest appearances with Paul at the Potters Bar Hotel, Cyril at the Black Bull, and Ted at the Queen's Head. He had also done one whole gig with Harry King's band, when Gavin had been away on holiday. This was his first ever paid gig on trumpet with an established jazz band. It went well, too. He had neglected for too long his mentor Len Adams and therefore made a concerted effort to pop along to the Alex on Sunday evenings, when he wasn't seeing Marlene or going to Wood Green Jazz Club. He knew in his heart that he shouldn't be making music his number one priority while he had a girlfriend who was not similarly obsessed. He couldn't help himself, though. Nothing, at that stage, could be allowed to get in the way of his clearly defined goal, which by now was tantalisingly close. In any event, theirs was a platonic relationship, to all extents and purposes. However, he was feeling more than a little guilty. If only she wasn't such a considerate, forgiving sort of a girl, never given to any kind of unseemly outburst. She always kept her cool. Just every so often, she would ask whether there was any possibility of Martin giving up one of his music evenings to see her instead, particularly if it happened to be the weekend. Her acceptance without any sort of complaint of Martin's varied reasons for not being able to do this made him feel worse than ever. He guessed, accurately, that she must be saddened by his lack of commitment.

Things came to a head, all about Christmas Eve. Cyril had managed to get some extra money from the landlord of the Black Bull for a 'Christmas spectacular', as he had put it. He had asked Martin to do the whole evening, for which he would be paid thirty shillings. Marlene had wanted Martin to come and have a meal with her parents, at home. She had also asked whether Martin minded drinking just one bottle of beer. Her parents only had the odd tipple at Christmas and didn't approve of regular drinking. Martin made his choice. It was the wrong one, and Marlene reacted, for the first and last time. She telephoned Martin to say that, although he *had* asked her to come to the Black Bull, a place that she normally would not have set foot in, she really wanted him to come to Little Berkhamsted. It was Christmas, after all.

"Please, just this once," she implored. "I have bought you a Christmas present!"

Now there was a hint of a sob in her voice. Martin was at a crossroads. This had come suddenly, without warning.

"I have promised Cyril that I will do his gig. It's too late to back out now."

This, he knew, was pathetic. Hadn't Kathleen warned him that he was not treating Marlene fairly? Such a nice girl too, she had added. Distressingly, he could hear her sobs over the telephone, quite clearly now.

"I love you," she said tearfully.

Next, he heard, in the background, her mother's voice: "Marlene, don't upset yourself, come away from the phone. *Marlene!*" Suddenly, there was a 'click', followed by the dialling tone.

He stood there in the hallway, holding the receiver to his ear, as if the telephone might reconnect of its own volition. Then he walked away, out of the front door, and around the corner to the Arkley Hotel, where he proceeded to get drunk.

All the staff at Guinness Mahon received a 7.5 per cent Christmas bonus with their December salary. In Martin's case, this amounted to £52/10s. He had some extra cash saved up over the year and in total now had £80 to spend on his next car. If he waited until January, twelve months after he had joined the bank, there would be even more, when his pay rise came through. Over the Christmas week, he bought the *Exchange and Mart,* the *Barnet Press,* and the local papers for the Potters Bar, Southgate, Enfield and Finchley catchment areas. He spent some of Christmas Day poring over the small ads and making notes. Christmas was never going to be anything special, what with him being in the dog house after the way he had treated Marlene. His parents were very disillusioned with him. He was not proud of what he had done, but in the few seconds when he could have changed his mind during that last fateful telephone call, he knew that he was not going to marry Marlene. Given the temporary disconnect between Martin and his parents, it would have been a waste of time asking his dad for a loan, so he had to be able to finance the car, the road tax and the insurance on his own. He had set his heart on a Sunbeam-Talbot 90. Ever since he had owned the Talbot 10, he had started to notice this elegant, post-war product from the Rootes Group. The body shape reminded him of a Mark 2 Jaguar. It had a white steering wheel with the Talbot lion in blue on the horn boss. It had a column change. It had comfortable, wide leather seats. It had a grooved metal dashboard with an impressive array of instruments and knobs. It had a fitted tool compartment in the boot. It had a reversing light. Oh, it was so desirable!

There were about half a dozen 90s listed in all. Prices seemed to be between £110 and £150, depending on whether it was a trade or private sale. There was just one within Martin's budget, a 1950 model, listed at £75 and located in Barnet. He dialled a number that he had written down about a month back, and not used up until now. "Happy Christmas, Brian. How's it all going up there in Cambridge?"

"Martin! Happy Christmas to you too. It's still a bit chaotic, but we're getting there. This is a surprise!"

"Actually, my old friend, can I pick your brains?"

"Ah, I knew there had to be an ulterior motive for you ringing – when did you ever ring to wish me a Happy Christmas?"

Martin told him about the low-priced Sunbeam Talbot, and wondered whether Brian could shed any light, or whether it was probably just a rust bucket. Brian explained that the 1950 model would be a mark one, nothing like the later versions. For a start, it had a smaller engine. And the suspension was leaf sprung, whereas the later cars had independent front suspension.

"Tell you what, give me a ring after you have looked at it, but I reckon you could knock him down even further.

Most people want a mark two or three, so they're not terribly popular." He went on to say that, even so, it was a post-war engine, with overhead valves, etc., and would be a lot more powerful than Martin's previous car.

It was maroon coloured, with a matt finish. "You'll find that if you give it a good go with Simonize, it will come up nice and shiny." Thus spoke its owner.

"Can I just have a look around the underneath, please?"

Brian had briefed Martin to check the areas prone to rust: the sills, the wheel arches and the spare wheel compartment. There was surface rust in all these places, but nothing was rotted through. Then it was a drive round the block. As the owner drove the car away, deliberately fast, Martin felt the rush of acceleration push him back into the seat. This one thing alone convinced Martin that he just had to have it. There were no obvious mechanical defects, it steered and braked well, the interior was in good condition, except for a water stain around the edge of the sunroof. It was now or never. "Would you be prepared to accept £65, do you think?" Martin had rehearsed this sentence in his head.

"Well now, I'll split the difference with you: £70, and no less."

They shook hands and Martin arranged to collect it the next day.

St Albans council had given Owen a date for his new home. Meanwhile, Martin offered to drive them both to the White Hart on the first available Sunday lunchtime that would feature a 'bit of a jazz blow'. Owen had been in touch with Alec. It could be no more than a trio, due to restricted space. Also, other than a free drink, no one, other than Alec would be paid. Well, that was what they had been expecting anyway. Along the wide, straight St Albans Road, Martin put his foot down. The speedo said seventy-two. "It's not flat out yet, either," he informed an impressed Owen. Once at the pub, Martin parked next to Alec's Rolls Royce. "Best two cars in the car park," he said, with some pride.

The Hammond organ occupied half of the small stage. Once Owen had assembled his drum kit, there was just about enough room for Martin to perch on a chair on the edge. In the bar were a few regulars, not particularly interested in whether there was music or not. Alec had put the word around though, and was hopeful for some jazz fans. Alec was clearly in charge, and he called the numbers, all safe middle-of-the-road tunes that he hoped most people would recognise, such as 'When You're Smiling', 'My Blue Heaven' etc. Neither Martin nor Owen had heard Alec on the organ before. His piano playing at Potters Bar, backed up by Brian on the bass, had been rhythmic enough for an impromptu jazz ensemble. Now, with two keyboard manuals and a whole array of bass pedals, he was a different prospect altogether. Everything seemed languid and 'palm-court' like. Owen did his best to counteract this lack of rhythmic pulse, but it was a struggle. Martin didn't really mind either way. If it was up to him to produce some sort of sensible jazz performance over a syrupy background, it was all grist to the mill. As good a music lesson as he would have had if he had paid for it. The dichotomy reminded him of a Charlie Parker LP he had recently acquired: *Charlie Parker with Strings*. He had bought it out of curiosity, and it *was* a curious recording!

A few more people had arrived by the time that they took a break. None of them seemed to be into jazz, but were keen to make their requests: "'Ere, mate, what about 'Twist and Shout?" The requests continued in the same vein, after a willing Alec had acquiesced: 'Do You Want To Know a Secret?', 'Take These Chains From my Heart', and even 'Rock Around the Clock' (Martin's starting point in music!) and so on. Martin eventually decided to pack his trumpet away and retire to the bar. Owen soldiered on with a strange expression on his face. Maybe it was concentration, maybe he was struggling with his conscience; being acutely aware that it was no longer a jazz session.

"Thought it went well, lads," said Alec, when it was all over.

Martin was about to say something, but Owen restrained him by a touch on the arm.

"Yes, I reckon we could make something out of this once I have moved up here," he said.

On the way home, Owen explained that he wanted any kind of work, jazz or not, a sentiment that Martin completely agreed with.

"However," said Martin, "considering what it was supposed to be, I don't think jazz accounted for more than a third of what we did. On Sunday lunchtimes, I can always go to Islington and sit in with Harry King's lot. Even as a sitter-in, I would get to play more jazz than today, all in all."

"Well, what do you want to do then?"

"Oh, look, it's a good thing that Alec persuaded the pub to try it out. I don't *mind* carrying on, but could we *please* try to make it mainly jazz, with a small amount of the other rubbish thrown in, rather than the other way around?"

Owen promised to see what he could do.

CHAPTER 34

Bert Alto

Spring 1964

Martin had a new girlfriend. Once again, the Royalty had come up trumps. She had gladly accepted his offer of a lift home to Enfield, especially when she found out that he had a Sunbeam Talbot. Martin was in two minds whether to ask her for a date. He had developed some degree of self-awareness at long last. His track record with women had been disastrous and he had no stomach for yet another bitter ending, with him, once again, being the cause of it all. Perhaps just the one date, he thought. If the signs were not good, he could end it straight afterwards, and no harm would have been done. Yes, that would be sensible!

The following Tuesday they had arranged to meet in the saloon bar of the Crown and Horseshoes, which was reached by crossing a footbridge over the New River in Enfield. After Martin had fetched the drinks, they carried on with the usual exchange of details, following their initial chat on Saturday. The revelation that she worked in a record shop in the high street led Martin to muse, most inappropriately, about staff discounts. Wisely he kept such thoughts to himself. There would be a better time for an 'innocent' enquiry. Eventually Carole asked Martin about how things ended with his previous girlfriend. For a brief moment, a lie pushed itself to the forefront of his thoughts, which he immediately despatched to the cranial waste bin. Instead he said, "Carole, I had to make a choice between doing something that she wanted to do, or going out on a gig. It was not the first time this had happened, and it *was* Christmas Eve. That was the end for her. I could not make the sort of sacrifice that she asked for; not even once! I didn't feel good about this by the way. I did beat myself up a bit afterwards. The worst thing is that she was such a kind and considerate sort of a person, not someone to be let down in the way I did."

Carole, to begin with, said nothing and looked away, so Martin continued: "By the way, I'm glad that you asked this. I might not have volunteered it. That's a weight off my mind."

She looked back, straight into his eyes, her own burning fiercely.

"Maybe you did let her down, but anyone who doesn't like music is missing one of the greatest pleasures in life, and those who *make* music are special people who have a need to perform. That's what I think, anyway. And so does my dad!"

"Your dad?"

"Yes, he used to be a dance band pianist. I have grown up with music for breakfast, dinner and tea. My dad once said that there is only about 1 per cent of the population who have any musical talent, and it is therefore their duty to entertain the other 99 per cent as often as possible. Maybe he said it just to placate Mum." She laughed at this last bit.

Phew! Martin immediately relaxed and took stock. Carole was quite shapely, with brown eyes, dark hair and a sort of mischievous face. He had noticed that she laughed a lot and imagined that she could be a lot of fun.

"Would you like to come out again, and maybe go and

hear some jazz?" he asked as they parted. Yes, she would. "Anywhere in mind?"

"How about Wood Green Jazz Club, to hear Alex Welsh?" was his suggestion. She had never been there, and said that she would be looking forward to it. The following Sunday, he called to pick her up as arranged.

"Come in and meet Mum and Dad." They seemed two pleasant, unremarkable middle-aged people. He realised that he was being given the 'once over' though. Sid, Carole's father, shook Martin's hand. "Carole tells me that you are a musician. Trumpet, I believe?"

"Yes, although piano was my main instrument and, to be honest, I am still a lot better pianist than a trumpet player."

Sid was interested in this. "Played with anyone I might have heard of?"

"Oh, I doubt that very much. The last band I played with was called Austin Royce and his Music. But I have guested at the Potters Bar Hotel with Paul De Bois."

Sid chuckled. "Austin Royce! Some of these band names, eh? But Paul – was he the guy who got done for drink-driving by telling the police that he was sozzled before they had even asked him?"

"Yes, the same!"

At the Fishmongers Arms, time simply flew away. Carole was at least as enthusiastic about the music as he always was; if not even more so. On the way home, Martin asked whether there was any live music in Enfield. "Yes, there is. Sunday evenings in the Cricketers. I don't know what it's like though. Do you want to give it a try next week?" Martin asked whether she minded if he brought his trumpet with him; just in case it turned out to be the sort of thing where sitters-in were encouraged. Carole said that she would be disappointed if he didn't, and added that she was keen to hear him play.

Owen was by now a St Albans resident and Martin usually went to the White Hart for the Sunday lunchtime session. Thankfully, Owen had managed to convince Alec that it should be mainly jazz, no matter what the customers wanted. This initially resulted in the loss of a few of them but, on the other hand, gained some new ones once the word had got around about the jazz. There were even sitters-in. Martin, on one glorious day, found himself in the role of the established trumpeter, happily allowing another to do what he himself had been doing for the last two years!

During the interval, Owen told Martin that he had made contact with some venues where he thought he could get bookings for Austin Royce.

"But Brian is in Cambridge," Martin said.

"Well, you have got a good left hand, so we can manage without a bass. How about adding a clarinet? I have spoken to Brian Simmonds, and he is up for it. Look, we could do some of that Benny Goodman Trio stuff, that you keep raving about. He's the nearest thing to Goodman I've ever heard. What do you think?"

Yes, Martin thought, *we bloody could*. The prospect of that kind of a trio was exciting; even though he would be on piano, rather than his chosen instrument.

"Yes, let's do it; count me in," was what he said.

He met Carole that same evening in the Cricketers, almost next door to the pub where they had their first date. There were several alcoves in the saloon bar, the largest of which had one continuous bench along the back wall.

Seated in the right-hand corner was a piano accordionist. There were very few vacant seats in the pub, even though it was only seven o'clock. However, Martin found a couple towards the back of the bar. He had brought his trumpet, but was glad to be able to secrete it quickly under the table before anyone noticed. As soon as they were seated, with their drinks, a weasel-featured chap in his early forties walked in, went up to the bar and said, "Can I have my pipe, please?" Carole and Martin looked at each other; both wearing quizzical expressions. The barman reached down below the counter and handed him an instrument case. The 'pipe' turned out to be an alto saxophone. "First time I've heard it called that," offered Martin. "I've heard non-musicians call clarinets 'liquorice sticks', but this is a new one!"

The music started – just the two of them. The first tune was 'Blue Skies', then it was 'Autumn Leaves'. Carole giggled and whispered, "Next up is going to be 'White Christmas'." Martin thought that he was going to get on just fine with Carole, not only the daughter of a musician but blessed with a sense of humour too. After an hour, there was an interval during which Martin introduced himself to Bert, the alto player.

"Do you allow sitters-in?" he asked, having explained that he was a trumpet player.

"Let me introduce you to Ernie. It's his gig. I'm just make-weight. I'm sure it will be OK though," he added. Ernie, the accordionist, was delighted that Martin had asked to join in.

"Mavis, is it possible for you to move along a bit? We've got another musician joining us."

They all squeezed up along the bench to make room.

After Martin sat down next to Bert, Ernie suggested 'Yes Sir, That's My Baby'. He did know it. Not only did he know it, but it seemed to him that he knew it slightly better than Bert. Carole was beaming at the end of the number and applauded much too vigorously. The majority of the tunes were what Martin had either played before or had heard often enough to be able to busk them. Every so often he was plunged into unknown territory too. Strangely enough, he found this didn't bother him. If the sax played the melody, he seemed able to find some reasonably safe complimentary phrases. All the 'lessons' he had learned from sitting in and using his ears were at last beginning to pay off. Not only that, he was fairly sure that he was making at least as good a fist of it as the sax player. It wasn't jazz in the strictest sense, but both Bert and Martin were given carte-blanche to improvise solos whenever they wished. Some of the tunes were of the Old Time Music Hall variety, but Martin wasn't fazed. He already knew them, from those interminable gigs at the Victory Hall with Austin Royce. After half an hour, he thanked them both for the blow, but they weren't expecting him to leave. He explained 'sotto voce' that he had only recently met someone, and didn't want to leave her all on her own.

"You can really play, can't you?" Carole was already in grave danger of becoming his number one fan. "I honestly don't mind if you carry on for the rest of the evening. *I'd* enjoy it anyway." But Martin had resolved to stay with her.

"Carole, I hardly know you yet, so it would be nice to sit here and chat for a while. Anyway, I've done enough playing for one day, what with the lunchtime gig. Hey! Your glass is empty; same again?"

After closing time, Ernie and Bert came over to have a few words. Ernie spoke: "We both liked your playing. How would you be fixed for joining us every week, or whenever you can make it? It went down well with the regulars, and I've just spoken to the landlord. He can give us a bit more dosh. What do you think?"

What did he think? *What did he think?* He needn't have said anything; the expression on his face would have been enough. Bert added: "I'm glad you can help me out – it's good to have a fellow front line instrumentalist. I have been playing for quite a few years but, to be honest, I'm a slow learner. Sometimes I only have a hazy idea of how the tune goes so, between us, we should be able to make a better fist of it. Here, I'll give you my number just in case you need it." He wrote 'Bert Alto' on a beer mat followed by a telephone number. From that day forward, Martin knew him only as Bert Alto, the man who kept his 'pipe' behind a pub counter.

When they were on their own again, Carole said: "I must be your fairy godmother. You *said* that you were looking for regular work. Looks like you've found it!"

"Looks like I have," said Martin.

THE END

CODA
Whitstable 2015

They were still laughing as he finished his tale about backing Frankie Vaughan in a pit orchestra. Tony had certainly had a colourful musical career! He, Jon, Robert and Martin were monopolising the small area known by them, and only by them, as the 'Chestfield Bar'. It used to be separated from the main bit of the pub by a door, long since gone. They were enjoying their usual Friday night wind down session, after the working week. Music was all that filled Martin's week nowadays. It had been ten years since he last sat behind an office desk. The other three still toiled for various masters, although in Tony's case only when it suited him.

As Tony and Martin had both spent a lifetime in music, mainly as semi-professionals, there was often a good deal of chewing the cud over the 'good old days'. Between them they had played most forms of music at some time, apart from symphony orchestras and present-day aberrations such as heavy metal, garage and rap. But the common denominator was jazz, an all-consuming passion for both of them. It was a regular source of amusement for Jon and Robert that, whatever Martin had done in the past, Tony could usually be relied upon to top it with something along the same lines, but more amusing, or more significant.

On this particular Friday evening, the conversation had moved towards recollections of encounters with the great and the good, both triumphs and failures. Martin mentioned that he still had the programme for the 1991 Boulogne English Music Festival where his own band had shared the bill with Yehudi Menuhin. Tony wasted no time in recounting the time when a senior member of the Royal Family had asked him to shut up! Martin went on to say that he had once sat in on piano with Nat Gonella. Tony then eclipsed this by his recollection of the time when Buck Clayton complimented him for his big tone on the trombone. Martin had played a season at Warner's Holiday Camp on the Isle of Sheppey, but Tony had played a summer season at the famous Gaiety Theatre in Douglas, and so on!

Jon asked Martin at what age he started playing the trumpet. "Well, I actually bought my first instrument, a beaten up old Salvation Army cornet, when I was eighteen or nineteen, but I didn't really start playing until about twenty-one and even then, only sporadically. My main instrument in those days was the piano. Nobody wanted to book me on trumpet while I was a better pianist."

"Bastards!" Tony interjected.

"And, I guess, pianists were in shorter supply than trumpet players," Martin continued. "They still are, actually. I reckon I must have been about twenty-eight before I started to get more gigs on trumpet than on piano."

Tony then followed up with the story of *his* first big break, an audition for a stage band, and how, just by playing the part exactly as written, he got the booking because all the others, some of whom were very well known, tried to show off by adding their own embellishments.

"I had a few lessons while I was living in Worthing for a while," Martin continued. "Let's see, I think that would have been around about 1962. After that, it was a question of trying to get noticed. I did the rounds, you know, sitting in with all kinds of bands. A lot of them were traditional jazz bands; we were in the middle of the Trad boom. You may have heard of it? But I wouldn't have minded what kind of a band wanted me if it meant regular work. Eventually, after a lot of blood, sweat and tears, I did start to get some bookings." He stopped in mid-narrative, looking bemused. "Blimey, I've just realised all this was over fifty years ago. Half a century!"

Robert wanted to know what Martin was doing in Worthing. "Technically, working for Lloyds Bank Registrar's Department on a secondment from my main branch in Knightsbridge. Do you know what though? Those few months were probably the best of my life. We were all very irresponsible and immature. Can you imagine it, about forty of us, all about the same age, living the life of luxury in four-star hotels at the bank's expense, money beyond the dreams of avarice – well, enough, anyway, to pay for my first decent trumpet. Plenty of available young women in our group too! And if that wasn't enough, I nearly got seduced by my boss in the office. She was quite tasty, as I recall."

Tony was on the point of describing his summer season in the Isle of Man, but, by now, Martin had their undivided attention. "Going back to what you originally asked, Jon, I did my first ever gig on the trumpet while I was there. It was the department's Christmas party. A bit later, they offered me a permanent post, and had I accepted and moved down to Worthing, I would probably have picked up regular work as a trumpet player years before I did in the end."

As the memories of times long past came flooding back, Martin had got well and truly into his stride. He moved seamlessly from the story of his emergent trumpet playing to other things, now leaping to the forefront of his memory.

"When I think of some of the stunts we pulled!" He continued by telling them about the Friday night raves, the midnight swim in the freezing winter sea, the waitress at the hotel whom everyone lusted after and could have been his for the taking, Biggleswade's pick-up technique at the Chinese jazz club, the *real* people of East Worthing. They wanted to hear more.

He continued with tales of Barnet; the gig at the country club where they swapped pianos, the riverboat shuffle, his first car and having to plan routes where only left turns were possible, forming Austin Royce and his Music (Jon particularly liked this, as an old car enthusiast). He talked about some of the characters – Ted Nottage, totally outrageous, Benny Farr, the lounge lizard, Paul De Bois, the 'humble apologist', Bert Alto, and more. He slipped back a couple of years to the skiffle group he had when still at school. "Yes, my first ever band. Say what you like about skiffle, but so many musicians started like that; just strumming a few chords."

"And they still do," Tony interjected. "They're called rock stars now!"

This reminded Martin of a joke. "What's the difference between a jazz guitarist and a rock guitarist? Well, a rock guitarist knows three chords and plays to 5,000 people, whereas a jazz guitarist knows 5,000 chords and plays to...!"

Tony then told a story about playing with a rock band, after which Jon turned to Martin.

"Any more?" he asked.

"Oh, I'm bored," Robert helpfully interjected.

"No, no, that's enough, it would take too long and... (noticing the near emptiness of their pint glasses) I am preventing the further intake of refreshment!"

"You should write a book about it," was Robert's closing comment.

"Maybe I will," said Martin, as Jon ordered another round of drinks.